I0659694

THE
Long Slide
HOME

KATE McMURRAY

Published by
DREAMSPINNER PRESS

5032 Capital Circle SW, Suite 2, PMB# 279, Tallahassee, FL 32305-7886 USA
http://www.dreamspinnerpress.com/

This is a work of fiction. Names, characters, places, and incidents either are the product of author imagination or are used fictitiously, and any resemblance to actual persons, living or dead, business establishments, events, or locales is entirely coincidental.

The Long Slide Home
© 2015 Kate McMurray.

Cover Art
© 2015 Aaron Anderson.
aaronbydesign55@gmail.com
Cover content is for illustrative purposes only and any person depicted on the cover is a model.

All rights reserved. This book is licensed to the original purchaser only. Duplication or distribution via any means is illegal and a violation of international copyright law, subject to criminal prosecution and upon conviction, fines, and/or imprisonment. Any eBook format cannot be legally loaned or given to others. No part of this book may be reproduced or transmitted in any form or by any means, electronic or mechanical, including photocopying, recording, or by any information storage and retrieval system, without the written permission of the Publisher, except where permitted by law. To request permission and all other inquiries, contact Dreamspinner Press, 5032 Capital Circle SW, Suite 2, PMB# 279, Tallahassee, FL 32305-7886, USA, or http://www.dreamspinnerpress.com/.

ISBN: 978-1-63216-971-6
Digital ISBN: 978-1-63216-972-3
Library of Congress Control Number: 2015906568
First Edition August 2015

Printed in the United States of America
∞
This paper meets the requirements of
ANSI/NISO Z39.48-1992 (Permanence of Paper).

Readers love the Rainbow League series by KATE MCMURRAY

The Windup

"…the chemistry between the MC's and their sexy love making was smoking hot, so it all balanced out in the end."
—The Blogger Girls

"I can only urge you to read this book and discover for yourself the skills and talents Kate McMurray shows her mastery of."
—The Novel Approach

"*The Windup* is an upbeat, fun contemporary set in New York."
—Prism Book Alliance

Thrown a Curve

"I loved the emotion of the story… anyone who is a sucker for sport related romance is going to eat this one up."
—MM Good Book Reviews

"I do look forward to reading the next installment of The Rainbow League as I am dying to find out how the love triangle wraps up!"
—Joyfully Jay

By KATE MCMURRAY

Blind Items
Four Corners
Kindling Fire with Snow
Playing Ball (Multiple Author Anthology)
The Stars That Tremble • The Silence of the Stars
A Walk in the Dark
What There Is
When the Planets Align

THE RAINBOW LEAGUE
The Windup
Thrown a Curve
The Long Slide Home

Published by DREAMSPINNER PRESS
http://www.dreamspinnerpress.com

In memory of Bob Thomas.

Author's Note

The Long Slide Home deals with some themes that are a little heavier than the previous books in the series, and I wanted to acknowledge that. Not every domestic-violence survivor has a Nate in their life to rely on, but there are resources out there if you should ever find yourself in a situation that feels inescapable.

Please visit the National Resource Center on Domestic Violence (http://www.nrcdv.org/) or RAINN (https://www.rainn.org/).

Chapter 1

NATE HAD pressed the buzzer for apartment 4D several thousand times in his life, but it felt different now. He took a deep breath and pressed it with his thumb, waiting for the telltale static squawk of the ancient intercom system. Eventually Mama Lulu called out, "Hello?"

"It's Nate."

"Come on up, *mi hijo*."

When the buzzer sounded, Nate pushed through the door and went up the stairs, the same way he had nearly every day from when he was six until he was eighteen. By the time he got to the fourth floor, he was out of breath, a little out of shape after being lazy all winter. He dutifully knocked on the door. Luisa Ruiz—Mama Lulu to everyone—answered, her round body resplendent in a floral dress, waving her arms to welcome him into the apartment.

It was chaos inside, but then, it always was. Even though all of the Ruiz children had fled the nest, here were two more. Nate recognized them as Lourdes's kids, Lulu's grandchildren. Mia was not quite two, toddling around in a frothy pink princess dress complete with a little plastic tiara. The baby—Nate couldn't remember the baby's name and hated himself a little for it—wore a onesie covered with footballs, and was having a grand old time in his bouncy chair on the kitchen table. The baby also sucked on a blue pacifier. No gender ambiguity for these kids.

"Uncle Nate," Mia said, opening her arms to give him a hug.

He knelt to hug her back. "Hi, sweetie."

"I'm babysitting," Lulu explained.

"Ah." Nate stood back up and patted Mia's head.

"What brings you here, Nate?" said Lulu. "No, wait, sit at the table."

This was part of the ritual too. Nate would come in and sit at the kitchen table, and within moments some sort of food would appear before him. Mama Lulu was never happier than when she was feeding people. This time it was a bowl of paella, yellow rice with bits of chicken and chorizo and maybe some kind of fish in it. Nate's mouth watered, so he took a forkful. It was salty and savory and delicious.

Mia toddled over and climbed onto one of the other chairs. When she sat, the table came up to her nose, but this didn't seem to bother her.

"Now," said Lulu, plunking down a glass of lemonade in front of Nate, "talk to me. It's bad news, yes?"

Nate sighed. Just being inside the Ruiz home made him feel many times better, so much so that he almost didn't want to bring up his reason for visiting in the first place. But he'd come here seeking comfort, so he said, "I was in the neighborhood. Mom's in the hospital."

"Oh, Nate. What happened?"

He rubbed his forehead. "The cancer's back."

Mama Lulu's face fell.

"I'm not sure how I feel about it," Nate said.

Mama Lulu rubbed the back of Nate's hand. He loved that he didn't have to explain. Lulu already knew that Nate's mother, Rebecca, was cold and stoic, that she and Nate weren't very close, that her working so many hours when Nate had been a boy had driven Nate into the Ruiz home to begin with. The cherry on top was that Rebecca was devoutly Catholic and Nate's homosexuality had never quite sat well with her.

Of course, the Ruiz family was Catholic too, but matriarch Lulu was everything Rebecca was not: she was warm and welcoming and loved her children fiercely and without condition. When her son, Carlos, Nate's best friend since first grade, had come out, she'd given him a hug and carried on with her day. And Nate had never felt unwelcome here. Even though he wasn't blood related, he had been a part of the family since his elementary school days.

Nate's mother was currently in the hospital being treated for breast cancer that the doctors had apparently not completely excised the first time. Now it had spread to other parts of her system. Of course she hadn't told Nate about it, not at first. Only when she started coughing up blood did she decide it might be a good idea to call her son and ask him to take her to the hospital.

He put his fork down. Mama Lulu stroked his head.

"I don't want bad things to happen to her or anything," Nate said, "but we're so distant these days that, I don't know. I think I should be sadder than I am?"

"You feel how you feel, *mi hijo*."

"Yeah. Well, anyway. The prognosis is not good. The doctors are saying she may not last the summer." He shook his head, more frustrated than sad. "Her doctor won't say it, but I get the feeling this might have been more treatable if she'd gone to see him sooner. She has insurance now. I don't understand why she would wait so long. The oncologist told me she must have felt unwell for months while the cancer progressed. Months!"

Mama Lulu smiled sadly at Nate and stroked his hair some more. "Maybe she thought it was just the flu. Maybe she did not want to admit to herself that the cancer was back."

Nate swallowed and picked up his fork again. He ate a piece of chorizo. In many ways, he was grateful to his mother, who had always kept a roof over their heads even if it meant working two jobs, who had helped pay for his college, who bought him new clothes every year. But Lulu Ruiz continued to show Nate every day that there was a lot more to being a mother than paying for stuff.

Rebecca had once come to Ruiz family functions. The big Puerto Rican family certainly knew how to throw a party. Often Rebecca would arrive quietly and then sit on the edge, awkwardly eating and not talking to anyone. Around the time Nate turned sixteen, she'd started begging off, and once Nate left home, she stopped going entirely.

Bottom line was that Rebecca may have been Nate's mother, but he'd long felt that the Ruizes were his real family.

"She has a few months left," Nate said. "Then I'll have to say good-bye."

"That's never easy."

"No."

"Abuela!" little Mia said.

"You want some *arroz con pollo*?"

Mia screwed up her face in confusion. Nate guessed that Lulu's Spanish dishes were not in her diet or vocabulary yet.

"How about some animal crackers?" Lulu offered.

Mia nodded enthusiastically. Lulu got up to fetch the box from the counter. She offered Mia her high chair, which Mia adamantly refused. So Lulu put some animal crackers on a plastic plate and then placed it in front of Mia. Mia had to reach above her head to pick them off the plate, but she sat there, crunching happily.

As Mama Lulu walked around the table and settled back in her chair, she asked, "Have you talked to Carlos about this?"

"Ah, well. I haven't really talked to Carlos much at all since he moved in with Aiden."

Lulu made a disapproving guttural noise and pushed back from the table. "Why is that?" she asked, her voice wary.

"I may have let it be known that I don't really like Aiden and I thought Carlos was making a mistake, and now Carlos hardly talks to me. You must know that."

She nodded. "He hasn't said as much, just that you had an argument. You really told him you thought moving in with Aiden was a mistake?"

"I did."

That hung in the air. Nate supposed he didn't need to explain why. Lulu had always been extraordinarily intuitive.

"I worry about him," Lulu said. "Carlos loves Aiden, I know that, and Aiden seems like a decent man, but I just don't...." She shook her head. "There's nothing wrong with him."

"No. There isn't." Well, except that Aiden was the man Carlos went to bed with each night, not Nate. And Nate just got a bad vibe off him, but Nate was so crazy with jealousy that he didn't trust his instincts. Carlos had never really shown bad judgment with men in the past—his exes were mostly good guys with whom things just hadn't worked out, or that was how it seemed before Nate's heart decided he and Carlos should be together. So Nate should have trusted Carlos's judgment, but something about Aiden.... "I've never been able to put a finger on why I don't like him, but I don't. Besides the obvious reason. I don't know. And probably I'm saying too much."

"It's all right, Nate. I appreciate your honesty."

He ate a few more forkfuls of rice and watched Mia carefully chew on her animal crackers. The baby—was his name Jorge, maybe?—had fallen asleep in the bouncy chair and looked serene, his little pacifier bobbing occasionally as he sucked on it in his sleep.

"It's funny," Lulu said. "I always thought you and Carlos would end up together."

It hurt Nate to hear that, like a punch in the stomach. It was a recent thing, wanting Carlos, and it had sprung on Nate quite suddenly two summers ago when they were both single for the first time in a while and Nate started thinking, *Maybe....* Carlos had been his best friend forever, his family, and they cared about each other deeply. Nate had always thought Carlos objectively attractive—he had that tall, dark, and handsome thing going for him, for one thing, and he was in good shape and a little obsessed with proper grooming. He wore too much cologne, but Nate had come to miss the cloud of it that always surrounded Carlos.

One day, though, Nate and Carlos had been tossing a ball back and forth in Central Park and Nate had noticed how much Carlos's brown eyes sparkled, how neat his eyebrows were, how plush his lips looked; he'd seen musculature he hadn't noticed before, strength, physique. He noticed that Carlos actually had quite a nice ass, that the swishy way Carlos walked was kind of seductive, that Carlos's husky voice could sometimes make Nate hard even if he was talking about unsexy things like baseball or work.

Of course, within weeks of Nate discovering all of these things, Carlos had discovered Aiden.

"I thought we would end up together too," Nate said.

He realized suddenly he'd spoken out loud and put a hand to his mouth.

Mama Lulu stared at him.

"I'm so sorry," said Nate. "That was an inappropriate thing to say to his mother. I swear, I've never even made a move on him."

Then Lulu laughed. "Oh, Nate. No. It's all right. Carlos loves Aiden, but something nags at me when I see them together. I don't know what. Aiden may be a good man, but I do not think he's the right one for Carlos. But Carlos will not be dissuaded. I made my peace with it. If this is what Carlos wants and Aiden makes him happy, who am I to stand in the way?"

"And arguing with him just makes him more stubborn."

Lulu balked but then nodded slowly. "Yes, he is that way. These are matters of the heart, though."

Still, Nate hadn't been able to shake the idea that this was his fault somehow. Instead of talking about his feelings like a mature adult, he'd lost hope and let Aiden claim Carlos. Then he'd acted like such a pill about it that Carlos had stopped talking to him. He worried that being an ass about Aiden had spurred on Carlos's stubborn streak, and even though Carlos himself had been having second thoughts about moving in with Aiden, Nate agreeing it was a bad idea had seemed to inspire Carlos to do it anyway.

"It's too late now," Nate said. "They have happy domestic bliss and I have nothing."

Lulu sighed. She put some more animal crackers on the plate in front of Mia. Then she said, "So dramatic, *mi hijo*. You have plenty. You are just having a rough year. No matter what your relationship with your mother, it can't be easy seeing her sick. And I know you care about Carlos, so stop picking fights and make up with him."

Nate nodded. "No, I should. I will."

"You boys have been such good friends for so long. I do think you could make each other happy, but this is the way life has dealt the cards. It is hard for me to talk about since you're both my boys." She tilted her head. "I would not give up hope just yet. But there are other fish, Nate. I know there is a man out there who will make you very happy."

"Thanks, Lulu."

"And if you need anything, you obviously know where to find me. We'll get you through this, okay?"

"Yeah." Nate couldn't tell if she meant his mother's illness or his feelings for Carlos. Picking Door Number Two, he said, "I mean, you know, I care about him, but he's made his decision."

Lulu frowned. "It seems that way."

"So I'm dating. I'm moving on." Although that was an exaggeration. He'd been on a lot of first dates in the past year, but none of the guys measured up.

"Good. Eat your rice, *mi hijo*."

CARLOS WAS tired of having the same fight. He mentally prepared himself for the inevitable "I don't know, what do *you* want to do?" conversation that would stretch on and on because lately Aiden was so noncommittal about everything. They could go out or they could eat leftovers, Aiden didn't care. He'd eat sushi or pizza. He'd go get a drink if Carlos wanted, but he didn't care if they went here or there.

Carlos figured he'd start with an easy question. He walked into the living room, where Aiden was lounging on the couch in just his underwear, flipping through the TV channels.

"You want to go to Mason and Patrick's wedding with me?" Carlos asked.

Aiden shrugged. Of course. "We've been together almost two years and I'm still just a plus one?"

"Actually, you were explicitly invited." Carlos flipped over the invitation envelope and showed it to Aiden. It was addressed to Carlos Ruiz and Aiden Smith.

"Oh."

"It's not until August, but the RSVP date is about a month away, so we should probably let them know."

"Yeah, yeah."

Was Aiden even paying attention? "I just figured, you know, I'd ask without assuming, since these are really more my friends than yours and you don't love weddings."

Aiden finally turned to face Carlos where he stood at the arm of the sofa. "Are all the Hipsters going?"

Carlos interpreted that to mean *Is Nate going?* "I haven't asked, but I assume so."

"I'll go."

All right. One item off the list. Carlos put the invitation on the little table behind the couch. Next up, that afternoon. "Don't know if you remember, but Rainbow League sign-ups are today." Carlos and Nate had joined the Rainbow League together, back when they'd still been the sort of best friends who talked daily, and they played for the same team. He'd met Aiden through the league, in fact; they'd been together since they first made eyes at each other two years before.

"Oh, yeah! I almost forgot." Aiden sat up. "And Will finally finished setting up the damn website, so we can register online this year."

"I thought it might be fun to head into the city. Drop by the park. Ty and Josh are in charge of sign-ups again this year."

Aiden tilted his head as if he were considering that. "I suppose if we went, it would be easier for you to switch teams in person."

"Wait, what? Switch teams?"

Aiden crossed his arms over his chest. "Don't you think it would be more fun if we both played for the Queens?" He spoke in a patronizing tone, as if he had just asked if it would be better for Carlos to avoid spicy food if it was upsetting his stomach.

"Okay, first of all, we never talked about that. Second of all, why would I switch? Your team already has a good player in my position. Actually, all of the outfielders on the Queens are pretty good. And third, you don't think it would be weird if we played for the same team? Couldn't that get awkward?"

"For who? We'd spend more time together."

Carlos pressed his lips together to keep from pointing out that they already spent almost all of their time together outside of their respective jobs, to the point where Carlos hardly ever saw his friends anymore. "Aiden. I wouldn't make you leave your team. These are my friends and I want to continue to play alongside them. I'm sure it's the same for you and the Queens."

Aiden looked a little angry now. "Sure."

"Let me have this. I've played with the Hipsters for five seasons, you know? And I mean, just because we consolidated living spaces doesn't mean we have to consolidate our whole lives, does it?"

But even after that little speech, Carlos worried that the real issue here was Nate. Carlos didn't know why, but his best friend and his boyfriend hated each other. Aiden thought Nate was jealous, but Nate wasn't into Carlos in that way. But then Nate kept saying he didn't like or trust Aiden, but not for any specific reason. He and Carlos had gotten into it last summer because Nate felt ignored while Carlos spent all of his spare time with Aiden. That had some logic to it, since Carlos really had been neglecting their friendship. Carlos had promised to try harder, and he had, but then he'd also finally relented to Aiden's increasingly frequent pleas to move in together, and now here they were in Aiden's Brooklyn apartment that they hardly ever left.

Carlos wanted to scream.

He loved Aiden, he did, but he couldn't figure out how to maintain his freedom without pissing off or hurting Aiden, and he didn't remember Aiden being quite so needy before they moved in together.

Aiden was glaring at him now.

"We can have separate social lives sometimes," Carlos said. "It doesn't mean we don't love each other. Besides, I invite you along to all of the Hipsters' events, don't I? You don't even want to come half the time."

Although he usually came anyway. Probably to keep an eye on Nate. As if leaving Carlos alone would be all the invitation Nate needed to make a move. Which, please. It wasn't like Nate hadn't had an opportunity in the nearly thirty years they'd been friends.

"Fine," Aiden said, though he didn't sound pleased.

Was this weird tension between them just relationship growing pains or the sign of a bigger problem? They'd only been living together about six months, and at first, Carlos had been happy, but lately it was just tension and arguments—and fine, pretty hot sex—but none of the joy Carlos had felt when they first got together. Aiden was too noncommittal or too irritable most of the time. And Carlos missed his friends, especially Nate, but he stayed away for fear of rocking the boat.

That was a problem, wasn't it?

Carlos groaned. "Just come with me to the park, okay? We'll chat with whoever's there, maybe get a drink at Barnstorm after. What do you say?"

"Sure, if that's what you want to do."

Carlos dug his nails into his palms rather than shout or throw himself out the window. He said, "Yeah. That's what I'd like to do."

Aiden stood. "I'll get dressed, then."

"Yeah."

Six months ago, Carlos would have made a sexy joke about how Aiden could go to Manhattan in the altogether and turn a few heads, if only Carlos wouldn't get jealous, or something like that. But he wasn't feeling like he wanted to joke just then.

From the bedroom, Aiden called, "Is Nate gonna be there?"

"I don't know, but I doubt it."

This was not going as well as he'd hoped, basically. And Carlos had no idea how to fix it.

Chapter 2

THE FIRST practice of a new baseball season had long been one of the most exciting days of the year for Nate, but this year it brought him a lot of dread. He hated all this tension between him and Carlos, and he worried about the distraction. Would it fuck up his game?

With some reluctance, Nate walked to the Prospect Park ball fields, where the Hipsters had their weekly practices. Scott, the Hipsters' team manager, stood near the backstop, a clipboard in his hand. Mason, Ty, and Ian were already there, sitting on a bench and lacing up their cleats, while Joe was wriggling into his pads. No sign of Carlos yet. With a huff, Nate dropped his stuff near the bench.

"Hey, Nate," said Josh, walking up to him. "How's your pitching arm feeling?"

"Pretty good," Nate said, stretching said arm out a little. He smiled. "Good enough to throw a hot one past you."

Josh laughed. "Not much of an accomplishment. I'm a little rusty. I tried to get Tony to throw some balls at me last weekend, but he interpreted that the wrong way and, well...." Josh shrugged.

"Didn't know he meant *base*balls," Ty said, glancing up at Nate.

"Yeah, I got that," Nate said, but he laughed anyway. "Sucks for you, because Mason and I went to the Upper West Side batting cages last weekend and I still got it." He preened a little for his onlookers.

Ty stood and slapped Nate on the back. "I'm glad. Missed you at sign-ups, bro."

"Aw," said Nate. "Sorry, guys, but I got tied up with some work stuff. Figured I'd take advantage of the fact that Will finally got the website up. It took a whole thirty seconds, so I opted not to bother getting on the subway."

Ty raised his eyebrows. "I never thought I'd say this, but I think website sign-ups might be a bad thing for the league."

"How so?" Nate asked.

"You missed some drama at sign-ups," Josh supplied with an eye roll.

"I'm surprised you haven't heard about it already," said Ian from his spot on the bench.

This meant it likely involved Carlos. "What happened?" Nate asked.

Ty glanced at Ian. "Well," he said slowly, drawing the word out in his Texas accent until it had a few syllables. "Aiden and Carlos came by. Apparently Aiden thought it would be a good idea to try to get Carlos traded to the Queens. Did Carlos not tell you about this?"

"No. I've been swamped with work. I haven't talked to Carlos all week." That wasn't strictly true, as a good chunk of Nate's evenings had involved sitting in front of his television surfing channels while playing puzzle games on his phone. But it wasn't like Carlos deigned to speak to him much lately.

Ty's eyes went wide. "Oh. Well, yeah. Aiden got a little belligerent with Josh."

Josh grimaced. "Well, not *belligerent*, but he wasn't the friendliest."

Nate looked around, still not seeing Carlos. "Did Carlos agree to the trade?"

"Oh. No," said Ty. "The Queens' right fielder had already signed up for the season. Josh and Will wouldn't make the trade."

"And," said Ian, "Carlos made it pretty clear he wasn't in favor. So he should be here any minute, if that's who you keep scanning the field for."

"So Aiden was just being a jerk?" Nate asked.

Ty slapped Nate on the back again. "All right. I think we all agree that ship sailed when they moved in together, so take this with a grain of salt, okay? But yeah, Aiden was being kind of a jerk. Don't give it any meaning, though. Aiden's usually an all right guy. I think he really wanted to be on the same team as his boyfriend, but they couldn't make that happen. Can't say I blame him." Ty shot Ian, his boyfriend of two years, an adoring look.

Nate had to fight to keep from rolling his eyes. "Mason's not on the same team as his freaking fiancé, though. That works out fine, right?"

"It does," said Mason. "I kind of think it's better. The rivalry is fun. Plus, you know, Patrick has the guys on his team he's played with for years and I've got you guys. We all have rhythms and habits. It'd be a shame to break that up."

There were nods all around. Nate took Ty's spot on the bench and pulled his cleats out of his bag. Carlos appeared at the edge of the field then, fast-walking toward them, probably aware that Scott would chew him out for being late.

Which is what happened; Carlos arrived and promptly got a stern lecture about arriving to his practice on time, although by Nate's watch, Carlos was actually three minutes early.

Nate wondered if he should just bite the bullet. Carlos actually dropped his stuff next to Nate's as if it were just any other practice and not the first after six months of bullshit. Nate finished with his cleats and stood. To Carlos, he said, "Hi."

"Hi," said Carlos.

Nate stalled. This was so hard. Nate gazed at Carlos's familiar face, one he knew as well as his own reflection. For years they'd been able to communicate just by meaningful looks. Nate hated that Carlos lowered his eyelashes, his gaze at his feet, rather than looking up at Nate. Nate deserved it—he'd been an asshole about Aiden, and he regretted that at least insofar as it had driven Carlos away—but this still sucked.

"Nate," Carlos whispered. "Can we just—"

But before Carlos could finish, a hush came over those assembled, diverting Nate's attention. A guy made his way across the baseball diamond, and everyone just stared. He was breathtakingly handsome. He had a Mediterranean look to him, with olive skin and thick black hair. His face was perfect—wide eyes, nice nose, pouty lips, square jaw nicely lined with stubble. His body was a museum-quality sculpture of muscular perfection; his round, corded muscles were clearly outlined by the tight T-shirt and track pants he was wearing. Nate watched with interest as he approached. He might have drooled a little.

"Who is *that*?" Carlos asked.

"Oh, did I not mention?" said Ty. "Shane had to take this season off since he and his husband made the foolish choice to adopt an infant, so we had to fill the spot. That's Andreas."

"Good Lord," Nate sighed. When had he ever seen a better-looking man? Murmurs of assent rippled around him.

Andreas arrived at the clump of assembled athletes.

"Hello, how are you?" Andreas said a little stiffly. He had a faint accent Nate identified as… vaguely European.

"Hi!" Nate said brightly. "Welcome to the Hipsters."

Andreas grinned. Carlos frowned.

Practice got under way with Scott leading the whole team through some kind of improvised yoga moves, which was awkward in the sandy grass of the ball field. Andreas effortlessly twisted his body around. Lord, he had a great ass. Nate wanted to reach over and grab it, though he refrained and patted himself on the back for being so strong-willed. Then Scott made everyone run laps while he yelled at them about off-season weight gain. Finally, they all lined up while Nate and the two other pitchers took turns putting the batters through their paces.

For part of the cycle, Nate pitched to Carlos.

Carlos walked up to the plate and put some swagger in his step, swinging the bat around and waving at an imaginary crowd of cheering fans.

"Stop showboating and hit the ball," said Scott.

Carlos grinned at Nate. For a second they shared a private joke, and it was like nothing was wrong with their relationship. Carlos lifted the bat. Nate knew how to make Carlos succeed, knew his strengths and weaknesses as a batter. If Nate threw a fastball right over the plate, Carlos could hit it, but a knuckleball or Nate's recently perfected curve would get away from him. Nate wondered for a moment if he should try to help Carlos hit or challenge him. He threw a fastball, which Carlos hit easily, sending the ball sailing into the outfield.

Scott said, "Do that again."

Nate looked at Carlos from across the field. Carlos patted his batting helmet and resumed his stance. Nate could feel his gaze from forty-five feet away, and though he couldn't see his face clearly, he could imagine those eyes narrowing in concentration, and the determined set of his jaw.

So he pitched the curve, which went a little wide but still stayed within the strike zone, and Carlos miscalculated where it would end up and swung too low. The ball whizzed right over his bat.

Carlos shook it off and resumed his stance.

Nate threw the curve again, part of him wanting to trip Carlos up but part of him hoping Carlos would hit it this time. Carlos caught the edge of it, sending a grounder toward third.

Scott golf-clapped. "Nate's trying to trick you with curve balls. Glad you got that last one. Next!"

Carlos pulled off his batting helmet and sent Nate a surprised look before getting back in the line.

As they wrapped up, Scott said, "I'm going to assume you all remember the mechanics of the game. Most of you are not new here. All but one of the players rejoined this year, so that's great. Uh, hi, Andreas." Scott gave a little wave like he, too, was intimidated by Andreas's beauty. "Anyway, we could have done better last season if we focused more and Joe hadn't been out with a twisted ankle half the season."

"It's better now, if anyone cares," said Joe.

Scott sighed. "I think we can do well this season if you guys stay focused and we don't let any team drama get in the way. And I understand Mason got engaged to one of the SoHoMos in the off-season, but don't make the mistake that this means we'll go easy on them."

"If anything, the opposite is true," Mason said with a shrug.

"Right. Well. I just wanted to say, I like you guys. I think this will be our year. Just don't goof off, okay?"

Everyone thanked Scott, who for all his mean bluster really was an excellent coach—determined to win, knowledgeable about the game, and able to back off when a teammate was in genuine distress—and went to pack up their stuff. Everyone chatted and laughed and changed out of their cleats and tried to decide where to go next.

Ty said, "Let's go to Excelsior." That was a Park Slope gay bar that was a common postpractice watering hole.

"Yeah, okay," said Nate.

"I gotta get home," Carlos said, hooking his thumb back in the direction of his apartment north of the park.

Nate found that disappointing. They'd barely seen each other at all in weeks and had hardly talked to each other today, and now Carlos was leaving. Nate missed him, missed his company, missed his usually cheery demeanor—particularly now that he looked sort of sad.

"You sure?" Nate said. "I'll buy you a beer. Maybe we can talk the guy at the bar into putting on the Yankees game. They're playing Tampa today. Eh?"

"Nah, sorry. Maybe next time." Carlos shot Nate a look that was… plaintive? Sad? Something was wrong here, and Nate wanted to get to the bottom of what that was.

Although that wasn't his job anymore, was it? Not now that Carlos was with Aiden.

Behind him, Ty said, "Andreas, do you want to come with us for a drink? It's kind of a team solidarity thing."

"Yes, I would like that."

"You go, Nate," Carlos said. "Have fun. I'll see you around, okay?"

"Yeah."

Still, Carlos hesitated. "Everything's okay, right? Mom told me you stopped by."

Rebecca's prognosis had not improved; she was resting comfortably at the hospital, but Nate knew her days were numbered. He'd mostly pushed the matter out of his head, but it came raging back now, an unpleasant reminder that she was slowly drifting away at a hospital up in the Bronx and Nate was currently standing on a ball field in Brooklyn. He'd visited her the day before and had a stressful conversation with her oncologist, who was trying to determine if her condition had improved enough for her to go into hospice care instead of the hospital. There'd been a lot of talk about what next steps the doctor could take in her treatment; Nate didn't know how to decide what to do.

So he'd pushed it out of his head, which wasn't exactly healthy.

He forced a smile for Carlos. "Just visiting. Everything's okay."

Carlos pursed his lips, a sure tell that he didn't believe Nate.

"Go home to your man," Nate said. "I'll catch you later."

"Are you sure?"

"Yeah."

Carlos nodded, frowned, and waved at everyone. He turned slowly and started walking toward the north exit of the park, dragging his feet a bit as if he didn't want to go.

"*Is* everything okay?" Mason asked.

Nate paused while Carlos moved out of earshot. "My mother's ill, but…." Nate shook his head. "Not much I can do about it."

"Well, if I can do anything—"

"She has good doctors." Nate thought that sounded sufficient.

Mason gestured toward everyone else walking west toward the bar. Andreas wandered over.

"You played professionally?" Andreas asked Mason.

"For the Yankees, yeah. I'm retired now. Hurt my foot."

"But you still play for this league?"

"I love baseball. I could never give it up entirely. Amateur baseball is not as hard on my leg, although I have to sit out games sometimes." Mason stared at his foot as if it annoyed him. "My fiancé is being very strict with me this season. He made me promise not to play if my leg bothered me."

Andreas chuckled. "Must be nice to have that."

Mason smiled. "It is. I mean, I'd rather play, pain be damned, but he's right. He's looking out for me. And yeah, that is really nice."

"How are wedding plans going?" Nate asked.

Mason shrugged. "My mother and Patrick's mother have teamed up and taken over the planning, so heaven help us all. I just wanted to do something quiet, maybe get married at city hall and have a little party after, but now that the moms are involved, it's turning into the wedding of the century."

"It will never be as insane as Carlos's sister Lourdes's wedding. Two big Puerto Rican families trying to outdo each other." Nate shook his head. "Her dress was so big it needed its own zip code. At least you don't have to deal with that."

"Carlos? The man who just left?" Andreas asked.

Nate nodded. "We've been friends for years. Grew up together basically. I know his family well."

"But he has a boyfriend who is not you?"

The words, in Andreas's weird accent—German, maybe?—sounded like an accusation. Nate bristled a little, saddened by it. By rights, Nate should have been Carlos's boyfriend. He certainly loved Carlos more than he thought Aiden possibly could. But his teammates were right. That ship had sailed.

"Carlos is in a relationship with a guy from another team," Nate said.

Andreas smiled. "Keeping it in the league. I heard that happens a lot."

Mason laughed. "Yeah. I think that's the point more than baseball."

"That is good, because I do not have a lot of experience with baseball. With men, though…." He winked at Nate.

Nate didn't know what to make of that. Was Andreas… flirting with him?

Well, hell. Why shouldn't Andreas flirt with him? He wasn't so hard on the eyes. And why shouldn't he flirt back? Certainly saving himself for Carlos was a futile endeavor. So Nate smiled at Andreas. Their eyes met. A little sizzle of mutual attraction passed between them.

Nate smiled wider. "Let me buy you a drink at the bar," he said.

Andreas grinned. "Yes. Happily."

CARLOS KNEW it was irrational, but his blood was on fire as he made his way across the meadow toward the north exit of the park at Grand Army Plaza. That stupid European guy and his stupid good looks, smiling and flirting with Nate. Where did he even get off....

Lord, was Carlos jealous?

Of all the stupid things! Carlos groaned out loud as he realized that he was, in fact, seriously jealous. It shouldn't have mattered. Nate was single and certainly deserved to have a handsome man in his life. Carlos was with Aiden, who was right now waiting for him at home so they could have dinner together. This was good for Nate, the way things were supposed to be. And yet....

Carlos crossed Grand Army Plaza, dodging strollers and clumps of people and bicycles whizzing by. Getting across the tangled traffic circle around the big arch in the middle of the plaza was like playing Frogger, so Carlos took his life into his hands as he did it, but he got to the other side successfully and walked the three blocks to the apartment he shared with Aiden.

He liked the apartment okay. He'd grown up in the Bronx and lived in Manhattan most of his adult life, so he wasn't a stranger to the city, but Brooklyn, where he lived now, was a different thing. His neighborhood was populated by twentysomethings with trust funds who could afford the overpriced apartments and hipster cachet, and families with babies, and while he appreciated the new restaurants and shops opening up along Vanderbilt Avenue, something about this place still didn't feel quite like home.

He let out a heavy sigh as he unlocked the main door of his building and went up the stairs to his apartment. Aiden was home, sitting on the sofa with his laptop open in his lap, typing away.

"Hey," Carlos said, dropping his gym bag on the floor near the door.

"Hi," said Aiden. "How was practice?"

"Fine. I actually hit a curve ball today, so that was kind of cool."

"Oh, congrats." Aiden typed for another moment, fiddled with the trackpad mouse, and then closed the laptop. "What do you want to do for dinner?"

"I don't know, *papi*. You were the one who insisted I come home after practice so we could eat together. I guess we could buck trends and cook."

Aiden laughed as if this were the funniest thing he'd ever heard. "Let's just get something delivered and eat here. What do you want?"

Carlos sighed. He spent the next ten minutes negotiating. By the time they settled, Carlos was no longer hungry. He hopped in the shower while Aiden waited for the food, and he thought the whole time he was getting clean that *none* of this really felt like home. Aiden's apartment was nice and full of comfy furniture and anything Carlos could want, but it was all Aiden's stuff. Aiden was the one who wanted to live together, but it was Carlos who had sacrificed to make that happen.

He'd been living with a roommate in Chelsea before the move to Brooklyn. His place had been a few blocks uptown from Nate. He and his roommate had barely interacted except when rent was due, but that was okay, because Nate was in the neighborhood and all it took was a phone call or text message and they'd sit together on somebody's couch, stuffing their faces with pizza or Thai food and talking over a baseball game.

When was the last time that had happened?

Carlos had left most of his furniture behind and come to Brooklyn to live with his boyfriend because it seemed like the next logical step in their relationship. So now here he was, using Aiden's shampoo in the shower and the woodsy-scented soap that dried out Carlos's skin because Aiden didn't like the smell of the stuff he usually liked, and deep in his gut, Carlos hated all of it.

He missed his old life. He missed Nate.

But he'd made his commitment and he had to follow through. Besides, he loved Aiden, and they'd been together a long time, and he owed Aiden this, didn't he? Carlos was thirty-three years old, definitely old enough to settle down. This was the way life was supposed to go, wasn't it?

When he returned to the living room a little while later, the pizza had arrived and was enjoying a prime spot on Aiden's cheap kitchen table. Aiden was in the process of pulling plates out of the cabinets. Carlos took a moment to smell and savor the greasy spiciness of the pepperoni, thinking of a thousand nights with Nate and pizza and baseball and comfort and anything that wasn't this queasy uneasiness he felt now. The smell reminded him of everything he'd given up to make this happen. It had been a sacrifice he'd wanted to make for Aiden, but was this relationship worth the cost?

"All clean?" Aiden asked with a smile, his teeth gleaming under the yellowy kitchen lights. He was handsome and charming and loved Carlos, which Carlos had to remind himself of now that he was full of doubt again.

"Yeah. Sparkling clean." Carlos smiled too, but he didn't feel much joy as he sat down to eat.

Chapter 3

THE FIRST game of the season against the Park Slope Strollers had been an easy victory for the Hipsters. Nate had tried being friendly and polite with Carlos but had gotten gruffness and monosyllables for his trouble. And now, despite the victory, Scott seemed determined not to let the team rest on its laurels. He was extra shouty at the next practice.

Carlos was late again, which was an alarming trend, not only because he was bound to get in trouble but also because it was so unlike him. Carlos was usually super punctual; it was a habit from having grown up in a big chaotic family where someone was always late for something.

He looked downright upset as he set his bag down near the bench.

Nate didn't want to let it go anymore. He knew something was wrong, could read it in the way the sadness rippled off Carlos, and he was tired of pretending everything was fine. More than that, he missed his best friend, and he was tired of the ache in the pit of his stomach that seemed to grow every time Nate and Carlos occupied the same space without really speaking to each other.

"Hi," Nate said.

"Hi," said Carlos, and it was a strained sound.

"You okay?" Nate asked.

"Fine," Carlos said tersely.

Nate grunted. "Come on, Carlos. Used to be we could talk about anything. You're clearly upset about something. I doubt it's just that you're late and Scott is coming over here to lecture you about it."

Carlos looked so tense it was like his limbs were trying to push their way back into his body. "I could have said the same to you a week ago."

The accusation, and the venom with which Carlos leveled it, took Nate's breath away.

Carlos's whole body went slack. "I'm sorry. I didn't mean...."

"No, you're right. We're both...."

"Carlos!" shouted Scott. "I told you to be here on time. Everyone needs to get here promptly so we can start practice at exactly two o'clock." He pointed to his watch.

"I know. I'm sorry."

"Just don't do it again." Scott turned his attention to everyone else. "You bums better be ready to start in five minutes."

Carlos plopped down on the bench and pulled his cleats out of his bag. He took his sweet time putting them on and fiddling with his laces. Nate just stood there, unsure of what to do or say. It was hard to long for someone sitting right there in front of him, and yet Carlos was like sand through his fingers. He wanted to make Carlos smile. He wanted Carlos to be his old self. Even if Nate couldn't have Carlos the way he wanted, he still wanted his friendship, and it didn't even feel like they had that anymore. He would give anything to get it back.

"Nate," Carlos said, lifting his head and finally looking Nate in the eye. "This is so stupid."

"I know," Nate said.

"Why is this happening to us? Why are we like this now?"

Nate had some theories, but he said, "I don't know, but I hate it."

"Me too. Can we just—"

"I'm so sorry," Nate blurted. "For what it's worth. For all the things I said. I know I was a jerk—"

"You were looking out for me."

That hung there for a moment.

"I was, that's true. But I shouldn't have… I mean, I still said some shitty things."

"That's also true." Carlos sighed and rubbed his forehead. "I probably did too."

It felt like an opportunity. Nate didn't want to let this moment of civility go to waste. He wanted to find a way for the two of them to talk to each other. Maybe Carlos would never be with Nate in the romantic sense, but Nate could cope with that if he could get his best friend back.

Nate said, "Can we… I don't know. Put this behind us? Make this less awkward? Is that possible?"

Carlos let out a breath. "I sure as hell hope so. This sucks, *papi*." He sighed. "All of it sucks."

Nate couldn't begin to guess what "all of it" included, but the words seemed to break the tension. Nate plopped down next to Carlos on the bench. "Yeah, it does suck. A lot."

Carlos nodded slowly. "Get a drink with me after practice? We'll talk, okay?"

That seemed promising. "Sure, but do we have to go to the cowboy bar?" Nate had a lot of bad memories tied up in that place, a Western-themed gay bar called Spokes. Plus it was right near Aiden and Carlos's residence, so Aiden was likely to show up.

Nate expected Carlos to make an argument in favor, but instead he said, "No. There's a sports bar on Vanderbilt that shows the Yankees games. They make a great burger. Want to go there? Yanks are playing Baltimore tonight."

Nate wanted to hug Carlos. "Yeah. That sounds great. I, uh, have some things I should tell you."

"I figured." Carlos tugged on the laces of his cleats and nodded to himself. "Me too. Also, it's weird that you'd go to see my mother before you talk to me."

"I'm sorry about that too."

"I know why you did. We'll talk later, okay? I can feel Scott's laser gaze from here."

Carlos jogged over to where Scott was herding everyone into lines to start warm-up exercises.

Practice was mostly uneventful, everyone going through the motions but playing pretty well. Slightly above average, even. The batters did a decent job getting their bats around everything Nate threw at them. The infielders' reflexes seemed to be in top shape. The prospect of talking things out with Carlos after the game certainly made Nate feel lighter, like maybe they'd soon find their way out of this awful purgatory.

Other things that didn't hurt: Andreas prancing about looking beautiful, his accent making the baseball jargon sound lovely and foreign. He wasn't very good, probably the worst player on the team, but he could run fast, and Lord, he was pretty.

Andreas was the last up for batting practice, and he held his hand up as if he were testing the wind. Nate just watched, captivated by the beautiful man with the perfect bone structure, even if what he was doing looked like a parody of baseball.

"All right," Scott said from behind the backstop. "Try to keep the bat level as you swing it. You keep slicing it high. You'll never hit the ball that way." He made eye contact with Nate and gave the signal for a fastball.

So Nate tossed a ball at Andreas and watched as Andreas stuck his ass out too far and then swung the bat too high to get anywhere near hitting anything. The ball soared past Joe, squatting in the catcher's position, and clanged against the backstop, close to where Scott had threaded his fingers through the chain link fence. Scott yanked his hands away in alarm.

"Try again, pretty boy," Scott said.

"Don't stick your ass out so far," Nate said. "Bend your knees a little, keep your back straight. Yeah, like that."

"It's a nice ass, though, yes?" Andreas asked.

It was. Nate relaxed his arms for a moment and checked it out.

"Stop looking, Nate," said Scott.

Nate shook it off and laughed. Then he lobbed a fastball at Andreas, straight over the plate. Andreas caught the end of it, but it spiraled out foul and landed a few feet in front of him.

Scott shook his head, his expression dazed, as if he weren't quite sure what to do with Andreas. "That's a wrap," he said. "Get the hell out of here, everyone."

As practice wrapped, Ty walked up to Nate and slapped him on the back. "Nice pitching today."

"Thanks."

"Even against the hot German."

Nate scanned the crowd of guys packing up their stuff. Andreas was smiling at Joe, who was miming hitting a ball, perhaps giving Andreas pointers.

"I pride myself in not letting a nice ass distract me," said Nate.

"Sure. And good looks alone will not win a baseball game." Ty pulled a ball out of his pocket and tossed it in the air. He caught it again deftly. "So I heard that they're gonna close Excelsior."

"The hell you say."

Ty held up his hands. "The landlord raised the rent above what they could pay. Just like every other fucking business in this neighborhood. Plus, you know, gay bars in this city seem to be going the way of the dodo unless they're in Chelsea or Hell's Kitchen."

"That blows."

"I know. I mean, if nothing else, Excelsior always throws a good party during Pride. Brooklyn Pride has turned into a family-friendly street fair full of kids." Ty crinkled up his face in disgust. "But the Excelsior party is always a good time."

"I take this to mean the parenting bug hasn't bit you and Ian yet."

Ty's eyes went wide. "God, no. Can you see us as parents? No."

Nate laughed. "So is Excelsior definitely closing or is this just a rumor?"

"Just a rumor right now. Still, I think we should take advantage of it while it's still here. Come get a beer with us after practice?"

"Not this time, Tex," said Nate. "I have to talk to Carlos about something, so we're going to go somewhere showing the Yankees game. I'll see you Tuesday, though."

"More beer for me." Ty slapped Nate on the back again.

People divided as Carlos approached Nate. He motioned toward one of the park exits, so Nate fell into step beside him. He realized quickly enough that Carlos was headed up a path that would exit the park at Grand Army Plaza, away from where everyone else was headed.

"I didn't get a chance to ask you about this last week, but I heard Aiden wanted you to join the Queens," Nate said.

Carlos laughed. "I guess word travels."

"So it's true."

"Yeah, it's true, and I told him he was being ridiculous. I don't want to leave the Hipsters."

"Good. The team wouldn't be the same without you." Plus, if Carlos joined another team, he and Carlos really would never see each other.

"Thanks." Carlos coughed. "So that Andreas."

Nate laughed. "Christ, he's hot. I don't even care if he can play ball. I just want to look at him."

Carlos bristled. "Empty head."

"Mmm. Don't care."

Carlos turned toward him, making an expression Nate couldn't interpret, before he looked back ahead of them. "Anything going on between you two?"

Nate shrugged. "Eh, not really. After practice last week, I bought him a beer and we chatted and flirted for a while, but we just left it there. He's from Berlin originally. Here on a work visa to do something for some international bank. Not finance, though. Some kind of customer relations job that sounds like glorified party planning to me. It wasn't really clear. Anyway, apparently the bank encourages its employees to pursue athletics. Something about work-life balance. So he joined the Rainbow League for the only reasons anyone does."

"Sex?" Carlos asked.

Nate shrugged. "I mean, I assume so. If ever there were a more noble athletic pursuit…."

Carlos laughed. "Yeah. You like him?"

"I don't know. I mean, you're right, he's dumb as a post, but he's really pretty."

They walked together for a while without speaking, just enjoying a comfortable silence. After a couple of minutes, Carlos said, "So what's going on with you that you needed help from Mama Lulu?"

Nate sighed. "Mom's cancer is back."

Carlos sucked in a breath. "How bad?"

"Metastasized to her lungs. Seems to be spreading. Doctors think she's got until the end of the summer."

"Oh, Nate. Oh, *papi*, I'm so sorry."

Nate shrugged.

Carlos nudged him with the heel of his hand, an old gesture that felt alarmingly familiar. "Oh, don't shrug it off. I know you and your mom aren't that close, but this can't be easy for you."

Nate let out a breath. He didn't like the direction the conversation was taking. He wanted to talk about Andreas more, because it was easy. If Andreas made Carlos jealous, as Nate suspected he did, that was something Nate could hold on to. It was less important. But part of him needed to talk about this too. No sense in continuing to push it aside. "No, you're right. It sucks. On every level it sucks. I mean, first of all, it's like a reminder of how hard it is for me and Mom to talk these days, because she didn't say boo until the situation was dire." Nate kicked a rock. "It sucks because hospitals are the worst, and I know she's in pain and she looks awful. Sitting with her is draining. I've been going to see her every other day or so."

"Oh, Nate."

"And it sucks because dying is expensive, and she's already in debt from the last round of treatment." Nate had to stop for a moment. He put his hand out and leaned against a tree. "Visiting her has been maybe the hardest thing because I just don't know what to say. So we sit there being awkward."

"Nate."

Nate looked right at Carlos. "It sucks too, because I used to be able to tell you anything, but things are weird with us lately, and I didn't know if I could call you to talk or what. I really could have used a friend, but I didn't feel like you were mine anymore."

Carlos turned to face Nate. He frowned, and then his whole expression fell. Before Nate knew what was happening, Carlos had pulled him into his arms and was holding him in a tight hug.

It was perfect in a lot of ways. Carlos's body was warm, the right amount of hard and soft, and it had a familiar shape and scent from hundreds of hugs over the years. Nate rested his chin on Carlos's shoulder and hugged him back, pulling in comfort from their touch.

"Nate, *mi hermano*, please, call me anytime, okay? You need anything, I'll be there. Things *are* weird, but I've missed you a lot these last few months."

"I've missed you too."

"I'm still your friend, no matter what. Okay? I'll always be your friend."

"Yes. Me too. I'm here for you too, you know. If something's going on."

It was deliberately leading, but to Nate's chagrin, Carlos didn't bite.

"Come on, let's go watch the Yankees game, okay?" Carlos pulled back from the hug.

"Yeah. Thanks, Carlos."

"Anytime. Seriously. Don't be a stranger anymore."

Chapter 4

IT WAS one of those fights that went on for three days. It started on Friday, when Carlos tiptoed home after a night out with Nate and a couple of guys from the Hipsters, kind of an impromptu "Hey, we never got around to doing this!" engagement party for Patrick and Mason at a bar in Hell's Kitchen. As he figured a dutiful boyfriend should, Carlos texted Aiden on his way to the bar to say he was going out with his Hipsters teammates and that he'd probably get home late. No big.

Later he and Nate stood on the corner of Fifty-Fourth Street and Ninth Avenue, trying to decide if it was better to get a cab or take the subway, when Carlos pulled out his phone to check what time it was. He had eight texts and a missed call from Aiden.

"Whoops," Carlos said, still a little drunk.

Nate took the phone and scrolled through his alerts. "Um. Your boyfriend? Controlling much?"

Carlos grabbed his phone back. "He's probably worried I got hit by a bus because I didn't reply to his texts." Without bothering to read them, Carlos texted, *On my way home now.* Then he followed Nate toward the subway.

He didn't actually read any of those texts until he was walking from the train to his apartment. They alternated between concerned and hostile, from *U ok? Where R U?* to *Text me back, asshole!* Carlos couldn't tell if that one was kidding. The last text Aiden sent read *You better get your ass home ASAP. We need to talk.*

Carlos was annoyed now. Where did Aiden get off? Carlos had missed his texts, yeah, and he planned to apologize for neglecting to look at his phone, but *coño*, Aiden needed to calm down.

Aiden was fuming when Carlos got home, his face red, his anger practically coming off him in waves. Carlos held up a hand and said, "Chill out, *papi*. I'm sorry I missed your texts, but—"

"Are your friends more important than me?"

"Of course not. I just forgot to look at my phone. It was in my pocket, but I didn't feel it vibrate."

"Was Nate there?"

Carlos rolled his eyes, tired of having this argument. He flipped up his hand again and said, "I'm going to bed. We can talk about this after you've cooled off."

Carlos made it three steps before Aiden grabbed him hard and slammed him against the wall. "Don't walk away from me. We need to talk about this."

Carlos shoved him away with enough force to make Aiden stumble back. "What we need to talk about is how you turning into a raging jerk has nothing to do with me missing a couple of text messages. I went out, I didn't look at my phone, I'm home now. Nothing urgent happened while I was out, did it?" He looked at Aiden expectantly while he rubbed his arm. It fucking hurt where Aiden had grabbed him.

Aiden glared. "No."

"So calm down. I'm going to bed."

Aiden stayed in the living room for a while after Carlos brushed his teeth, stripped out of his clothes, and crawled into bed. He was halfway to sleep when Aiden walked into the room. Aiden slid into bed and wrapped an arm around Carlos.

"I'm sorry," Aiden said against Carlos's hair.

"I'm sorry too. You better now?"

"Yeah."

But clearly Aiden had lied, because they got into it again at breakfast. Aiden apologized for overreacting but held firm that Carlos was in the wrong for going out and not texting him to begin with.

"I *did* text you," Carlos pointed out.

This led to a semantic argument about whether Carlos always had to text Aiden back, and then Aiden explaining that he only got mad because he was so worried.

Tired, Carlos rubbed his forehead, put his cereal bowl in the sink, and said, "Honey, this is never going to work if you fly off the handle every time something like this happens. When I'm out with my friends, I don't want to be focused on my phone. Just like I don't answer texts when you and I are out together either."

"Unless it's Nate."

Carlos rolled his eyes. "This again? Really?"

They were apart for the afternoon while Carlos was at Hipsters practice, though he came home promptly afterward at Aiden's request. He felt a little resentful, like Aiden forced him to leave his friends in order to walk into a war zone, but he swallowed his anger and decided to let Aiden prove he wasn't an asshole.

Carlos thought Aiden had dropped it, but he brought it up again at dinner. "Nate's in love with you, you know."

Carlos let out a long-suffering sigh. They were eating miscellaneous leftovers. Carlos had part of a piece of lasagna and some leftover pad thai on his plate, having lost the battle for the chicken parm and spaghetti to Aiden.

Rather than getting into it, Carlos just said, "Really?"

"He is."

"You know that's not true, and anyway, it doesn't matter. Our relationship isn't like that. And I'm here with you, aren't I?"

"You weren't last night."

"Yeah, but I was out with a bunch of my teammates. Nate and Mason and Ty and Ian and Joe. Patrick was there too. He's kind of touchy-feely. You going to accuse him of being in love with me too?"

Carlos said it to get a rise out of Aiden, which: mission accomplished. He knew Patrick and Nate weren't even in the same ballpark. Nate had been friends with Carlos since kindergarten; they had history and, yes, a friendly sort of intimacy. But it was brotherly. They could communicate wordlessly because they had for so long. They had whole conversations about the Yankees that basically went "Hey, did you see—" "Yeah, did you hear—" "Dude." "Bro." They understood each other. Which was how Carlos was so sure Nate was *not* in love with him, because if he was, he would have made that abundantly clear.

Aiden threw his fork at his plate, and it clattered loudly. Carlos jumped.

Still, he grunted, trying to convey how aggravated he felt. "Nate and I are like brothers. There's nothing going on between us. He's not in love with me. I'm not in love with him. You need to let this go. I'm not discussing it anymore." Then he stood up, dumped his plate in the sink, and left the room.

Aiden was so snuggly sweet that night that Carlos was certain he'd finally seen the back end of that argument.

But then again, Sunday afternoon: "He's already texted you, like, eight times today."

Carlos didn't even need to ask who. Besides, Aiden wasn't wrong; Carlos and Nate had been texting through that afternoon's Yankees-Red Sox game. Before Aiden, they probably would have sat together on Nate's couch or in a bar to watch this game, but since Aiden was being an untrusting douche, Carlos had opted out of that more often than not lately. Just like he'd opted out of going out with the Hipsters after practice, something he missed. Texting was a poor substitute for Nate's company—for any of his friends' company.

"We're watching the game," Carlos said, holding up his phone.

"So, wait, you text Nate about fucking baseball, but you can't be bothered to text me when you go out just to let me know you're all right?"

"Not this again."

They were off to the races then, Carlos stuck in a marathon of bickering with Aiden while surreptitiously texting Nate and watching the game—he finally had to say, *Sorry, bro, but Aiden's trying to pick a fight with me, gotta shut it down.* Then he tossed the phone on the coffee table.

"Let it go, Aiden. It was one mistake. Are you really going to make me pay for it forever?"

Aiden sighed. "No." But on his way out of the room, he knocked a book off a shelf, and it hit the ground hard, its pages splayed out. Carlos heard something else thud in the bedroom, loud enough to make him hop out of his chair, but as he waited for his pulse to resume a normal pace, he opted not to investigate. Let Aiden have his hissy fit, even if it caused property damage.

By the end of that night, Aiden still looked like he wanted to pick a fight. Carlos didn't have the energy. Instead, he got in bed, pulled the covers up to his armpits, and rolled onto his side, away from Aiden.

Aiden sat heavily on the bed. "I'm sorry. I guess my jealous streak is worse than I thought."

"Could have told you."

"I didn't know I could get this irrational. Just the thought of you and Nate… I mean, I can picture you kissing, and I can't get that image out of my head."

"I wish you would stop with that shit. I have never, in my whole goddamned life, kissed Nate. Hug, sure, but never kiss. Our relationship isn't like that. You have to trust that and let this go."

"I'm trying."

"Try harder. Don't take your shit out on me."

"No, I won't. I'm sorry."

"Okay, then."

Carlos hoped that was the end. He didn't think it really was, though.

REBECCA'S DOCTOR was waiting outside her room when Nate got to the hospital Sunday afternoon. He was scribbling some notes on a clipboard.

"Everything all right?" Nate asked.

"Oh, Mr. O'Sullivan. Yes. That is, nothing has changed. She was having some trouble breathing this morning, but we've modified her medication and that seems to have helped. You can go in and see her."

"Thanks, Dr. Lefkowitz."

The doctor moved to leave, but then something occurred to Nate. "Is there anything I can do? To help her, I mean. Would she be more comfortable at home?"

Dr. Lefkowitz shifted his jaw. "In my opinion, her condition is too unstable to move her home. That is… you live in Manhattan, do you not?"

"Yes, but I'd be willing to move in with her for a little while if I needed to." Willing, but not eager. He would do what he had to in order to help his mother, whatever it took to make her comfortable, though the prospect of relocating to the Bronx, even on a temporary basis, made him uneasy. The morbid thought occurred to Nate that any such move would likely be short-term, at least. He felt like a shitheel for thinking that way. He also felt guilty because he liked the distance between him and Rebecca when he was home in another borough. It allowed him to forget this was happening for a little while.

So it wasn't that he relished the doctor letting him off the hook exactly, but he was somewhat relieved when Dr. Lefkowitz shook his head. "She needs round-the-clock care. Her blood pressure has been uneven. When she has trouble breathing, she tends to panic. She's in a great deal of pain and the medication we're giving her for it makes her groggy. But you know all this."

Nate sighed and glanced at her room. "I know. I just... if there's something I can be doing to help make her more comfortable, please tell me what it is."

Dr. Lefkowitz nodded. "Keep coming to see her. She needs to know she has people who care about her."

"Okay. I will do that."

"A week ago I thought hospice was an option, but…." The doctor breathed in and out uneasily, as if he were deeply unhappy about this situation. "I'll be honest. I'm sorry to say, she seems to be declining slowly. Her condition is stable, but I can't predict how much longer that will be the case. Probably not that much longer."

"I understand," Nate said, feeling strangely numb. The news felt meaningless considering how unstable she looked to him. And none of this was news; the doctor had already told him the previous week that he'd be surprised if she made it another two months. Once they'd determined she was too weak to handle chemo, this whole process became waiting for the inevitable.

"She's sleeping, but you should go in and see her. Sit with her for a little while. Talk to her if she wakes up. All right, son?"

"Yes. Thanks, Doctor."

Nate couldn't comprehend what "stable" could mean in the context of what he saw when he entered his mother's hospital room. He was grateful the other bed in the room was empty. They couldn't afford a private room, but there was already so much death and sadness around the oncology ward that Nate didn't think he could take the presence of another cancer patient in this space. And now here was his mother, lying on the bed, asleep but not looking especially peaceful. Her skin seemed to lack any color and her gray-streaked blonde hair was tied away from her face in a messy ponytail. She had tubes in her nose, an IV in her hand, machines measuring her vitals.

This was stable? Stable to Nate would have meant the ability to leave the hospital, but he realized with horror now that she probably never would. To have to die in such a place…. He didn't wish that on anyone.

He sat in an ugly orange chair next to the bed. He took one of her hands. Her skin looked like crepe paper, but it felt soft against his fingers. She sighed in her sleep.

"I hope you *are* comfortable, Mom," he said softly.

She wheezed and then opened her eyes. She gazed at him for a moment. "Nate."

"Hi, Mom. Good afternoon."

"What, um, what day is it?" She struggled to sit up against her pillows.

Nate reached over and adjusted the bed so she could sit comfortably. "Sunday."

Her eyes widened. "I missed church."

Nate hesitated a moment before he spoke, gathering the energy, because the coming discussion already exhausted him. "You're in the hospital, Mom. You can't go to church. But I imagine Father Egan would be willing to come here to the hospital. Would you like me to talk to him?" Nate couldn't imagine anything worse than talking to the homophobic priest who presided over his mother's church, but if it would bring her comfort, he'd do it.

Rebecca looked around the room and seemed to remember all at once that she was sick and in the hospital. "Oh.". She closed her eyes briefly and then looked at Nate. "Would you tell him I'm here?"

"I will." But maybe he could do it over the phone so as not to look the judgmental prick in the eye.

Not that Nate was bitter.

Rebecca nodded and laid her head back on her pillows. "How is baseball?"

"Good. I can throw a curveball now without beaning the batter, so that's progress."

She smiled. "How's work?"

He patted her hand. She just wanted small talk, and he appreciated that. So they chatted about nothing meaningful. It felt surreal to be here with her in the hospital and talk like they used to in the evenings when she made dinner. On nights he hadn't gone to the Ruiz apartment, he would come home and sit in the kitchen while his mother made dinner. They'd talk about their day then. She'd ask what he was learning in school, what books he was reading, what his friends were up to. It felt strange to remember that now, like it had happened in a different lifetime. Had they been close once? He supposed they had, when Nate had been very young. When had they become so estranged?

Once Father Egan had gotten certain ideas into Rebecca's head, Nate supposed, although the priest wasn't the only problem. Nate and his mother didn't have much in common. She wasn't interested in baseball, he didn't read the same kinds of books she did, and often they had very little to talk about. His love life was a forbidden topic; she would feign interest in who he was dating occasionally but always got that look on her face like she disapproved of whatever he was doing, so he stopped trying.

No sense in dwelling on that now. She had only a limited amount of time left, and he wanted to make it as good for her as he could. No rehashing old arguments or deliberately making her uncomfortable, though he'd done plenty of that over the years. He didn't see the purpose of it now.

When a nurse stuck her head in to remind him that Rebecca needed rest, Nate leaned down and kissed his mother's cheek. "If you need anything, Mom, please tell me, okay?"

She nodded. "Can you bring more books the next time you come? I've read all the ones you brought last time." When Nate glanced toward the side table where he'd been putting them and saw no books, she said, "I let one of the nurses have them. She shares them with the other patients."

"Oh. Yeah, of course. No problem. I'll bring you more books. Anything else?"

"That's all I can think of. Thank you."

"You're welcome. I'll be back Wednesday because I have a game Tuesday. I'll bring you some books. Is that okay?"

"Yes, that's fine. Anytime you can come is fine."

He nodded. "All right. Have the nurse call me if you can think of anything else."

"I love you, Nathan."

"Yeah. Love you too, Mom."

Chapter 5

CARLOS CARRIED a box that smelled faintly of hairspray into a salon. He looked around at everyone busily painting or unpacking boxes. They were setting up Patrick's new space, a salon in the East Village that he was opening with his friend and new business partner Valerie. Carlos didn't know this for sure, but he was pretty sure Mason was the primary investor in this particular business. Not that it mattered; Carlos was just here as physical labor.

"Put that box over at the second station." Patrick pointed.

Carlos complied. When he opened the box to unpack it, Ty wandered over. He gave the box a wary look. "I suppose this is what you'd call 'product.'" Ty made finger quotes. His Texas accent was thick.

"It's not so bad," Carlos said. "A little gel in your hair? You might look pretty slick."

Ty touched his head. His red hair was cut short these days. "I don't think so."

Carlos laughed.

Patrick breezed over and shooed them both out of the way. "No, no, the hairspray goes on the top shelf, like this."

Ty held up his hands and backed up. "There anything else in the van?"

Patrick handed him the keys. "Why don't you go check instead of getting in my way?"

"Might as well come with me," Ty said to Carlos.

So Carlos followed Ty outside and down the street to the van they had rented to move Patrick's equipment and supplies to the new salon. As Ty unlocked the back doors and opened them, Carlos's phone buzzed in his pocket. It was a text from Aiden.

"Dear Lord, how much styling shit does that kid need?" Ty asked. He leaned forward and grabbed one of the two remaining boxes. "You gonna help or what?"

"I gotta text Aiden back or he's gonna get pissy."

Ty stood back up, leaving the box behind, and narrowed his eyes. "He's gonna what now? He's been texting you all morning, hasn't he?"

Carlos sighed and rolled his eyes. "Aiden and I had kind of an epic fight last weekend over the fact that he texted me about forty thousand times while I was out with you all Friday night and I failed to answer any of those texts because I didn't feel my phone vibrate. Now if I don't respond promptly, he gets mad."

Ty leaned back a little and crossed his arms. "You had an epic fight about some fucking text messages?"

"I know. Just… let me answer him. He's just checking up on me."

"Checking up on you?"

Carlos looked up from his phone. Ty's face had gone wide-eyed with surprise.

"What?" Carlos asked.

"No offense, darlin', but it seems to me that your boyfriend has a wee bit of a controlling streak."

"Yeah, I… yeah." Carlos frowned at his phone, which buzzed with another message.

"Not one of his more endearing traits, I take it."

Carlos sighed. "No. And we've been fighting a lot lately. He just… I don't know. He was so sweet and amazing when we first hooked up, and I really thought living together would be okay. It was fun at first, but lately we just bicker all the time. But that's kind of normal, right? Relationships have ups and downs. I mean, you and Ian fight, don't you?"

"Sure, we fight sometimes. Not too often. Also, I think sometimes Ian picks fights with me entirely so that we can have wild makeup sex." Ty winked. "I mean, nothing better than makeup sex, am I right?"

"That's kind of gross, Ty."

Ty laughed and shrugged. "Hey, just saying. But you know what else? Do you see Ian checking up on me right now? Nope. That's because if I say, 'I'm gonna help Patrick move his smelly styling products into the new salon,' he gives me a kiss and says, 'See ya later,' and trusts that I'm doing what I say I'm doing. Is Aiden really trusting you if he has to check up on you so often?"

Carlos sighed. Ty was merely saying what Carlos had been thinking all week. "I just don't want to fight anymore."

"You sure Aiden is really the right guy for you if he's making you this miserable?"

Carlos honestly wasn't sure anymore. And he was amazed by Ty's insight, which felt right on the money. But he said, "I'm not miserable. It's just... adjustment. I'm still getting used to living with him."

"Right, sure."

"At least Nate's not here."

Ty balked. "Christ. What did Nate do now?"

"Nothing. Aiden thinks Nate is in love with me, so he's crazy jealous and he gets especially weird when I hang out with Nate."

Ty laughed, a big boisterous body laugh that had him bent over for a moment. "Oh Lord. You boys have some drama to work out."

Carlos wondered what was so funny.

Ty recovered from his fit quickly. He sniffed and reached for the box again. "Look. Every relationship is different. I'm not saying Ian and I are a model of anything. All I know is that, yeah, Ian and I fight sometimes. Sometimes it's about stupid shit. Ian likes everything to be in specific places, and I forget and put things away wrong sometimes. That kind of thing. Sometimes we argue about more important stuff too, but we always try to find a resolution. Because you know what? We live together and get in each other's way sometimes, but we love and trust each other too, and at the end of the day? There is no one I want to be with more than Ian. I'm the luckiest guy in New York because I go to bed next to him every night and I wake up thinking about him and I wouldn't have it any other way. Can you say that about Aiden?"

Carlos didn't know. Actually, if he was honest, the person he thought about at the end of the day the most often was probably Nate, especially through their weird estrangement and makeup. And what did that say?

"Maybe that's something to think about," Ty said softly, as if he'd heard Carlos's thoughts.

"Yeah," Carlos said.

"All right, then. So instead of twiddling your thumbs, why don't you grab that other box? The sooner we finish getting Patrick settled, the sooner we can break for dinner. I want a big sandwich from that place on St. Mark's in the worst way."

"YOU'RE THROWING curveballs on purpose."

As Nate watched, Carlos took a deep breath and resumed his stance. He was glad Nate had picked up a new pitch and was having success with it, but that success was frustrating because Carlos couldn't hit these balls.

"Anticipate it," Nate said. "Assume it's going to go a little to the right."

"It looks like a fastball from here."

"Then I'm doing it right. Try again."

Scott looked on, his eyebrows raised. Nate wondered if he was stealing Scott's thunder by coaching Carlos, but he kept at it anyway. A line of Hipsters waited to bat, but none of them looked especially anxious to face the dread curveball.

Nate wound up and pitched to Carlos, who furrowed his brow in concentration, leaned a little to his right, and connected his bat with the ball. Foul tip, sure, but at least he didn't whiff it.

"Next!" called Scott.

Carlos tossed the bat in the air. It clanged against the backstop as he walked around it to get back in line.

He'd been like that all day, irritable and unhappy, easily frustrated. Not that Carlos was the most easygoing guy Nate knew, but he usually wasn't quite this out of sorts. When Nate had asked earlier, Carlos had said, "Eh, Aiden and I have been fighting a lot."

It shouldn't have given Nate hope. He was so far beyond hope at this point. Carlos clearly preferred staying with the boyfriend he seemed to fight with all the time. Ship had sailed. Nate had lost.

The fastball he threw Ian, who was next up at bat, might have been a little aggressive.

"Jesus, Nate," Ian said as he hopped out of the way.

"Eighty-seven miles an hour!" crowed Scott, who perhaps had missed the point. He held up the speed gun and waved it in the air triumphantly.

Andreas sauntered up next. He sent Nate a wink before he lifted his bat. Nate's heart fluttered a little. He wasn't quite sure what to make of Andreas beyond his being hot and flirty. And not that he was even in Andreas's league, but if Andreas asked him out, it would be pretty hard to say no. Actually, now that Nate thought about what it might be like to get his hands on that ass….

Although there was Carlos, scowling at him from behind the backstop.

After practice, everyone descended on the cowboy bar, which Nate almost opted out of on the assumption Aiden would show up. But Carlos hung on his arm and said, "I haven't been able to do this in so long. You have to come," and Nate couldn't say no. Carlos had smiled for the first time that day as he'd asked. That was irresistible.

"Are you coming, Andreas?" Nate asked his would-be paramour.

"Oh, my dear, unfortunately no. I cannot make it tonight. Next week, though."

Lord, his voice was smooth as butter. It took a moment for Nate to realize he'd been denied. He almost didn't mind. "Next time," Nate said, convincing himself it was something to look forward to.

Andreas leaned over and kissed Nate's cheek before he left. Oof, he even smelled good.

"Come on, Romeo," Ty said.

"Is Aiden coming tonight?" Nate asked.

Carlos grunted. "Yeah. When I told him I was coming out with you guys tonight instead of going home and that he could suck it, he insisted on coming along."

"Charming," said Nate.

As they walked through the park toward the bar, Ty offered to restrain Nate if needed. Nate hoped Carlos didn't hear. Although honestly, of all the controlling bullshit. Was Carlos not autonomous enough to go out with his friends without boyfriend supervision?

Aiden was indeed sitting at the bar when they walked in. Carlos went straight to him and gave him a quick peck on the lips. "Hi, *papi*," he said with a smile.

Nate almost walked out.

"Come on," Ty said, hooking an arm around Nate's and leading him to a table in the back of the bar. "Don't get bent out of shape."

"I should be over it," Nate said.

Ty let go of his arm and shrugged. "You feel what you feel."

It had gotten worse lately. When Carlos and Nate weren't talking, it was easier to be angry, to push his feelings aside, to wallow in the fact that Carlos and Aiden were a couple and Nate had lost. But when they were actually in good standing with each other, when they saw each other frequently, that old yearning got worse. Tasting what things could be like had reignited his craving.

Hell, this had been going on for two years. Nate was a fucking idiot.

It had been rough, that moment when he realized his feelings had shifted from friendship to something more romantic, when he started picturing cohabiting with Carlos, when he jerked off thinking about what sex between them would be like. That dimension of their relationship would probably only ever exist in his head, but he wanted it so bad he could taste it. And apparently absence had only made his heart grow fonder, because despite being angry and irritated with Carlos, he wanted Carlos now more than he ever had.

"Why can't I just move on?" he asked Ty quietly as they sat down. "I felt nothing but friendship for him for years and years. Then all of a sudden, two years ago, we're both single at the same time for a change and I looked at him and thought, 'Well, hey, I'm attracted to him.' I guess it wasn't sudden or anything, but just... I mean, we'd both dated plenty of other people. And of course, as soon as I get there, Carlos turns and goes out with Aiden."

"It sucks, man," Ian said, sitting down next to Ty. He leaned his head on Ty's shoulder. Seeing the happy couple didn't really help Nate.

No, being around happy couples made Nate feel sad and bitter. As most of his friends were happily coupled, it was somewhat inescapable. It nagged at him. But geez, when had he become this person? He didn't really begrudge other people's happiness. He hated that he'd become so jaded.

He'd tried. He'd gone on dates. This past winter he'd had a six-week affair with a hedge-fund manager who liked spending his money on Nate, and that was kind of fun, but that guy had been about as deep as a cookie sheet. And then there was Andreas.

Nate let out a sigh.

"You'll meet the right guy," Ian said.

"Yeah," said Nate, not believing it. "Hey, I want a beer. You guys want anything?"

"Sure," said Ty. Ty predictably rattled off the name of the Texas-brewed beer the bar had on tap, and Ian said he'd have the same.

So Nate got up and walked to the bar, where Carlos and Aiden were being nauseatingly sweet with each other, Aiden's arm hooked around Carlos's waist. They were talking with their faces close to each other. Nate ordered beers for himself, Ty, and Ian.

While he waited for the bartender to pour, he glanced back at the happy couple—just in time to see Carlos jerk backward suddenly, out of Aiden's hold.

"Really? Are we still arguing about that?" Carlos said.

Aiden looked up and met Nate's gaze. His eyebrows came together in a point.

Nate hoped the bartender would figure out how to pour faster.

Carlos turned around. "Nate, you should—"

"I don't want to get involved." Nate held up his hands.

Carlos turned back to Aiden, so Nate couldn't see his face. His body language was tense, though. Nate didn't like that, felt defensive about it. Part of Nate wanted to march in and rescue Carlos from a situation that was clearly making him unhappy.

But was it really? Was Carlos actually upset? Maybe they were just having a brief bit of tension, but he was otherwise happy. No, of course that was what it was.

The bartender finally finished pouring the last beer. Nate breathed a sigh of relief and carefully picked up all three glasses.

He sat with Ty and Ian, and they talked, mostly rehashing practice and their last game. Ty and Ian had plenty of praise for Nate's pitching, but Nate's attention was still on Carlos. He and Aiden seemed to argue quietly for a few more minutes, but eventually they must have made up, because they were making out. Just like old times.

Nate sighed. "I think I'm gonna go home," he told Ty and Ian, standing up.

"You can't keep letting him make you feel this way," Ian said.

"Easy for you to say. He's not the love of your life."

"Nate."

Nate waved his hand. "It's fine. I should go up to the hospital and see my mom before it gets too late anyway."

He spared a glance for the happy couple on his way out of the bar. After all this time, it shouldn't have hurt so much. But it did.

He was tempted to text Andreas, whose number he'd scored that first night they'd had drinks after practice. Maybe mindless sex with a hot guy would take his mind off this. But no, that would only be a temporary solution. Besides, Andreas had ditched drinks with his teammates. He was probably busy, or maybe even fucking somebody else. Not that taking the subway up to the Bronx to see his mother was exactly a happy distraction either.

He wanted to scream. He stood on the subway platform and wanted to shout until he was hoarse. He stayed quiet, though, and as the train pulled into the station, he tried to accept his fate.

Chapter 6

WHEN CARLOS got home from Tuesday night's game, in which the Mermaids soundly defeated the Hipsters, Aiden was sitting on the sofa staring intently at the TV.

"How was the game?" he asked, venom in his voice.

For the first time, in that single moment, Carlos thought, *I can't do this anymore*. "Fine," he said.

Aiden nodded. "Mermaids beat you?"

"Of course." The Queens had played the Mermaids the week before, so Aiden knew full well how unbeatable they were. The Mermaids were one of the Rainbow League's two all-female teams, and they consistently made it to the finals every year.

"You go out after?" Aiden asked. "You're home kind of late."

"Well, I had *a* beer. Nate wanted to commiserate over the fact that we got pounded so badly." Carlos had deliberately invoked Nate—Nate had actually kept his distance most of the evening, and it was Ty who had insisted Carlos should stay for one drink—because now he was spoiling for a fight. They needed to have this out so they could put it behind them, or Carlos needed to leave.

"Nate," Aiden said.

Which, bingo.

"Yup."

Aiden grimaced and shook his head. "You spent time with Nate."

"He's my friend. My best friend." Carlos worried he was being too defensive, but Aiden's tone indicated he was displeased with the situation. So Carlos plowed forward. "I've tried explaining that he's no threat to you and you choose not to believe me, so it's not my problem anymore. I'm sick of defending our friendship."

Aiden stood up. "It's very much your problem if you're spending so much time with him." He took a couple of steps toward Carlos.

"Look, you trust me or you don't. I tell you that there's nothing between me and Nate except friendship, which is the goddamn truth, and you believe it or you don't. If you don't believe me, well, we have a problem. I can't keep having this argument with you. I can't."

Aiden looked angry, but he blew out a breath, making the fringe of hair on his forehead fly up comically. Carlos might have laughed if he wasn't so angry. "Fine," Aiden said. "I believe you. It's him I don't trust."

"Aiden—"

"I don't care. He has feelings for you."

"It doesn't matter how Nate feels if I'm in love with you, does it?" Though Carlos still didn't believe it could be true. Nate had only ever looked at Carlos with friendship in his eyes. They were close, sure, but it wasn't sexual or romantic.

Not that Nate was bad-looking, because actually, Carlos had thought for a while that he was pretty sexy, and if Nate were interested....

No, he couldn't go down that train track. He was with Aiden, who loved him, whom he loved. He was just frustrated right now because of the fatigue from this fucking endless fight.

"I guess you're right," Aiden said.

"See? Can we get past this? Because if we can't, maybe I shouldn't be here anymore."

Aiden's eyebrows came together and he pressed his lips into a thin line before he said, "So you want to leave me."

"No! No, I don't want to, but I don't have it in me to defend myself or Nate anymore. I need you to trust me. If you don't, what kind of relationship do we have?"

"Because you really want to be with Nate."

"No, I don't. Goddammit, Aiden, how can you—"

"How can *you*? I love you, Carlos, but I just don't trust—"

"Then maybe I *should* leave."

"No, baby. No. I just get mad about Nate because I love you so much." Aiden stepped closer to Carlos and ran a hand down his arm.

"You have a strange way of showing it."

"What, you don't believe me?"

Carlos about lost it. He groaned. "God, you frustrate me."

"Because things would be so goddamned perfect with Nate, wouldn't they?"

"Damn it, Aiden. I just can't. There's nothing going on with me and Nate! Get that through your skull!"

"And you'd rather spend time with your teammates than with me!"

"You and I just spent almost all weekend together! I see you all the time! We live together. We spend a lot of time together."

"Yeah, fighting."

"Whose fault is that? If you didn't—"

"Oh, don't even. Don't even get started. I'm not the one at fault here. I'm not—"

"You never let things go! You never—"

Carlos felt the sting before he realized what had happened.

Aiden had slapped him.

He relived the moment as if it were in slow motion as he stared at the floor. Aiden's face had gone red and then he'd hauled off and slapped Carlos right across the cheek.

Carlos took a step back. "That's it. I'm out of here."

He checked his pockets for his wallet and keys, and then he headed out the door.

NATE WAS halfway asleep when the buzzer for his apartment started blaring like a fire engine. It took him a moment to realize the sound was in his apartment and not outside. At first he dismissed it as kids horsing around—not the first time he'd gotten a prank buzzer—but something about the insistence and repetition with which it buzzed made him get out of bed and answer it. He hit the intercom button and said, "Hello?"

"It's Carlos. Can I come up?"

Nate hit the door button without a second thought.

When Carlos knocked a minute later, Nate opened the door and found him standing there, still in his Hipsters uniform T-shirt and the jeans he'd changed into after the game, his hair disheveled, with a cut on his cheek that hadn't been there earlier in the evening.

"Can I stay here for a few days?" Carlos asked.

"Yeah." Nate blinked at Carlos sleepily. "Of course. Come in."

Nate ushered Carlos inside and looked him over. Carlos didn't have anything on him—no overnight bag, no jacket, nothing. He looked rattled.

"Are you okay?" Nate asked, still not quite firing on all cylinders. What the hell was happening here? "What's going on?"

Carlos gestured to his face. "Aiden hit me."

"He *hit* you?" Nate thought for a moment that his half-asleep foggy brain was keeping him from truly understanding the situation, although the word "hit" had him on his toes, ready to pound the stuffing out of Aiden.

"I mean, not in an abusive boyfriend way or anything. We were having a fight that got heated and I think he just got overexcited. He's never done it before. I didn't think he had a violent bone in his body."

"He hit you."

"Just a slap."

"On your face, by the look of it." Nate reached over and ran his thumb lightly over the cut on Carlos's cheek. Carlos winced.

"He wears a ring on his right hand. Gift from his mother. Must have nicked me with it."

Nate's heart went out to Carlos as he imagined how terrifying it must have been to feel the full brunt of Aiden's rage. Nate felt some of that rage when he was in Aiden's orbit, but then, Aiden didn't much like Nate. Nate could only imagine what the brute force of Aiden's anger would feel like. And Carlos was here now. He'd done the right thing by leaving Aiden. And he'd left without taking any stuff with him, so he was probably seriously freaking out.

Nate pulled him into a hug and held him close. "Stay as long as you need to."

"Just a day or two, probably. Until Aiden cools off."

"You're going *back?*"

Carlos sighed and pushed away from Nate. "Please don't. I can't deal with another huffy, stubborn man tonight."

"But… he hit you."

"I'm aware. And I don't know what I'm going to do yet. I told him I can't keep having the same fight. I think we're just going through a rough patch. Maybe it will get better. Maybe it won't. But I'm the one who has to figure it out. I know you're not exactly Aiden's biggest fan, but you have to let me work this out on my own, okay? I can't take anyone else pushing me around right now."

Nate let out a breath, trying to keep his emotions from bubbling over. He felt so much now: fury at Aiden, sympathy for Carlos, frustration at his inability to help. "Okay. Couch is yours. Like I said, stay as long as you need to. You're always welcome. You want something to wear?"

Carlos looked down as if he were just now noticing he'd never gotten around to changing out of his uniform. "Yeah, that would be good. Just sweats or something to sleep in. Maybe I can borrow some clothes in the morning? I'll go home tomorrow while Aiden's at work and pick up some things."

Nate nodded. He and Carlos were about the same size and had been swapping clothes since they were kids, so that wasn't anything new. "Anything you need. I've got an extra toothbrush too, I think."

"Thanks, Nate."

"For what it's worth, I'm sorry you have to go through all this."

Carlos nodded sadly. "Yeah. I really thought… well, I don't know what I thought." He sat on the couch. "Not that anything like this would happen."

Nate went back into his bedroom to grab a pair of sweats for Carlos to wear. He tried not to feel hopeful about the imminent dissolution of Carlos's relationship with Aiden. This was much worse than anything Nate had ever imagined. Nate had been suspicious of Aiden from the beginning, thinking he was a bad match for Carlos and was bound to do him harm eventually. He hadn't anticipated actual violence. Really, he'd been telling himself for most of the past year that his antipathy for Aiden was born of jealousy, not anything Aiden was doing. He wasn't sure how to feel about his hunch being on the money after all. Carlos had done the right thing by leaving, but Nate wasn't sure if it was right for him to say so.

He pulled out a pair of sweats and then a pair of jeans and a T-shirt. He grabbed an extra blanket from the closet and a pillow off his bed. As he carried these out to Carlos, he felt heavy.

It wasn't how this was supposed to go.

Although what was "this"? This was Nate helping out a friend. It wasn't romance; he had no hope for the future he wanted. It was just Carlos, Nate's oldest, dearest friend, a man Nate loved more than himself, a member of his family. They were bound together by years, by love, by baseball. This was Nate being there for Carlos the way he always had been, the way Carlos would have been there for him had their positions been reversed.

Carlos sat on the sofa, looking dazed, staring at his phone.

"He's texted me about twenty times." Carlos turned his phone off and tossed it on the coffee table.

Nate wanted to hold Carlos, wanted to touch him and comfort him. He wanted to make Carlos, their lives, everything okay. But this situation, it wasn't okay. Nothing about Carlos sitting on that sofa was okay.

"Think these jeans will fit you?" Nate asked.

"You're skinnier than me these days, *papi*. I bet Mama Lulu yells at you to eat more every time she sees you."

"She does usually feed me."

Carlos smiled faintly. "Me too. Let me see." He motioned for Nate to pass him the pile of stuff. He settled the blanket and pillow in his lap, then put the clothes on the coffee table. He checked the label on the jeans and whistled. "Wow, when did you start buying classy jeans?"

Nate shrugged. "They fit well."

Carlos unfolded them and held them up. He turned them around. "Oh, yeah. I recognize the pattern on the pockets. They do make your ass look good."

Nate felt a flush go through him. "You noticed that, huh?"

"Hard not to."

"Worth every penny, then."

Carlos chuckled. "They might be a little tight on me, but I'll manage." He put the jeans down. He leaned into the sofa and rested his head on the back. He looked up at Nate. "What the fuck am I going to do?" He looked utterly lost, his face a tangled mess of confusion.

Nate moved into action. "Right now, you're going to change out of your uniform and then you're going to sleep on my couch. In the morning we'll get breakfast at the café on the corner because I know you like their scones."

Carlos nodded thoughtfully. "That is true. God, I miss living in this neighborhood. Brooklyn's got some good stuff, but it's not the same."

Nate swallowed, not allowing himself to feel pain or hope, focusing all of his attention on Carlos and what Carlos needed. "After tomorrow, who knows? You'll figure it out. I know you will."

Carlos rubbed his eyes. "I'm so tired."

"I'll leave you alone to sleep. Holler if you need me."

"I will. Thanks again."

"Anytime." Nate took another deep breath, trying to keep calm. "For what it's worth, I'm glad you came here. I'm here for you, okay?"

"Yes." Carlos leaned back on the sofa and closed his eyes. "You're a good friend."

Nate couldn't speak, so he nodded and went to his room.

Chapter 7

CARLOS HELD his breath as he unlocked the door to Aiden's apartment. To *his* apartment. It was the space he'd called home for the last several months. Since Aiden had been there for a few years before Carlos moved in, it still felt like Aiden's space, though Carlos had certainly put his own touch on the place.

Aiden worked a typical nine-to-five job in HR at a publishing company, so, figuring he wouldn't be there, Carlos snuck over during the late morning. There was still a chance, though; maybe Aiden had called out sick just as Carlos had.

But he hadn't; the apartment was empty. Carlos took a deep breath and walked to the bedroom. He grabbed his old backpack and stuffed in three days' worth of clothes, his shaving kit, and all the other sundries he needed.

It was just temporary. He kept reminding himself that. He'd only be staying with Nate a few days. Something was up with Aiden and he was acting like a strange angry alien, but he'd be better soon enough. Everything would go back to normal. Carlos wouldn't leave him without giving him the chance to prove the night before had been a fluke. They'd been together two years quite happily, aside from Carlos's reservations about living together. And look how that had turned out.

Although if they couldn't live together, their relationship didn't have much hope, did it?

He sighed as he looked around for whatever else he might need if he was going to stay at Nate's for the rest of the week. He wasn't really that jazzed about sleeping on Nate's lumpy couch for several more days, but he couldn't afford a hotel—not in New York—and he preferred Nate's company to anyone else's. He supposed he could have crashed at his mother's, and she kept a room open for anyone in the family who needed it, but she was all the way up in the Bronx. That was a very long ride to his job. Plus, he didn't want to worry her. Nate really was the best person to crash with, the only person he'd thought of when he decided he had to get out of this apartment. And for extra bonus points, Nate lived close to Carlos's job.

Feeling mildly guilty for just leaving, he thought about leaving a note for Aiden, but instead he sent a quick text: *Gonna stay with a friend for a few days. Text if you can talk rationally.*

He was tempted to turn his phone off as he went back outside and toward the subway.

Staying with Nate? Aiden asked.

Yes if you must know. On his couch.

A long delay—a few minutes at least—passed before Aiden texted back, *I love you. I'm so sorry. Come home.*

Not yet. Then Carlos did turn off his phone and descended the stairs to the subway.

THE YANKEES game was on the TV, but all Nate saw was indiscriminate blobs moving around on the field.

He'd been home from the hospital for about a half hour, but his mind was still up in the Bronx, fretting about the fact that his mother had wheezed through most of their visit. And yet the doctors seemed unfazed. He also couldn't get out of his mind the look on Dr. Lefkowitz's face when he'd said there was nothing more they could do. There really was nothing. No treatment would get rid of the cancer. Any treatment to slow down the pace of the metastasizing cells would probably only make her sicker in the short term. Surgery would kill her. Nate hadn't expected different news. And yet it was all the more disturbing to hear from a doctor in no uncertain terms—not for the first time—that his mother would die, and it would happen soon.

The sound of a key in the lock brought everything back into focus. Carlos came in and shot him a wary smile. "You okay?"

Nate shrugged and sat up a little straighter on the sofa. "Saw my mom today."

"How is she?"

"The same." That wasn't really a lie. Nate took a deep breath and decided to tell the truth. "I didn't really get to talk to her much because she was having trouble breathing. Her doctor told me that there isn't really anything more they can do for her besides make her as comfortable as possible while we all wait for the inevitable."

Carlos's face crumpled in sympathy. "I'm so sorry, Nate." He sat on the couch next to Nate and put a hand on his thigh, which certainly got Nate's attention.

Nate stared at Carlos's hand. "Well, I think I can say without reservation that this is basically the worst summer ever."

Carlos pulled Nate into a hug. It was a little awkward because they were both sitting, but Nate hugged him back, happy for the touch. Carlos smelled like his usual overcologned self, which Nate found comforting. His skin was warm where it touched Nate's. Nate sighed and sank into the hug.

"Thanks, Carlos."

"Of course. Anytime you need a hug, come to me."

Nate eased away. "How are you?"

"I'm tempted to block Aiden's number from my phone, but otherwise I'm all right. I got some clothes and stuff from my place today." He rubbed his face, which currently sported a few days' worth of stubble. "I need a shave in the worst way."

Nate thought he looked handsome, truth be told. "You look rugged."

"Ha."

"No, you do. I bet you'd look good with one of those close-trimmed beards. Like, remember that guy Luke who used to play for Hell's Kitchen? The one with permanent five-o'clock shadow?"

"Oh yeah. Didn't Will date him?"

"Oh." Had he? "Maybe. I don't remember. I just remember wondering a lot how he got his scruffy beard so perfect all the time." Nate rubbed his own face. "I can't grow a beard at all. It just comes in patchy and weird-looking. It's like puberty forgot to bestow that particular aspect of masculinity on me. But you. You'd look hot with a little scruff."

Carlos scrunched up his nose and shot Nate a look that indicated he thought Nate was crazy. "Shut up."

"Hey, whatever. Just saying."

Carlos turned toward the TV. "What's going on with the Yankees?"

Carlos at least knew how to lighten a mood. Nate was grateful to him for being here, even under these circumstances, because he didn't think he could get through the situation with his mother on his own.

"I've only been sort-of watching," Nate said.

"Oh, *mi hermano*, have you just been sitting here spacing out? Are things really so bad?" Carlos took Nate's hand and intertwined their fingers.

"Talk to me about baseball," Nate said, watching Carlos's face.

Carlos looked at the screen. He squinted. "Looks like the Yanks are up one run, bottom of the fourth. Uh, Robertson seems to be pitching. Gardner's about to bat." He looked at Nate and squeezed his hand. "This lineup is not so terrible as the last couple of years, yeah? Think they have a chance this year? Or are they gonna be total bums again?"

Nate turned back toward the TV. "Somehow Baltimore is unstoppable. Six games ahead, last I checked. I don't know if we'll win the division, but we've got a good shot at the wild card. I like this rookie they keep playing in right field. Lambert, I think is his name. Although that guy Banks is trouble. Did you see the fight he got into with the ump over the weekend?"

"Three-game suspension, which he deserves. That guy's a punk."

Nate sat up a little straighter. "Well, the ump kind of deserved it. It was a fair ball. Banks hit home before the ball did. Mr. Magoo would have ruled it safe, but the ump called the out? That's bullshit."

Carlos chuckled. "Right, I forgot your secret aggressive streak. I know you are always secretly pleased when a Yankee batter hits one of the Red Sox with a pitch."

Nate couldn't keep the smile off his face. "That's not really a secret. And it has the drawback of putting a guy on base." He turned back to the TV. "Seriously, though, what do you think of the Yanks' prospects? Been a few years since we even made the play-offs, but this could be the year that breaks the streak."

"Yeah, could be. Assuming they don't fuck anything up."

"Might be a tall order after last season."

"Eh, they won the other night against the Blue Jays. You see that play Sanchez made in the ninth?"

Nate squeezed Carlos's hand back, happy for the distraction. "Yeah, it was a thing of beauty."

Chapter 8

CARLOS WOKE up on Nate's couch for the third morning in a row. His first conscious thought was that his back hurt, probably because he'd twisted himself and the blanket into a pretzel over the course of the night. He grunted as he tried to straighten himself out without falling off the couch. He managed to roll onto his stomach as Nate walked out of the bathroom.

Nate's apartment was not large. It had one bedroom, one bathroom, the living room, and a microscopic kitchen. To go from the bathroom to his bedroom, Nate had to pass through part of the living room, which he did so now wearing only a towel. Carlos watched him, unaware of anything besides Nate's pale skin, his musculature, the mole on his shoulder, the light dusting of hair on his chest, the way his hips did that V thing that pointed toward his….

Oh, yikes. Carlos was staring, wasn't he? Nate was—well, not naked but as good as, and his body was… sexy. Appealing. Arousing.

"Sleep okay?" Nate asked.

"Uh." Carlos was glad he was now on his stomach so Nate couldn't see his rapidly hardening dick.

"Give me a few minutes and I'll scare up some breakfast."

Carlos propped himself up on his elbows and watched Nate go into his bedroom, pulling the towel off as he closed the door. Carlos got the briefest glimpses of Nate's ass as the door closed. It looked so… smooth and… grabbable.

Ay Dios mío, what was wrong with him?

Nate came back out a minute later, dressed for work. "By breakfast, I meant cereal. I assume you're going to your office today?"

"Yeah. Guess I have to."

Nate went into the kitchen and started banging around. Carlos rolled into a sitting position, pulled the blanket over his lap, and made a show of rubbing his eyes while he waited for his erection to subside. This was dumb. Nate wasn't the man Carlos wanted. Sure, he looked good even in his casual work clothes, dark jeans and a nicely tailored plaid shirt, and... oh, there was his ass again, covered in denim this time, but *still*.

Carlos hopped up and ran toward the bathroom inside of three seconds.

When he walked back to the kitchen a minute later, Nate had poured two bowls of cereal and was giving Carlos a weird look. "You okay?"

"Fine. Just noticed I had to pee all of a sudden."

"Right. Well. Cereal's up."

They ate together and talked about nonsense. Carlos was only half in it, fretting now about Nate and his grabbable ass.

Later, as he walked to the subway headed toward his office, he reasoned that maybe he was just hard up. He hadn't had sex in a couple of weeks now, since he and Aiden had been fighting for so long. He was just horny and Nate was the closest male. Of course Carlos was feeling a pull toward him. Just proximity. No big.

Carlos strolled into the Center for New Civil Rights Policy, the nonprofit he'd been working at for the past few years, ever since he'd quit his corporate law job in a blaze of glory. He felt like a cliché sometimes, one of many people who had joyfully triumphed over law school only to discover that the actual practice of law sucked out loud. His law school class boasted a good number of ex-lawyers. But Carlos had settled into this job advising a group of activist types, and he found the work rewarding, though he'd had to take a pretty serious pay cut. He supposed he was kind of their dream lawyer, being both gay and Latino, since most of their work was done in the interest of the civil rights of all manner of lesser-represented members of society.

He walked past his assistant, Sonia, who immediately stood and trailed him into the office.

"Did something happen with you and Aiden?" she asked.

"Why?"

"He's called here about eight times already this morning."

"Eight?"

She shrugged. "I'm exaggerating a little. More than once, though."

"I'll take care of it. Anything else?"

"Nothing pressing. You've got that meeting at eleven with Linda Marsden."

"All right, thanks."

He sat at his desk and stared at the phone for a long time. He turned on his computer, contemplating whether to call Aiden as his e-mail loaded. No, he wasn't ready yet. But what if something happened? He didn't want to talk to Aiden unless he'd come to his senses. Unfortunately, now he was obsessing, and before he finished reading the first message, he had picked up his phone and was dialing Aiden's cell phone number.

"Carlos, thank God," Aiden said as soon as he picked up.

"Please stop pestering my assistant."

"You wouldn't take my calls."

"I needed time. I wish you would respect that." Carlos took a deep breath. "We're talking now. What do you have to say?"

"Okay, I know you're mad. And I am so sorry I hit you. That was wrong of me. Very wrong. I feel awful about it. I overreacted, okay? I just, I don't know, lost my mind. Temporary madness. I swear to you, I'll never do it again."

Carlos believed him. The remorse in his voice was palpable. But he knew he couldn't cave. "All right. But the bigger issue is your weird jealousy. I'm really sick of fighting about the same things over and over."

"I'm sorry, it's just… I love you so much. I want you to stay with me. The thought of you with someone else makes me feel crazy."

Carlos didn't find that especially reassuring. "I wish you would just believe me. If I tell you that you have nothing to worry about and I'd never cheat on you, that should be the end of it. If I want to spend time with Nate, who is my very good friend, I need you to let me do that without losing your mind. I need you to trust me, or this is never going to work."

"If I promise to try, will you come home?"

It wasn't like Carlos wanted his relationship to fail. He wanted to go home to his boyfriend. Two years together was no joke, and he wanted this man he'd fallen for, whom he'd invested time in, whom he'd built a home with, to be able to welcome him home.

"I want to."

"Please, Carlos. Please come home."

Carlos took a deep breath. "Let's have dinner tonight."

"Dinner. I can do that. Come to Brooklyn?"

"Yeah. I'm not making any promises, but let's talk it out a little more, okay?"

"Yes," Aiden said. "I want that. We'll talk it out. Everything will be great."

They made arrangements, and Carlos felt pretty good about it. They'd figure it out. Things seemed a bit less bleak.

ONE OF Nate's favorite TV guilty pleasures, a dishy cable cooking competition show, was on the screen, but he wasn't really seeing it. It was coming up on 11:00 pm and Carlos still wasn't home.

Although geez, it wasn't like Nate's apartment was Carlos's real home. Maybe it *should* have been. Nate wanted it to be. But Carlos had his own life with his own plans, and Nate getting all bent out of shape with worry was ridiculous, because it wasn't like Carlos was his boyfriend. Nate had no reason to do anything except chill out and watch TV.

Except he was worried. His fretting was a full-on cold sweat, stomach-churning panic as he imagined Carlos beaten to death and left for dead in a gutter or a dumpster or something, and he was never coming home, and oh, where the hell was he?

The key turned in the lock a moment later, thank goodness. Nate let out a breath and tried to stop panting as the door opened.

Carlos gave him a sheepish smile as he came into the apartment. The door slammed shut behind him as he put his stuff on the floor near the kitchen. His hair was disheveled, his clothes a little off kilter, and he....

Nate knew instantly what had happened. His heart sank.

"So I had dinner with Aiden," Carlos said, confirming Nate's suspicion.

"And?" Nate was angry on top of still being unable to shake his worry. Carlos should have known better.

Instead, Carlos shrugged like it was no big deal. "And I believe him when he says he's sorry. I wanted one more night away, but I'll get out of your hair tomorrow."

"It's really not an imposition, you know. You can stay as long as you want to."

"I want to go home."

That little plaintive thought spoken aloud, and all the longing in Carlos's voice, just flayed Nate. Carlos's home was not here in this apartment but across the river in Brooklyn, with Aiden. Realizing that felt like Carlos had ripped Nate's chest open so he could thrust the knife directly into Nate's heart. Not that Nate had any expectations here, but the finality of Carlos's decision hung in the air and reminded Nate that no matter how convinced he was that he and Carlos belonged together, Carlos disagreed, so what Nate most wanted would never happen.

"What's that look on your face about?" Carlos asked. "You think I'm making a mistake, don't you."

"It's not my place to—"

"Jesus, Nate." Carlos plopped down on the sofa next to Nate and reached over to touch his thigh. His hand was hot. It felt wrong there. "Don't be all polite. I want your opinion."

"Well, I mean, he *hit* you."

"I know. And I really think it was a fluke. He just lost his mind and overreacted. He's never done anything like this before and he's been nothing but apologetic since."

"How can you know it was a one-time thing? How can you know he won't lose his mind again?"

Carlos sighed. "Because I've been dating him for two years and living with him for six months and he's never demonstrated that he has a violent bone in his body? I think he just temporarily lost it and I believe him when he says it won't happen again. Maybe that's naïve, but I know him a hell of a lot better than you do."

Nate didn't like the defensiveness in Carlos's tone or that he'd caused it to be there. "That's true. I just worry."

"I know. And I'm glad. Not that you worry, but that you care about me so much. That means a lot to me."

Carlos's gaze settled on the middle of Nate's chest for a moment. Nate wasn't wearing anything special, just track pants and a Hipsters T-shirt from a few seasons back. Nate had put on a little weight since then and the shirt was on the tight side, but he couldn't fathom why Carlos was staring.

Except... oh, he blinked and seemed to focus again. Carlos wasn't staring at Nate, he was just staring.

"I can't sleep on your couch forever," Carlos said, looking up and meeting Nate's gaze.

"No, I know."

"I mean, my back would never recover."

Carlos was kidding and Nate knew it, but Nate still touched his shoulder. "Don't just move back in with Aiden because my couch is uncomfortable."

Carlos shrugged him off. "I'm not. I was kidding."

"I'll take the couch tonight if you want."

"No, it's fine. It's really not a big deal. And just one more night." Carlos took a deep breath and put his hands in his lap. "I do really appreciate you letting me stay here, but it's time to go home to my boyfriend if I want to salvage my relationship."

Nate wanted to protest. He didn't think Carlos should want to salvage the relationship. He wanted to point out how much better a boyfriend he would be than Aiden. He wanted to point out that the relationship might not be worth saving. But he said none of these things, he just nodded. Then he said, "The couch will still be here if things don't work out."

Carlos nodded. "Am I making a mistake?"

Nate didn't know how to answer beyond saying, "It's your call, really."

Carlos tilted his head and gave Nate an appraising look. "I appreciate your trying to stay out of it."

Nate grunted.

Carlos leaned close to Nate. He still pressed his warm hand against Nate's thigh. He looked directly at Nate's face, his gaze seeming to bore into Nate's eyes. "Come on, it's not like you to keep quiet like this. You never had a problem opening your mouth before."

"And look where it got me." Nate was finding Carlos's presence a little unsettling, mostly because Carlos smelled really good. Sort of musky and warm and also something that wasn't normally Carlos's scent.

Aiden's cologne, probably.

Damn.

Nate shook his head. "I get it. I'm an asshole. I told you from day one that I didn't really trust Aiden, and I don't know, maybe it was irrational, but maybe I was onto something. I mean, to hear you tell it, your last week with Aiden before you left was basically one big fight that ended with him slapping you across the face. Is that something a good boyfriend would do? No. Not in my opinion. But the last time I gave you my opinion about Aiden, you shut me out and barely talked to me for months. I don't want that to happen again. So I'll keep my mouth shut in order to keep you as my friend and in my life."

"Nate."

"And I realize I just told you plenty, but it's nothing you haven't heard before. I'm really done now."

"You're looking after me."

"That's… diplomatic." But true, in a way. Nate had wanted only for Carlos to be happy. Well, he wanted to be with Carlos, but if Carlos was happy, he supposed that was really the endgame. Nate still probably would have been a jealous monster if Carlos had fallen in love with a good man, but maybe he'd be able to cope with it better if Carlos seemed happy.

But Carlos didn't seem happy. And Aiden had slapped him.

"This is not so great for me either, you know. My boyfriend is jealous of my best friend. My best friend doesn't trust my boyfriend. The two of you can't stand each other. Do you know how much that just sucks?" Carlos leaned forward and put a hand on his forehead. "At least I can talk to you about it without you losing your mind."

Nate wasn't sure that was true, but for the first time, he realized that the big fight that had ended with Aiden slapping Carlos had probably been about Nate. Aiden was likely suspicious of Nate; Carlos had mentioned in the past that Aiden had accused Nate of being interested in Carlos romantically. Lord, he didn't know the half of it. "So what are you going to do?" Nate asked. "Did you and Aiden make peace?"

"Yes." Carlos hesitated just a hair.

Nate was aware suddenly of how close they were sitting. Close enough for Carlos's hot hand to be on Nate's leg, close enough for Nate to touch Carlos's face… to kiss him. But of course he couldn't, not if Carlos was headed back to Aiden tomorrow.

Nate smiled and put a hand on Carlos's shoulder briefly before he shimmied back and stood up. "I'm glad that all worked out for you."

"You don't sound it."

"What should I say? Really, all I want is for you to be happy. Does Aiden make you happy?"

"Yes." But there was that hesitation again.

"Then that's all that matters." Nate took a deep breath. "I'm going to bed. You need anything?"

"No."

"All right. Good night, Carlos."

"Night, Nate."

Chapter 9

A SHIVER went through Carlos. It wasn't a good shiver; it was like he suddenly had ice in his veins. He struggled to keep his hand steady enough to put the key in the door, but the effort just made him shake harder.

He still didn't trust Aiden. He wanted to be home, to be in his bed and near his stuff, to wear his own clothes instead of borrowing from Nate, to revel in familiarity. He wanted to try to trust Aiden again. But he didn't. Oh, he believed Aiden's apologies, believed Aiden was sincere, but he didn't know if their troubles were behind him or if frustration would make Aiden strike again or even if he was making the right decision by going back to Aiden. Part of him suspected Nate was right. About everything.

Nate had asked him if he was happy, but the truth was that he wasn't and hadn't been, probably for a while.

Carlos had always thought Aiden was a good man. Lately he'd made mistakes. He loved Carlos, and Carlos knew that in his gut, felt it in Aiden's gaze, in his actions. But maybe that wasn't enough.

Carlos took a deep breath and realized that while he believed that Aiden didn't think he would hit Carlos, Carlos didn't trust it wouldn't happen again. What would keep Aiden from losing his mind the next time they argued?

Carlos dropped his keys. He let them lie there a moment and thought about Nate last night, the way he'd tried to comfort Carlos. He'd leaned close, close enough for Carlos to touch him, to smell him. Just his hand on Carlos's shoulder had thrown Carlos into chaos. He couldn't want Nate. That wasn't the way his universe worked. He loved Nate, sure, but like a brother.

As he picked up his keys, though, Carlos started to think about all the ways Nate was *not* like a brother. The way his body looked, how it moved, how Carlos looked at it—he'd had some very unbrotherly thoughts anytime he caught Nate walking through the apartment in just his undies, or without a shirt, or the rare moments when Carlos got a peek of Nate wearing nothing at all. It had fired Carlos up. He *did* want Nate. That was the primary reason he couldn't stay at Nate's apartment.

He stood back up and put his hand on the door. He'd told Nate again that morning that he was certain he was making the right decision. Now that he was here, on the threshold of his own damn apartment? He was not sure at all.

He managed to successfully insert his key in the lock and get the door open. Aiden was there, standing near the little table off the kitchen where they ate meals.

"I thought I heard you out there," Aiden said. He smiled widely. "Welcome home."

"Thanks. It's good to be home."

Aiden walked up to him and took his backpack. He laid it on the big armchair in the living room. Then he returned to Carlos and put his hands on Carlos's waist. "I missed you," he said, all smiles, like nothing had happened, like Carlos was just coming home from a short trip out of town on business.

Carlos decided to throw himself at this. He put his hands around Aiden's neck and said, "Me too."

He went with it when Aiden ducked his head and kissed him. It was a nice kiss, soft and familiar. When Carlos pulled back, Aiden had a goofy expression on his face.

"I love you so much," Aiden said. "I hope you know that."

"I do. I love you too."

"Good. So I was thinking, for tonight, let's just have dinner at home. Get something delivered. But nothing too heavy, because I want to sex you up afterward."

Carlos laughed. "All right."

So they ordered from a local Mediterranean place and Carlos tried to focus his energy on Aiden. When they'd first met, Carlos thought Aiden could do no wrong. He was so fucking sexy, he had a great smile, and he seemed to get Carlos's sense of humor. Carlos had had an absurd crush, the sort high school boys got, and he'd dorkily mooned over Aiden for weeks. So when Aiden finally asked him out, his answer required no thought. Before he really understood what was happening, they were making out at Barnstorm after games and going out a few nights a week. They were almost perfectly sexually compatible, and the first few times they'd slept together had been mind-blowing.

It was natural, after two years together, for things to have cooled off. They didn't have sex as often anymore, and sometimes even when they did, it felt routine. Everyone got their rocks off, but it wasn't as exciting as it had been. So, too, did date nights start to feel tired and predictable. Well, maybe not lately. Aiden had morphed into another person, it seemed. But that wasn't really good, either.

So while Carlos finished off a piece of spinach pie, he watched Aiden, who seemed to be his old self. But Carlos also couldn't shake that image of Nate, his towel slipping from his hips right before he kicked his door closed, that tantalizing bit of his exposed ass. Aiden probably could have sat buck naked in front of Carlos right then, but a three-second glimpse of Nate's ass was suddenly more exciting.

Of course, Aiden was not naked, so maybe that was part of the problem.

Dios, Carlos was horny.

"What?" Aiden said with a mouth full of gyro.

"What?" asked Carlos.

"You're looking at me weird."

Carlos tried for a sly smile. "I was just thinking I'd like for you to be naked." It wasn't a lie.

Aiden laughed. "It's good to have you home."

"You think I'm kidding."

They abandoned dinner soon after that. It was only hours later, when Carlos decided to clean up the living room because he couldn't sleep, that it occurred to him that he'd thought of Nate the whole time he'd been fucking Aiden. And that was really fucked up.

ANDREAS HAD really shiny hair. Nate didn't know how he was able to hold up his end of a prepractice conversation with a man this goddamn beautiful, but somehow he was doing it. Mostly they were talking about how it was nice to finally have a sunny day after a week of gray skies and drizzle. The conversation was pretty low-stakes, so it gave Nate the opportunity to examine the sheen in Andreas's hair and how his nose was kind of pointy but a nice fit for his face, and Lordy, did he have a nice body. Nate pictured him naked, and that derailed him enough that he stuttered out a, "Wait, what?"

"I was just saying," Andreas said in his mildly accented English, "that I like the weather here better than in Berlin. That's where I grew up."

"Oh. Right. Huh. I bet they don't have a lot of baseball in Berlin." Nate wanted to kick himself. Everything he said sounded so stupid when talking to Andreas.

But Andreas smiled. "No. I played soccer in school. The Rainbow League has a soccer division in New York, but it doesn't start up until September, so I figured I would give this a shot. I watched a lot of Yankees games to understand the rules." He winked.

Nate thought for a second that he might pass out. "That's a good start," Nate said. "Watching the Yankees, I mean."

"They're your favorite team, yes?"

"Less flirting, more baseball!" Scott shouted.

Nate rolled his eyes and looked for Carlos, who seemed to be running late again. In fact, Carlos didn't arrive until they were about halfway through the warm-up exercises. He dropped his bag on the bench and looked sheepish as he pulled on his cleats. Scott reamed him out as he fell into the group and started stretching.

Nate wanted to ask what was going on, but Scott glared at him, so he kept his mouth shut.

They went through the motions of practice. Nate ran laps behind Andreas, who looked great from behind, all tight muscles and bubble butt. It was all Nate could do not to reach out and grab it. When they did a cooldown lap and started to form lines for batting practice, Andreas said, "I'm hot," and even though Nate knew what he actually meant, he muttered, "I'll say."

Scott decided to make the pitchers trade off this week and take turns batting when they weren't pitching. Nate hated batting. It really was a shame the Rainbow League didn't have a designated hitter rule. Nate had been getting regular lessons from Mason since the previous summer, so he'd gotten better, but he was still a much better pitcher than a hitter. He dreaded waiting in that line, but then Carlos got in it behind him.

While they waited, Nate said, "Everything okay?"

Carlos sighed. "Yeah. Aiden was being weird when I left. Not a big deal."

Still, Nate didn't like the sound of that. And it certainly *was* a big deal if it caused Carlos to be so late to practice. Everyone knew Scott was a time cop, and so for years, every member of the Hipsters had always arrived promptly five minutes before practice.

Maybe it didn't matter. Nate pushed it out of his mind and then proceeded to embarrass himself at bat, hitting only one of the five pitches Eddie lobbed at him, and even then not hitting it very far. He felt far more in his element later, when he finally got to pitch.

Andreas was all ass and a smile when he walked up to the plate, the sunlight glinting off his teeth as he lofted the bat. Nate didn't know how he was expected to pitch against such an assault, but he rallied everything he had and managed to get the ball over the plate without looking too stupid.

After practice, Andreas walked up to him. "You really are very talented."

Nate felt his face heat up. "Oh. Thanks."

"You're cute too. I like when you blush."

Well, yikes. Nate's ears were practically on fire. He wondered if smoke was billowing off his body. "Thanks. Um. You're, well. You probably own a mirror."

Andreas grinned. "Would you like to go get a drink with me?"

"Right now?"

"Sure. Or tomorrow. Or anytime. Unless you have a boyfriend?"

Nate glanced at Carlos, who was busy hoisting his bag over his shoulder. Carlos, who had gone back to Aiden after everything. Carlos, who even now was gesturing north toward his apartment while talking to Ty, indicating he would be going home to Aiden and not spending a night out with his friends. Carlos had made his choice perfectly clear. "Nope," Nate said. "No boyfriend. Let's go get a drink."

Nate put the rest of his stuff away and begged off when Ian asked if he was going out with them. "Andreas asked me out," he said softly. Andreas was talking to Scott a few yards away, but Carlos was in earshot.

Carlos said, "He what?"

"Is it so impossible to imagine that the smoking-hot German replacement player might find me attractive enough to want to liquor me up tonight? He said I'm cute."

"Did he really?" Ian said. He shot Andreas an approving look.

Carlos sighed. "No, it's not hard to imagine at all. Have a good time, Nate. I gotta get home. I'll see you all at the game Tuesday."

Carlos loped off. Ian watched him go for second before turning back to Nate. "Good for you."

"I mean, maybe it's just a process of elimination thing, since so many people on our team are coupled up."

Ian looked around the field. "I don't think so. Shane is still single, I think. And Zack."

"Oh."

"Could be he actually thinks you're cute. You should go for it."

Nate picked up his bag and smiled as Andreas approached him. "You know what? I totally will."

CARLOS STORMED into his apartment, anger ripping through him as he thought about that smarmy asshole Andreas making moves on Nate. On *his* Nate.

Of course, Nate was a free agent, since Carlos was right now in the apartment he shared with Aiden, and why shouldn't Nate have found someone to date, and why did it make Carlos feel so much rage?

Ugh.

On top of everything, a current of arousal moved through Carlos. He'd been watching Nate be sweaty and adorable all practice, and Carlos had finally admitted to himself that despite everything, he wanted Nate. He'd always liked Nate, since they were kids, but now he liked Nate in a sexy way, and he didn't know how to act.

Of course he was jealous. Jealous of a fucking German baseball player who, sure, was hot, but he wasn't actually any good at the damn sport, and really, Nate deserved so much better.

But it wasn't Carlos's place to do anything, was it?

"Hey, baby," Aiden said, walking out of the bedroom. "How was practice? I was about to text you."

"I need to fuck you right now."

Aiden looked startled. "What?"

"I want to have sex right now. I want to bend you over the couch and fuck you so hard." Because yeah, that could work. Fucking Aiden was always a good distraction. He just needed to focus on his own relationship and stop worrying about what Nate was up to. He and Aiden could have wild monkey sex right now and he'd be back to normal. No more of this stupid bullshit with Nate. Nate could fucking have Andreas because Carlos had chosen Aiden and he was going to make the most of it.

"All right," Aiden said. "But come to the bedroom. I just vacuumed the couch."

And wasn't that just fucking perfect. Carlos wanted to fuck but Aiden was talking about vacuuming?

"What about spontaneity?" Carlos asked as he followed Aiden into their bedroom. "Your lover just came home all worked up from baseball practice and wants to fuck, but you want to make sure we do it on a bed?"

Aiden turned and narrowed his eyes. "Worked up? From baseball practice? Was everybody naked?"

"No." Carlos couldn't figure out if Aiden was kidding. "No, just, you know. Running around. Getting hot."

"Getting hot and bothered because other men you find attractive were there?"

"Hey, I came home to you, didn't I?"

"Sure, you did."

Aiden whipped his shirt off over his head. Now they were in business. Carlos moved on him right away, running his fingers through Aiden's chest hair.

They spent the next few minutes ripping the clothes off each other. Carlos sensed that Aiden knew exactly what was going on, and Carlos felt bad about it—no man should ever be his boyfriend's consolation prize—but Carlos was so fucking hard and hot and he needed the sweet oblivion sex would give him.

But even that didn't provide much relief. A little later, when Carlos was pounding the stuffing out of Aiden and Aiden was moaning beneath him, Carlos realized that this was not what he needed. His body might have been here with Aiden, his cock hard and sliding in and out of Aiden's hot body, but his mind, his heart, were a few blocks away at whatever bar Nate had ended up at with Andreas. Would one of them invite the other home? Would they fuck like this? Could Andreas make Nate feel all the things Nate needed to feel, deserved to feel? Would Andreas take care of Nate after?

Carlos looked at Aiden's back. He watched Aiden flex and move. There was no mistaking Aiden's broad back for Nate's narrower one, no denying that the thick, dark hair on the man Carlos was fucking was

Aiden's, not Nate's. Carlos suddenly wanted to be anywhere but here. He couldn't fuck Aiden.

He didn't love Aiden. Not anymore.

Startled by that realization, Carlos pulled out and flopped on the bed next to Aiden. He was still hard and panting, but he was confused now and not sure he could carry on.

"You want to switch positions, baby?" Aiden asked. "This is better. I get to face you this way." Aiden straddled Carlos's hips and sank onto his cock.

And that was getting the job done. Aiden was objectively hot, and the sight of him stroking his own cock as he bounced up and down on Carlos's was stimulating. Carlos put his hands on Aiden's shoulders, hoping to get back into it, needing for this to work, because if Nate was off with Andreas, then Carlos clearly belonged here with Aiden.

Except he knew that wasn't really true. He knew as well that his heart wasn't in this anymore. He'd just… he'd get through this. He'd sleep on it maybe to make sure he wasn't just confused. Then tomorrow, he and Aiden would probably have to have a talk. Maybe Carlos couldn't have Nate, but that didn't mean he had to stay with Aiden.

"Stay with me, Carlos," Aiden said.

Carlos balked and bucked his hips, worried Aiden could read his thoughts, but then he realized Aiden was just trying to pull him back from his wandering mind.

Aiden threw his head back and closed his eyes. "Aw, yeah, right there. Oh, that's the spot."

"Aiden."

"Yeah. Yeah, say my name."

"Aiden." Carlos had to make this stop. The friction on his cock was enough to pull him over the edge if he could just get his head back in the game, but part of him didn't want to anymore.

Nate. Goddamned Nate. Fucking Nate. Always Nate.

"Aiden!"

"Oh, baby, I'm gonna come."

Carlos wanted out, but he was trapped under Aiden's weight and also the sweet pressure of Aiden's body, and then Aiden was coming and squeezing even harder, and despite himself, Carlos felt his balls tingling.

"Shit," Carlos muttered. "I'm gonna come too."

"Come inside me, baby. Come inside me, Carlos. Say my name."

"Aiden."

"That's right. You're mine, baby. Carlos, you're mine. Say it."

"Aiden."

"Oh, fuck."

Aiden leaned back a little and continued to slide on and off Carlos's cock, and then Carlos just lost it, thrashing against the bed as he came, trying to push Aiden off of him before it was too late.

And then it was over and Carlos lay there, mortified and angry at himself.

Then his cheek stung.

"You were thinking about him, weren't you?" Aiden asked.

Slap! Aiden hit Carlos's other cheek.

"What?" Carlos managed. "I—"

Aiden grabbed Carlos's shoulders and picked him up off the bed before slamming him back down. Carlos's soft cock slid out of Aiden, but Aiden was still straddling him, still had his weight pressed on Carlos so that Carlos couldn't move.

And Carlos panicked.

"You were thinking about Nate while you fucked me."

"I wasn't! I swear, Aiden."

"You fucking were." Aiden landed a punch to Carlos's midsection that was hard enough to make Carlos cough.

"Jesus, Aiden, I wouldn't—"

"You spent all afternoon at practice with your loverboy Nate. I know you stayed with him while you were away from me. Did you fuck him too?"

"No. No, I've never had sex with Nate."

Only Carlos didn't get all of Nate's name out of his mouth before Aiden landed another punch on his shoulder. Carlos was too shocked to react, too surprised to figure out how to cope with Aiden beating on him and telling him that he really wanted Nate and not Aiden.

A point Aiden really didn't have to reiterate with his fists.

"Aiden, stop it. Let me up. Let me get up. Let me go."

Carlos pushed at Aiden, who outweighed him by a good forty pounds. Aiden had Carlos pinned to the bed now and was letting out all of his fury on Carlos's body. He threw punches, slapped Carlos's face.

Carlos could only push and buck futilely, trying to get away, trying to escape this mess.

In a crazy burst of memory, Carlos saw the last two years of his life flash before him, the elation he'd felt the first time he'd hooked up with Aiden, Nate's misgivings about the relationship, Aiden's more controlling tendencies, his demands, the first slap, Nate's naked ass, Nate and Andreas, and now Carlos lying on his own fucking bed, Aiden beating him all to hell.

Who was crying now? God, Aiden was crying. Carlos had gone numb, had floated out of his body, had stopped feeling any goddamn thing, except he saw now that Aiden was crying and had finally slunk away to the other side of the bed.

Carlos rolled off the bed and managed to land on his feet. He ran to his dresser and pulled out a T-shirt and a pair of pants. He put them on, knowing he had to get out of here as soon as he could.

"I'm so sorry," Aiden said.

"Fuck you," said Carlos. "Was this what you really wanted? To drive me away? Because if you intended to keep me, I think accusing me of lusting after my best friend and then beating me up was not the way to charm me back into your good graces."

Aiden got off the bed and stalked over to Carlos. "So that's it. You're leaving."

"I can't do this right now."

"Oh, so you'll go see your loverboy Nate?"

"Fuck you, Aiden." Nate probably wasn't even home, or if he was, he was fucking Andreas by now. Going there was probably a colossally stupid idea, but Carlos couldn't think of anywhere else to go.

Aiden grabbed Carlos's arm.

"Let me go," Carlos said, trying to jerk away.

Aiden's fingers pressed into Carlos's arm hard enough to leave a bruise. Carlos's arm ached as he tried to pull away, but Aiden instead pulled Carlos close. He was still crying, but he looked angry too. "It's only because I love you so much. I can't stand the thought of losing you."

"Let me go, Aiden."

"No."

"This isn't love. This… whatever just happened here is not love. Love isn't violent this way. I need to get out of here."

"You're not leaving me."

"I am. Because it doesn't matter what I say." There was that weird, numb, floaty feeling again. It was like Carlos wasn't in his own body. With an amazing amount of calm, he said, "I've been telling you for a year that I'm yours and you shouldn't be jealous of Nate, but instead, you chose not to believe me."

"No, I—"

"It wouldn't matter if tonight while we fucked I was thinking about you or Nate or Abraham Lincoln. You would choose to believe your mad jealousy and not me. Well, I'm done. I can't have you not trust me."

"Carlos."

"And." Carlos summoned the last of his strength and his courage. "I could forgive one angry moment, but if you're going to make a habit of using me as a punching bag, then we're done here."

Carlos wriggled out of Aiden's grasp and grabbed his backpack from the corner. Without even looking, he grabbed clothes from his dresser and started stuffing them into the backpack.

Aiden came up behind Carlos again and grabbed his arm. Carlos shot his elbow back, aiming to hit Aiden in the stomach, but he missed. Instead, Aiden whirled him around, pushed him against the dresser, and punched him in the face.

Carlos's head shot back. Everything scattered and he forgot what he was doing and where he was. It was just pain and blindness. Silence.

When he came back to himself, Aiden was standing before him, sobbing and clutching at Carlos's shirt. He was muttering apologies and kept repeating that he loved Carlos.

This was not love, though. Carlos knew that now.

He didn't know exactly when it had soured, when Aiden had gone crazy. It didn't matter, because Carlos was done. He pushed a now-sniveling Aiden off him and grabbed his backpack. "It's over," he said. He took his keys, his phone, and his wallet on the way out the door.

His face stung as he rode the subway into Manhattan, toward Nate's apartment. He could tell people were staring at him, but he didn't give a shit, not now.

With stunning clarity, he saw now how manipulative Aiden had been all along. How Aiden had been separating him from his friends. How Aiden had been planting ideas about Nate and Nate's jealousy for almost as long as they'd been together. He remembered the night at

Spokes that Nate had gotten pissy with Aiden and Aiden had later suggested that Nate wanted Carlos. And that was fucking stupid because Nate didn't, but Aiden had wanted Carlos to think so. Aiden had wanted the assurance that he was Carlos's one and only, even a year ago. He wanted Carlos to move in with him even though Carlos hadn't felt ready. He'd objected to any bit of independence Carlos had tried to show since they moved in together, and had been intensely jealous whenever Carlos so much as contemplated going out with anyone who wasn't Aiden.

God, how had he been so blind? Had he really been holding on so hard to positive memories of Aiden from the early days of their relationship that he hadn't seen the terrible turn everything had taken?

Not that he was completely innocent. He shouldn't have initiated sex tonight. He felt dirty and slimy. It had felt wrong almost from the minute it had gotten started. It wasn't love, it was craziness, it was longing for something Carlos couldn't have, and Carlos was so unhappy about all of it and so ashamed and so….

Well, here was rock bottom.

He tried to push the thoughts of what he should have done, what he could have handled differently, out of his head. He shouldn't have fucked Aiden tonight. He shouldn't have gone back after the first slap. He should have listened to Nate. He should have opened his goddamn eyes and seen what was happening. Instead, he was now homeless and adrift, and all he had to show for it was a swollen face and a lot of regret.

Carlos wasn't going to let himself cry. He sat on the train stoically, shutting down his thoughts, counting down the stops until he got to Fourteenth Street.

Nate still lived in Chelsea, in that dinky little one-bedroom he'd been so proud of when he'd gotten it after college. Carlos had bounced around roommate situations, but Nate had been steadily renting this same place for so long he had an unheard-of deal. Sure, he was so far west he could easily spit into the Hudson and he had to put up with the constant hum of traffic from the West Side Highway, but it never seemed to matter to Nate. Solid, reliable Nate.

Unfortunately, he was also a good walk from the subway, and the pain finally hit Carlos as he made his way across Sixteenth toward Nate's place on Seventeenth off Tenth Avenue. As he walked, everything hurt. Carlos's face and chest ached, his shoulders and arms stung where Aiden had landed punches, and he started to doubt he'd even make it all the way as he walked the last two blocks. But he did.

Someone else was leaving Nate's building as Carlos got there, so Carlos went right in. He climbed the steps to the third floor and went down the hall to Nate's apartment. No light shone from under the door or through the peephole, so Nate was either not home or in his bedroom fucking Andreas. Carlos knocked, but as he expected, Nate didn't answer.

He sank to the floor and leaned against the wall next to the door. His body was screaming now, the pain unreal. Probably he should have gone to the hospital or something, but no, he needed Nate.

That was when he remembered he had a cell phone.

He pulled it out and managed to text *I need you* to Nate right before he finally broke and started to cry.

Chapter 10

ANDREAS WAS not the brightest bulb. Oh, he was bright and shiny and sexy, but he didn't have a lot of intellectual power behind his stunning blue eyes. Once Nate realized that, he was far less intimidated by Andreas's beauty. It made it easier to talk to him, of course, but it also made him less attractive the more they talked.

"So explain to me this designated hitter," Andreas said.

The beer—they'd had a couple of rounds now—was already making Nate feel a little fuzzy around the edges, but not so much that he couldn't recite basic baseball principles. "It's an American League rule. The short version is that pitchers are held in reserve just for pitching, so they don't have to bat. Instead, they appoint a runner to hit and run for them in the lineup."

"And why does this make people so angry?"

Nate shrugged. "Dunno. It makes sense to *me*. Of course, in the National League, there is no designated hitter, so pitchers have to hit. Everyone usually has to hit in interleague play and during the postseason too, depending on which stadium they're playing in." And watching pitchers who never had to bat try to hit the ball was a thing Nate derived a strange joy from.

"All these rules. And two leagues? How do you keep track of it all?"

"I just do. I know lots of other rules too." Nate was going for sexy, and he waggled his eyebrows, which pulled a grin from Andreas.

"You are cute."

"Thanks. Uh. Any other baseball questions?"

Andreas wrinkled up his face as though he were thinking. "I listened to the Yankees game on the radio yesterday. They kept talking about… sabermetrics?"

Oh boy. "Well, that's more complicated. It's basically an analysis of statistics that some scouts think is a better way of telling whether a player will help win games or not. Instead of looking at how fast a guy runs or how many home runs he can hit, they look at how many walks he gets and his on-base percentage, that kind of thing. I mean, there's a lot more to it, but that's the gist."

Blank stare.

Nate sipped his beer. "Baseball is really all about statistics. It's math. You don't necessarily want the guy who hits hard, you want a guy on your team who gets on base, because statistically, he's more likely to score a run. Home runs are nice, but they don't always win games."

Andreas clucked his tongue. "So complicated. In soccer, you kick the ball in the goal and you get a point. It's easy and straightforward."

Nate laughed. He supposed that was one way to look at it. "But I mean, you work for a bank, right? You probably see numbers all the time. This is kind of like that."

Andreas shook his head. "I mostly see customers. Besides, you don't need to calculate how a man will spend his money to figure out his account balance."

"What?"

Andreas groaned and waved his arms. "I do not know. I don't understand baseball sometimes. It seemed so simple when I signed up."

Nate smiled at that. "It is. It's really only complicated to those of us who are fanatical about it."

After another round, Andreas started making noise about how he had a very nice place right here in Park Slope and wouldn't Nate like to see the exposed brick in the living room? Nate figured Andreas wanted to expose something else.

Andreas leaned close and said, "You are very sexy, Nate. I'd like you to come with me."

"I want to."

"But?"

"Well, see—"

Andreas cut him off with a soft kiss. His lips pressed gently against Nate's, and ran his hand through Nate's hair. It was nice, objectively, but Nate felt... nothing. There was no stirring in his body, no excitement, no fireworks. Suddenly he wanted nothing more than to get the hell out of that bar.

"I should go," Nate said. "Home, I mean. To my home. Busy day tomorrow."

"You don't like me."

Nate slid off his stool and stood up. "It's not that. I mean, you are sexy as sin."

Andreas smiled.

"But I'm just... I'm not a put-out-on-the-first-date kinda guy, I guess."

Andreas tilted his head. "All right. I will respect that."

"I'll, uh, I'll see you at the game Tuesday. Okay?"

"Yes. Bye, Nate." Andreas leaned over and kissed each of Nate's cheeks before shooing him out of the bar.

It didn't dawn on him to check his phone until he was nearly back at his apartment. As he walked the last block, he pulled it out and saw a text from Carlos.

I need you.

Nate's pulse went bonkers as he worried about what had happened. Something certainly had. It wasn't like Carlos to just send out a text like that.

Nate vowed to call Carlos as soon as he got to his apartment. The text must have come through while Nate was on the subway or he would have felt his phone buzz in his pocket, right? The time stamp only showed when the text was received, not when it was sent. Was Carlos in trouble? Had he been hurt? Was he okay?

He went into his building and took the steps two at a time, his hand already flipping to his contacts so he could call Carlos—

—who was sitting on the floor outside his apartment, weeping.

"Oh God," Nate whispered. He ran down the hall and knelt next to Carlos. "Hey, what's going on? Are you okay?" It was a dumb question; Carlos was clearly not okay.

Carlos looked up. "Nate?"

Carlos's eyes were red. His whole face was red, except for a blotch under his left eye, which was a purple blossoming bruise.

"Jesus, what happened?"

"I left Aiden."

Carlos was in rough shape. It was hard to take in the damage in the harsh fluorescent lights of the hallway. Nate reached over and helped Carlos to his feet. Carlos groaned as he stood. Nate held him as he fished his keys out of his pocket and got them inside. He steered Carlos to the sofa, where Carlos sat with a grunt.

By the looks of it, Carlos left Aiden after Aiden beat the shit out of him.

"Did he hit you?"

Carlos nodded miserably. "I didn't want to come here, because you might have been with Andreas tonight, but I couldn't stay there and I didn't know where else to go."

"It's okay. You're always welcome here. And I'm not with Andreas. It was just a drink. Or three, I guess, but I decided not to go home with him. But that doesn't matter. I'm here and you're here and you're safe now."

"I played this all wrong, Nate. I was mad and I went home and... I shouldn't have... but then Aiden...."

Nate sat next to Carlos on the sofa and put an arm around him. "None of this is your fault. If Aiden hit you, the blame lies entirely on Aiden."

Carlos nodded and cried.

"I told you, my couch is here anytime you need it."

Carlos nodded again. "God, I'm so tired."

Nate wanted to know what had happened, but he figured Carlos would tell him when he was ready. The more important thing here was to assess the damage.

"Where did he hit you?" Nate asked. "Or was it just your face?"

Slowly, Carlos shook his head. Then he let out a breath and his whole body sagged against the cushions. He laid his head on the back of the sofa, and Nate could see his face in good light now. His whole left cheek was red and a little swollen and he'd have a dandy of a black eye in the morning, so that was one thing. He had a tiny cut near the apple of that cheek too. It looked like Aiden had well and truly slugged him.

But then Carlos lifted up his shirt and pulled it off.

Nate's heart just shattered.

Carlos's chest was more of the same, red and splotchy with purplish spots that would probably be horrific bruises for a few days at least.

"Dear Lord," Nate mumbled, tracing his fingers lightly over the bruises.

"I don't think anything is broken," Carlos said.

No, thought Nate, *except for both of our souls.*

Well, and Aiden's skull when Nate got through with him.

But one thing at a time.

"It's just bruises," Carlos wheezed. "No broken bones. But it hurts like a mother."

"I'll bet."

A couple of cuts punctuated Carlos's torso too. Had Aiden been wearing that ring? Had the force of his blows alone broken Carlos's lovely, perfect skin?

Nate stood. "Wait here. Let me see if I can find something to help with the swelling."

Carlos nodded and closed his eyes.

Nate first went to his bathroom and extracted a first-aid kit. He knew, because he'd banged up his knee sliding into third at a game just two weeks ago, that it had plenty of Band-Aids and first-aid ointment inside. So that was the first thing. Then he went into his kitchen. He wished he'd had a steak to put on that shiner, but he'd been eating mostly vegetarian lately. He did have plenty of ice, so he put some in a couple of plastic baggies and then wrapped both in hand towels before bringing everything back into the living room.

Carlos was still sitting there, his arms splayed out at his sides, his head on the back of the sofa, his eyes closed, and the cuts and bruises were just as startling as they had been when he'd first taken his shirt off.

Nate dumped his bounty on the coffee table and then sat next to Carlos again. He grabbed one of the bags of ice and put it in one of Carlos's hands. "Here, put this on your eye. It'll help keep the swelling down."

Carlos nodded and did as he was told.

Nate next went to work on Carlos's chest. "None of these cuts look bad enough to need a Band-Aid, but I'm gonna put a little bit of this antibacterial goop on them anyway. It'll probably sting. That okay?"

"Yeah," said Carlos.

Nate opened the tube of ointment and put a dab on each of the cuts on Carlos's chest. Carlos hissed or winced whenever Nate touched him.

"You sure you don't need a doctor?" Nate asked.

"I don't think so. I don't want to go back outside."

"Because if he broke one of your ribs and it punctures your lung—"

"Nate. I'm all right. Just sore and bruised."

Nate inspected Carlos's skin for signs of any other injuries. "All right. Holler if you change your mind."

"I will."

Satisfied that he'd taken care of the worst of it, Nate sat up and put the cap back on the ointment. "Okay. And I hope you and Aiden are well and truly done, because I'm going to have to go kill him now."

Carlos sat up and took the ice off his face. "No. I mean, yes, I'm done with Aiden for good now. Don't try to kill him."

"What? You don't think I can take him? I know he's bigger than me, but I'm pretty scrappy." Nate held up his arms and flexed his muscles.

Carlos laughed. Mission accomplished.

"Don't," Carlos said, clutching his side.

Nate grabbed the other ice bag and pressed it against the worst of the bruises on Carlos's chest. "Sorry."

"Let me figure out how to deal with Aiden, okay? I told him it was over and then I left, but… there's so much to sort out and… I just can't right now. I got out. I'm not going back to him this time."

"Okay. Good."

Carlos sighed. "So I can sleep on your couch?"

"Actually, if you're this banged up, you should probably take the bed. I'll put clean sheets on it."

Carlos leaned back and put the ice back on his face. "You sure?"

"Yep. I can take the couch. I fall asleep on it all the time anyway. It's no problem."

"Okay." That seemed to satisfy Carlos. He nodded and relaxed again.

"And like I said, long as you need."

"Thank you."

Nate sighed. Now that the worst of the crisis seemed to be over, he leaned back on the sofa, too, and took a deep breath. This was… well, this was a lot to deal with quickly, but he was happy with how he'd handled it. Now the real horror of it started to sink in as he looked at those bruises and thought about what Carlos must have felt as Aiden hit him. It was hard to imagine. And even though Nate hadn't really liked Aiden, it was still hard to believe that he'd lost it to this degree. And yet here was the evidence of it, all over Carlos.

"Do me a favor?" Carlos said.

"Sure. Anything."

"Look in my backpack and see if I grabbed any sweatpants or boxers or something to sleep in. I just grabbed, I didn't really think about it."

"Okay."

Nate went to the backpack and opened it. Clothes burst out of it, mostly Carlos's vast collection of colorful T-shirts, but also some of his work clothes. Nate started pulling them out and sorting them into little piles. A lot of Carlos's underwear had made it into the bag, which made Nate slightly uncomfortable, mostly because he kept picturing Carlos wearing only those briefs and now was definitely not the time. There was a pair of jeans and a pair of sweatpants at the bottom. He grabbed the sweatpants and handed them to Carlos.

"The spare toothbrush is still where you left it," Nate said. "I'll go change the sheets."

Carlos sat up again and took the ice off his face. He moved his jaw around a little and then nodded and looked up at Nate. "Thank you again. I'm grateful. I'd get up and hug you, but…." He gestured toward his bruised torso.

"No, I get it. There will be plenty of time for hugs later."

Carlos took the sweatpants and peeled himself off the sofa. He disappeared into the bathroom for a while, so Nate busied himself packing up the first-aid kit and then changing his sheets. When Carlos emerged again, he'd changed into the sweatpants. He dropped the jeans he'd been wearing on top of his backpack.

"So what happened with Andreas anyway?"

Nate laughed, mostly out of surprise. He'd nearly forgotten Andreas existed. "Well, he's pretty, but dumb as a brick."

"Really?"

"I thought at first that it was just a cultural thing? Like he grew up with a different frame of reference than I did or something and he just didn't get my jokes? But then I realized not all the gears in his head were turning. He asked me back to his place after, but I begged off and came home. Good thing I did, eh?"

Carlos smiled faintly. "Yeah. You going to go out with him again?"

"Probably not. I mean, I thought about having sex with him because how often does a guy that hot ask you out? But I don't know. Not sure I could live with myself."

"You couldn't live with yourself if you had sex with a hot guy just for the sake of having sex?" Carlos sat back on the sofa. "You always were kind of a prude."

"Yeah, well." It was weird having this conversation with Carlos. They'd talked about their relationships plenty in the past, but something was different now. It could have been that Carlos was sitting there shirtless, and now that the initial shock of the bruises and cuts had subsided, Nate couldn't help but notice that Carlos had a very nice chest. "Did you know you have abs?"

Carlos looked down. "Oh. Yeah. Turns out if you actually go to the gym instead of *accidentally* leaving your gym bag at the office, your muscles develop."

"Ha."

"And I mean, technically you have abdominal muscles under that layer of potato chips and M&M's, you know."

"All right, funny man. Lay off. I may not have a six-pack, but I'm not too flabby. Have you seen my arms?" Nate, at least, could be proud of the fact that he'd developed the arms of an overworked MLB pitcher.

"I know, Nate."

"Just making sure. Anyway. You want to watch a movie or something?"

"Yeah. You have something funny and mindless?"

Nate raised an eyebrow. "Have we met? The only serious movies I own have explosions in them."

Carlos laughed softly. "All right. Explosions it is."

Chapter 11

CARLOS WASN'T ready to deal with the fallout. Nate was being a completely gracious host, and Carlos was happy enough to wallow in that as he started to heal, but he put off making a decision about how to deal with Aiden.

Except after two days of sleeping in Nate's bed—a bed that smelled like Nate, or whatever detergent he used, anyway, and made Carlos hard to the point where he had to jerk off in the shower every morning or risk walking around with a boner all the time—Carlos realized a lot of his important things were still at Aiden's. And Carlos's nonprofit salary was not going to pay for all new stuff, no matter how much he dreaded returning to the scene of the crime.

Still, he put it off. He knew he'd have to go and retrieve his stuff. He'd surely have to face Aiden again, particularly as their baseball teams were scheduled to play each other before the end of the summer. But he couldn't deal with any of that just yet.

Speaking of games, Carlos sat out that week's. He made Nate swear not to tell anyone what had happened and prayed his face would be healed enough that he wouldn't have to explain at the next practice, but as the purple bruise on his cheek morphed into a full-on black eye, he started to worry that was too much to hope for.

Nate joked that the black eye made him look like a badass.

Nate also offered to accompany him back to Aiden's to get his stuff while Aiden was at work, but Carlos still wasn't ready to go back to the apartment, so instead he bought a razor and deodorant and the lotion he liked from the drugstore near Nate's apartment and a sweater from the super trendy men's store on Eighth Avenue, because he'd also failed to pack anything with longer sleeves than a T-shirt. That whole week went that way, with Carlos buying things as it occurred to him that he really needed them, but this was no solution, because everything Carlos owned—his late grandfather's watch, a stack of photo albums of him and his sisters and Nate as kids, his favorite books, his nicer clothes, shoes that weren't sneakers, his laptop, really everything—was still at Aiden's. Assuming Aiden hadn't hauled it all to Prospect Park and torched it.

But, no, that seemed unlikely. Aiden had started texting Carlos Monday morning. Mostly he apologized and begged Carlos to come home, but sometimes he was accusatory or angry. Every time Aiden's name showed up on the display of Carlos's phone, Carlos felt like he'd been punched again. It wasn't until Wednesday that Carlos finally texted, *I can't talk to you yet. Please stop.* The "yet" was probably a mistake, in retrospect, because it likely gave Aiden hope. It shut him up for a couple of days, anyway.

Thursday night Carlos came in and found Nate puttering around his kitchen.

"So I was thinking," Nate said when Carlos cleared his throat to make his presence known, "that we could get Ian and Ty in on Operation: Get Carlos's Stuff Back."

"What? Why?"

"I know you don't want to face Aiden again. Maybe making it a team effort will make it more bearable. Ian and Ty live near Aiden, and Ty works from home during the day. We trust them. They just seemed like the natural choice."

Carlos nodded because he could see the wisdom in that. It would probably be easier to extract his things from Aiden's with some help. "Okay."

"Good. We can talk to them after practice Sunday. Then maybe go next week during the day? I'll take a morning off from work."

"Yeah. All right."

Nate went back to preparing whatever he was cooking. It looked like chicken breasts on a bed of rice in a big baking dish. And that was the sum total of what Carlos knew about cooking; he'd grown up in a household of women who yelled at him when he went in the kitchen, so he had never bothered to learn more than the basics. He could boil eggs and microwave leftovers, but that was about it.

"I'm trying a recipe I got from Josh," Nate explained. "Apparently this is one of Tony's favorite meals. It's a lemon chicken situation." Nate picked up a saucepan full of some kind of yellowy sauce and poured it over the chicken breasts.

Josh's husband, Tony, loved to cook and was always inventing new entrées. Carlos had been over to their house for dinner many times, often with Nate in tow. Nate seemed to like to cook, although Carlos had learned from their brief time living together that he got takeout just as often as he actually turned his oven on.

Now Nate bent over to slide the baking dish into the oven. He set the timer on his microwave. Then he leaned against the counter and grinned. "It has to bake about twenty minutes."

"Okay."

"I've only made this once before, so it might be terrible."

"I'm sure it'll be fine."

Nate nodded. "The shiner looks better."

Carlos touched his cheek. The bruising had started to fade, finally. "Yeah. Guess I'll live after all."

"I still think you should have taken me up on my offer to do your makeup."

Carlos shook his head. Nate had done drag briefly when they were in their early twenties, and was actually pretty good with makeup, but that had been a short-lived phase. He liked doing makeup and dressing up more than he liked performing or being the center of attention. He'd never quite gotten acclimated to the stage, so he'd let it go. But he was the first one his friends called on Halloween.

Carlos said, "As much as I wanted to show up at work looking like Divine...."

"Hey, give me a little credit. I wouldn't have made you wear the blue eye shadow."

"I appreciate that."

"I mean, I have this shade of green that would go way better with your complexion. And Patrick told me green was the hot color this season, so you'd be way trendy."

Carlos burst into laughter.

God, he loved Nate.

The realization brought him up short. He stopped laughing abruptly.

"You okay there?" Nate asked, pulling a couple of beers from the fridge.

"Fine. Just remembered something I forgot to do at work today."

Nate nodded and grabbed a magnet bottle opener off the fridge. He popped the tops off two bottles of beer and handed one to Carlos, all smooth and easy.

Everything with Nate and Carlos had always been smooth and easy. Nate had always known exactly how to get Carlos to laugh when things got too intense, always known just what to say to make Carlos feel better. They'd been friends for so goddamned long that they just got each other. No need to explain or pretend or do anything other than just be themselves.

Until the last couple of years.

Until Aiden.

It was hard not to feel sad whenever it occurred to Carlos that Nate had been onto Aiden from the beginning, that Nate had warned Carlos off, that Nate had never trusted Aiden. Carlos felt so stupid sometimes for not seeing the subtle, and then less subtle, ways Aiden had been manipulating him. He should have seen it, should have anticipated that everything would go south.

And Christ, did he regret letting Nate get him all boiled up so that he was practically lethal himself during that last encounter with Aiden.

But that was over now. Aiden would soon be in Carlos's past. But could Nate be a part of his future? In a romantic way?

Did he want that?

THE LEMON chicken dish came out well. The rice was rich and buttery, the chicken moist, the lemon sauce tangy. Nate was pretty proud of it.

Carlos was quiet as they ate, interrupting Nate's silence or nervous chattering periodically to ask for the salt or to comment on Nate's cooking. "You're not terrible at this."

"I can't even tell if that's good or not."

"It's fine, *papi*."

"Well, *I* like it. I guess I'll be able to look Tony in the eye again. I'd hate to think he steered me wrong."

Silence followed, punctuated only by the scrape of silverware on Nate's cheap plates.

"Are you all right?" Nate asked. "Are you worried about getting your stuff from Aiden's?"

Carlos chewed slowly. Eventually he said, "I'm worried about a lot of things."

"Do you want to talk about it?"

"Not really."

Nate simultaneously understood that sentiment and was frustrated by it. Certainly he didn't want to talk about his mother, or about what a mess his feelings about Carlos were now, so he understood Carlos's reticence. On the other hand, if something was wrong, Nate wanted to help fix it.

"You could press charges, you know. He did assault you. You could get his ass thrown in jail."

Carlos shook his head. "No, I… no. I don't… I don't even want to talk about it in private. I'd have to tell cops and lawyers and judges about… no. I don't want to press charges."

"Are you sure? Because—"

"Nate. I know you're trying to help, but stop. I don't want to press charges. I don't want anyone else to know about this. It was a one-time thing and it was partly my fault anyway, and I just don't want to." Carlos's voice rose in volume as he spoke. Finally he yelled, "Get that through your skull."

Nate balked in surprise. He leaned back in his chair, away from Carlos, and let that wash over him. "All right. I'm sorry. Just a suggestion. I thought it might help you get some closure."

Carlos rubbed his eyes with the palms of his hands. "I don't need closure. I need for this to not be happening to me."

"I know, but—"

"I get what you're doing. Thank you. But no thanks. I just want to move on."

Nate wanted to push it, but he pulled back. He ate some chicken and let silence descend. He wanted Aiden held accountable, wanted to see the man behind bars for what he did to Carlos. He wanted to argue that if Aiden beat up Carlos, who knew who else he might have beaten, who else he might beat up in the future. But he also wanted to go with Carlos's wishes, and if Carlos wanted that to be the end of it, then that was the end of it.

But the silence made Nate uncomfortable, and he hated to see Carlos unhappy and fuming.

So instead, Nate said, "Did Marisol tell you she went on a date with a banker? He works at one of the big national banks. I forget which."

Carlos's eyes shot up. "A banker? Marisol? My sister Marisol?"

"The same. She even told me she liked him."

"Marisol, who thinks all finance people are evil Gordon Gecko types? Who doesn't trust big corporate banks enough to put her money in them? That Marisol?"

"I know. I thought it was crazy too."

Carlos laughed softly. "First little Gabby gets engaged, then Marisol dates a banker. My sisters are strangers."

"'Little Gabby' is twenty-eight. That's a pretty good age to get married."

Carlos shook his head. "They grow up so fast."

Nate laughed. "Okay. Oh, I forgot the best part. The banker's name is Dirk."

"Dirk? What the hell kind of name is that? Only soap opera characters are named Dirk."

And they were off to the races. It was good to see Carlos talking and laughing, perhaps distracted from whatever was bothering him.

After dinner they draped themselves on opposite sides of the couch with whatever junk TV was on in the background, occasionally chatting while Nate texted with Marisol. Nate had made Carlos tell her that he and Aiden were done, but so far she was the only one who knew. She asked after him, so Nate said he was okay.

How is it having him there? she asked.

Weird, Nate texted back. Then, thinking better of that descriptor, he added, *Good but weird.*

I'll bet. Do you still lurrve him?

Nate laughed, more out of embarrassment than anything else. Marisol, of course, knew full well the extent of Nate's feelings for Carlos and had once even encouraged him to go for it, but Nate hadn't had the nerve. If he'd had it to do over, he would have said something two years ago, because surely asking Carlos if he could have feelings for Nate before Carlos went out with Aiden might have saved Nate a lot of heartache over the past two years.

Or it could have broken Nate's heart.

"What's so funny?" Carlos asked.

"Just something Mari said. She's making fun of me."

"Good girl."

I do still love him, Nate said to Marisol. *But I can't do anything about it now. Not while he's on the rebound.*

Good point, she said. Then a moment later, she texted again. *That sucks, man.*

Thanks. Very helpful.

She sent him back a smiley making a toothy grin.

"What do you think of the model with the beard?" Carlos asked.

Nate looked at the screen. He'd been half watching a modeling reality show with Carlos that featured a mix of male and female models. The one with a beard was an absurdly tall brunet with angular eyebrows, a banging body, and a cute face.

"He's hot," Nate said.

Carlos laughed. "Yes, they all are. No, he thinks he's straight, but he's forging a very close friendship with the blond guy. The openly gay one."

"You think the blond guy's gonna turn the one with the beard?" Nate couldn't remember any of their names, but he didn't think Carlos did either.

"I think the one with the beard doth protest too much and he's totally into dudes, but I'm not quite sure. Your gaydar was always better than mine. What do you think?"

Nate watched for a few minutes. The bearded guy got a little drunk and a lot flirty, hanging all over the blond guy. The camera flashed to some other people in the model house, whom Nate didn't really care about, and then back to Beardy and Blondie, who were sitting awfully close to each other. Then Beardy reached over, cupped Blondie's face, and kissed him. It was a soft, closed-mouth kiss, but it was still a kiss. And it was pretty hot.

"So," Carlos said. "Drunk and bicurious? Or into dudes?"

"Into dudes," Nate said. "He's a harness away from Leather Night at the Eagle."

Carlos laughed. "Yeah, all right. You really think he's hot?"

"Sure, in a conventional way. The blond guy's more attractive because he's a little weird-looking. The big nose, I mean, and the really long arms. What do you think?"

"I actually think the guy with the baby face is the hottest." Carlos paused. "That one."

The guy on screen now—who was, incidentally, extolling on whether Beardy was gay—had spiky hair and dimples. On the body of a professional bodybuilder. "His head and his body don't match," said Nate.

"True, but he's cute, and man, that body."

Nate touched his own belly self-consciously. He'd been even more of a slacker where the gym was concerned since his mother had been in the hospital, so he felt a little out of shape. Although he'd never had shoulders or abs like this guy Carlos was drooling over.

"You know all these guys are, like, nineteen, right?" said Nate. "We're thirty-three."

"So? He's legal. It's not lecherous."

"If you say so."

"You jealous?"

Nate knew intellectually that Carlos was teasing, but the comment still hit him close to his heart. He wasn't jealous so much as self-conscious about the fact that he didn't look like the sort of guy Carlos was attracted to. This guy, Aiden—all the evidence pointed to Carlos being into a beefier species of male.

"No," Nate said. "Just, you know. It's kind of squicky to lust over guys that young. No?"

"Just enjoy the eye candy. Don't think about it too hard."

Nate sighed. "That was sort of my approach to Andreas."

That seemed to bring Carlos up short. He frowned. "Is anything happening there?"

"No. Not since the last time I went out with him. I mean, we talked after the last game, but he hasn't asked me out again or anything. I think he'd be game to go out again, but eh. Not really feeling it. Like I said, he's pretty, but he's kind of an empty vessel." Still, even if Andreas had more synapses firing, Nate only had eyes for Carlos. He'd hardly thought of Andreas at all since the night Carlos had shown up on his doorstep. And having Carlos around all the time was only serving to make that worse.

Nate wanted Carlos in a tangible way, but the timing was awful. And Nate knew he couldn't act and trust that what they had was real unless he knew Carlos was acting because he loved Nate, not because he was seeking solace after what had happened with Aiden. Nate reasoned that he was stalling again, talking himself out of making a move on Carlos just like he had in the months before Carlos started going out with Aiden, but this was different. Nate was almost as terrified now that Carlos loved him as he was that he didn't.

What a goddamn mess.

Still, waiting was the right thing to do, Nate knew that. He'd wait until Carlos seemed steady on his feet again, and then he'd tell him how he felt. He had to do it this time. He couldn't just sit around waiting for what he wanted, because that wasn't how the world worked.

On screen, the models angsted about whether or not Beardy was secretly gay. Beardy himself was basically like, "Hey, I like chicks, but I don't know. I really like *this* guy. And gay people are sure treated badly in society, eh?" As if one gay kiss had given him enough experience to identify with that.

Nate sighed. That really only served to make him think of his mother and Father Egan. Nate could tell Beardy some things about being treated badly.

Carlos reached over and tapped his knee at the same time his phone buzzed with another text from Marisol. So Nate tried to forget about all of it and concentrate on trivial matters. Because if he thought too much about everything he was feeling, he'd surely fly apart.

Chapter 12

WHEN CARLOS came home Friday, Nate was sitting on the couch eating noodles out of a plastic container.

"Got you the massaman curry," Nate said, not taking his eyes off the TV.

Carlos dropped his bag next to the couch. Of course Nate had ordered his favorite Thai dish when he'd ordered Thai food for himself, because Nate knew him and was kind and considerate. Would Aiden have even thought of him if he'd ordered himself dinner? It probably wasn't worth thinking about.

He plopped down on the couch. "What are you watching?"

"*St. Elmo's Fire.*"

Carlos laughed. He'd forgotten how much Nate loved this movie. He picked up his curry and pulled off the lid, letting the spicy scent hit his nostrils. "This from the really good place on Twenty-Third?"

"It is indeed."

"Bless you, *papi.*"

They ate silently and watched the movie for a few minutes. They were just at the part where Ally Sheedy's character walks out on Judd Nelson and into the waiting arms of Andrew McCarthy.

"This movie is so weird," Carlos said.

"In what way?"

"So, okay, the first time I saw it? That bus trip in eleventh grade?"

"Yup."

"Right, so when I saw it that time, I think I sided with the wrong characters. Like, Emilio Estevez has a crush on Andie MacDowell, right, and when you're young, it seems cute, but now I think he's a total awkward creepster about it, and I can't even watch those parts of the movie. And when I first saw the movie, I was really sympathetic toward Andrew McCarthy. He loves Ally Sheedy, right? Has been wanting her for years. And here she finally is because Judd Nelson is an asshole. So of course, they have this moment and I was happy because he finally got what he wanted and, let's face it, he's a lot cuter than Judd Nelson."

"Agreed."

"So their love is meant to be, obviously. But then I saw the movie again years later and I thought Andrew McCarthy was actually kind of a pushy stalker in this part. Like, he's been in love with her for years but never said anything, and then she finally shows up all distraught from her breakup, and he shoves his tongue down her throat."

Nate said nothing. When Carlos glanced over, Nate was staring at him.

"What?" Carlos asked.

"You don't think this part of the movie is romantic?"

"Eh. I know how it turns out. She loves them both! Please. Pick a side, girl."

Nate laughed. "Threesome?"

"Gross, no."

"That's fine. In my head, I've written fanfic where the guys decide to toss Ally Sheedy aside and end up with each other. Who needs a woman?"

"Really?" Carlos ate a big spoonful of curry. He let it sit on his tongue for a moment to savor it. It was rich and spicy. So good.

"You remember that weird comparative literature class I took junior year in college?" asked Nate. "That professor fancied herself a Freudian, which seemed to mean she found queer sex in everything. Whenever we read a book with a love triangle, she argued that the two men were only fighting over the woman because they secretly wanted to be with each other."

"So you think Judd Nelson and Andrew McCarthy want to bang each other?"

"Not a clue. I just think it's a funny idea. A tidy solution. I mean, don't get me wrong, I love Ally Sheedy, just, you know. I don't want to fuck her."

"But you do want to fuck Andrew McCarthy?"

"Oh, yeah. Even current Andrew McCarthy. Have you seen him lately? He's aged well."

Carlos chuckled and ate more of his curry. He supposed these scenes with Andrew McCarthy and Ally Sheedy were kind of romantic. McCarthy's enthusiasm was cute. He was kind of intense, though.

"I guess," Nate said, "this part always speaks to me because I want to be loved the way Ally Sheedy is. I mean, Andrew McCarthy is so in love with her. She inspires him."

Carlos put his curry back on the table. He was about to get up to get a glass of water when Nate passed him a can of diet soda. Amazing. Carlos popped the top and took a sip.

"You'll find the right man, Nate." Of that, Carlos was confident. Nate was such a great guy, it defied logic that he didn't have that in his life yet.

"I wish I had your faith."

Carlos put the soda aside. Nate put his dinner back on the coffee table too. Carlos wondered at Nate's choice in movies now, embarrassed that it had taken him so long to see what was going on here. But suddenly he knew.

Nate had cast himself in Andrew McCarthy's role.

Which made Carlos Ally Sheedy.

But no, that was nuts. Nate didn't feel that way about Carlos. He'd never said a word about it. There had never been a vibe between them, neither had ever made a move, Nate had never indicated....

Or had he? Had Carlos just not seen it? Had Aiden been right all along? Was Nate jealous of Aiden? Was Nate in love with Carlos?

Holy shit.

A strange clarity came over Carlos. The way Nate had instantly disliked Aiden. The way he'd been surly. The way he'd been... jealous. Lately Carlos had attributed it to Nate being better tuned into Aiden's less desirable character traits, but what if Nate really had been jealous of Aiden all along?

But it wasn't just that. It was the fact that Nate was the person Carlos came to when he needed help, Nate was Carlos's favorite person in the world, Nate was Carlos's family.

Although Carlos was honest enough with himself to admit he'd been having some decidedly not family-oriented thoughts where Nate was concerned lately.

So what would happen if he....

"Hey, Nate?"

Nate turned toward Carlos and moved forward a little. Carlos leaned toward him and touched his face. He cupped Nate's cheek, and Nate's eyes went wide.

"What are you—" Nate said.

Carlos cut him off with a kiss.

NATE WAS kissing Carlos. *They were kissing*. And it was *good*. The kiss was spicy from all the Thai curry, first of all, but also Carlos's lips were so smooth and his mouth was hot, and oh Lord, Nate had wanted this for so long. Butterflies fluttered in his belly and tingles went up his spine and all those dumb things, but something real and tangible here made Nate's heart race. He lifted his hand to the side of Carlos's face and slid his fingers over Carlos's cheek as he deepened the kiss. He curled his tongue and licked into Carlos's mouth, really tasting him, learning what his taste was like. It was better than anything Nate had ever imagined.

Carlos leaned in harder, pressing Nate into the sofa cushions. Nate pushed his fingers up, touching Carlos's scalp, feeling the texture and surprising softness of Carlos's thick black hair. Flashbulbs seemed to pop before Nate's eyes, though they were closed as he feasted on Carlos's mouth. It was magic. It was mind-blowing. It was....

Kind of painful, actually. Carlos bearing down on him was pushing him against the arm of the sofa at an odd angle.

Nate put his hands on Carlos's shoulders and eased him away.

"Wow," Carlos said. He started to lean in for more, but Nate put his fingers on Carlos's lips.

"Let me sit up," Nate said.

Carlos immediately backed away to the other end of the couch. "Oh God. Was that... oh, you didn't want me to do that, did you? I'm so sorry."

"No, Carlos, wait. Sweetheart, I could kiss you all night. Believe me, there is nothing in the world that I would rather do. But my neck was at a funny angle." Nate rubbed it. And actually, now that rational thought was returning, he was saddened to realize that this was maybe not one of the smarter things they'd ever done together. He took a deep breath. "Carlos," he whispered.

Carlos frowned. "Was that... was it okay?"

"Yeah. Oh, yeah, it was more than okay. Carlos, I...." Nate wanted to spill all the beans just then, but it felt like too much to confess. Still, he said, "I've been wanting to kiss you for a long time. But you were with Aiden, so...." He shrugged. That seemed sufficiently casual.

Nate's insides churned. Maybe Carlos's relationship with Aiden had been the catalyst to make Nate recognize his feelings. Really, that had meant almost two years of utter misery as the man Nate loved above all others fell in love with somebody else. That Aiden was such an asshole made the wound that much deeper, Nate supposed. Carlos preferred Aiden to Nate and had made that quite clear.

Not that Nate had actually given him a choice, since he'd never said anything, something he'd been regretting for a while too. If he'd just said something before Carlos had hooked up with Aiden, maybe all of this mess could have been avoided.

And still, "You *just* broke up with Aiden."

Carlos sighed. "I know."

And Nate knew he was going to have to put himself out there to get stomped on. He didn't like it, didn't like sharing his feelings so openly with such high stakes, but keeping quiet had gotten him in this bind to begin with. "You should know, I've had some, ah, more than friendly feelings for you for a while."

Carlos's eyes went wide. "Nate—"

"Just let me finish. See, I never said anything because by the time I realized what I was feeling, you were with Aiden, and well, you seemed happy, and I didn't want to break that up. I wanted you to be happy, even if you weren't with me. Plus, you know, you're my best friend in the world and if I said, 'Hey, I like you *in that way*,' you could very well have laughed at me and broken my foolish heart, and then where would I be?"

"I would never have—"

Nate held up his hand. "That's neither here nor there. It's all in the past, right? The way I feel hasn't changed. So now you know. And I know that you apparently like me enough *in that way* to kiss me, so this is new, right?"

"'I like you *in that way*'? Are we in high school?"

"Whatever. You know what I mean." Nate took a deep breath. Oh, this was the worst, to finally be offered something he'd wanted for so long and not be able to take it. Not if he wanted to do this right. "Look, here's the thing. I want this to happen. So badly. I want to kiss you and… well, and all sorts of things. I care about you so much and I've been wanting…." Nate shook his head. "But you *just* got out of a relationship less than a week ago and it ended rather traumatically. If this is a rebound thing for you, I can't… I mean, if this were only fueled by you needing something other than Aiden just for right now, it would…." Nate let out a breath. It was so hard to say this, but it needed to be said. "It would destroy me."

Carlos's eyebrows came together. "Oh, Nate."

"What I'm trying to say is that, if we're going to, you know, change the fundamental nature of our relationship, I need to know that what you're feeling is real. So I want to kiss you. Hell, I want to be with you so much. But I think we shouldn't rush into anything."

Carlos opened his mouth and lifted a hand as if he were about to protest, but then his whole body sagged against the sofa. "I know."

"But you understand what I'm saying? Because I really do… care about you." He couldn't quite say *love*, and in this moment he wasn't even sure that was what this was. Oh, Nate knew he loved Carlos and would have put his life on the line for him, and he knew he lusted after Carlos, but whether those two things had fused together into a big romantic love was an open question. Because the practical reality of where their relationship could be headed had just presented itself, and once sex had more realistically entered the equation, Nate had gotten a little confused.

When something he'd wanted for so long was finally in front of him, it was hard to know what to do with it. It was hard to trust it.

"I get it," Carlos said. "I mean, for a while now, the last few months, I've felt not totally sure about Aiden, but I just… because you and I were friends, and then we weren't talking for a while, and I just… I don't know, Nate." Carlos ran a hand through his hair, leaving it spiked up every which way. "I care about you too. You know that. I'd do anything for you. But the way I feel about you now, it's all kind of new. If I'm honest, it's confusing."

Nate didn't know how to respond, but he didn't want to push too hard and fuck this up.

Carlos looked toward the TV, seeming to watch the movie for a moment. Nate waited, watching Carlos's profile. Eventually Carlos said, "I mean, Aiden and I had so little in common. We sometimes didn't have much to talk about. But I liked him and we were sexually compatible."

Ouch. Nate winced.

"I'm sorry," Carlos said. "It's strange to say that in this context, but I need you to know where I'm coming from. My most recent relationship was not the greatest, even when I was trying hard to convince myself it was. I mean, Aiden and I had such a hard time communicating with each other sometimes that I just let him tell me what to do because it was easier. And I see now where I went wrong there, that I let him manipulate me."

"I'm not Aiden."

Carlos let out a huff of laughter. "Obviously. I'm not saying you are. The opposite, in fact. When I was at my most unhappy, you were there for me. I could talk to you about baseball for three hours and feel better about everything, you know? And okay, so maybe I started to think that if I wanted to spend time with you just talking about baseball more than I wanted to spend time with my boyfriend, then there was something really wrong with my relationship."

Nate was surprised to hear that. "Really? You really thought that?"

Carlos shrugged. "Yeah, maybe. But it's so hard when you're in the middle of something to have any perspective. I made some mistakes. I misjudged the situation. I can see that now." He looked up and their eyes met. "You're right, though. My head isn't exactly screwed on straight right now."

"Heh, *straight*," Nate said, because he couldn't help it. Because his instinct was to make a joke.

Carlos laughed. "Nothing straight about this, is there?" He grinned, but then his face went slack and serious again. "No, seriously, I know I'm not in a great place right now. My emotions are pretty confused. And that's not fair to you."

"But I figure," Nate said, "that I'm here and you're here and it's all in the open now, yeah? We have feelings for each other. I mean, you do, right? Have feelings for me? That are of a romantic nature?"

Carlos nodded as he held Nate's gaze. "Yes. I had no idea, Nate, that you felt that way about me too. I'm… I'm happy for it."

Nate's heart soared, but he tamped it down. "Well, I do. But we should give it time, and if those feelings are still here later, we can act then. Right now should be about making sure you're okay."

Carlos nodded. He turned toward the TV. It was one of the scenes with Mare Winningham and Rob Lowe. Carlos pointed at the screen. "I always kind of liked them together. The straitlaced one and the bad boy."

Nate laughed. He wondered if movies had lessons about what to do when you'd fallen in love with your best friend, and then he *kissed* you and somehow you found the superhuman strength to say no. He doubted it.

Chapter 13

NATE COULDN'T help but think about old times as he went to bed the night after Carlos kissed him.

He thought about playing with Carlos's action figures on the floor of the living room at Mama Lulu's apartment. He thought about first days of school and summers playing baseball and starting college. He remembered their first season with the Rainbow League, a million practices and games, afternoons at Yankee Stadium, the winter Carlos more or less moved in with Nate because the heat in his apartment wouldn't come on, and so many family parties. So many memories, so many small moments, cumulatively left a warm feeling in Nate's belly and enough happiness to float on while he figured out what he really wanted to happen with Carlos now.

One memory stuck in his mind. It had been one of the greatest moments of Nate's young life and, as he had been for all such moments, Carlos was there to witness it.

When they were twelve, Nate and Carlos's Little League team made the World Series. They'd gotten a little bit of national media attention because everybody liked an underdog story. They were on a down-on-its-luck, poorly funded team from the Bronx. But they had the power of Nate's stellar pitching and Carlos's solid hitting, and they'd made quick work of the competition in the regional finals, including— as they found out years later—Mason's team from the other side of the borough. So now here they were at the Little League World Series.

They didn't win the Series, but they made it further than anyone had imagined they could, so the city decided to have a dinner in their honor when they returned home. And Don Mattingly had been a guest.

Nate had spent a good portion of the first ten minutes inside the hotel ballroom freaking right the hell out, because Mattingly, one of Nate's favorite baseball players ever, was just standing around casually chatting with people in all his mustachioed glory.

"Are you going to be okay?" Carlos asked. "You look like you're about to have a heart attack."

"Carlos. He's coming this way."

It was true. Don Mattingly was on his way over. He shook hands with a few of the other kids, but then he stopped right in front of Nate.

"I heard you pitched a shut-out in Game 2," Mattingly said.

Nate was paralyzed. He just stared, unable to speak. One of his heroes was standing right in front of him, and he could only open and close his mouth like a fish.

"He did pitch a shut-out," Carlos said. "It was awesome."

"That's great. Hard to do. You thinking about the Majors, kid?"

Nate did the fish thing for another few seconds, but then he swallowed and managed to say, "Maybe," even though it wasn't true. He had no particular desire to play professionally. But if Don Mattingly thought he should, well, he supposed his future plans weren't written in stone.

"It's so great that a team from the Bronx did so well," Mattingly went on. "Nate, right?"

"Yeah. Um. Thanks, Don Mattingly." Timidly, Nate held out his hand to be shaken, and then he was shaking hands with Don Mattingly. He vibrated with nerves the whole time.

"Keep up the good work, kids," Mattingly said before moving on to talk to somebody else.

"Holy shit," Nate wheezed when he was gone. "Oh my God. Did that just happen? Am I dead?"

Carlos laughed. "It happened."

"I'm never washing this hand." He held up the hand Don Mattingly had touched and stared at it with awe.

"You know, normal boys get excited about touching girls."

Nate scoffed. "Oh, whatever. Girls. Do you know what just happened? My hero just walked up to me and congratulated me on pitching a shut-out. If I never touch a girl, I'll still be okay with how my life went."

Carlos laughed, but Nate was serious. Some of his friends were starting to notice girls, but Nate noticed... something else. He wasn't ready to tell Carlos yet.

But then Carlos said, so softly Nate barely heard him, "I, um, may not be normal because I don't really think I'm into girls."

Nate froze, wondering if he'd heard correctly. Could it really be possible that he and Carlos felt the same way? That Nate wasn't the only kid in their class who felt this way? He didn't want to make a big deal of it, though, so he calmly said, "No. Me neither."

"Maybe it will change?"

"Maybe."

Carlos crossed his arms over his chest. "Or it'll be like Lourdes keeps saying." Carlos put a hand on his hip and posed like a girl. Then, imitating Lourdes's nasal voice, he said, "If you like Nate so much, why don't you marry him?" Carlos resumed his normal posture. "Man, she's annoying."

"Too bad you can't marry me, huh?"

"Who needs marriage?" Carlos pointed at Don Mattingly. "We have baseball."

"Yeah, we do." Nate held up his hand for a high five.

They came out to each other more officially a couple of years later, but Nate had known from that moment that he had an ally, someone he wanted by his side as he journeyed through life. It would take a couple of decades for Nate to work out that he felt that romantically, but even now he thought that if he had Carlos as a friend, he'd be all right.

BY SOME miracle Carlos's face had more or less healed by the time Sunday practice rolled around, but Carlos still let Nate apply a little makeup so that at least he wouldn't have to explain himself. That worked well enough until they were at Spokes afterward and Nate made Carlos explain to Ty and Ian why they had to sneak into Aiden's apartment.

"Not that it's even sneaking, because I still have a key," Carlos said as Ty and Ian gawked.

"I'll kill him," Ty offered. "That way we can be sure he won't be there."

"Get in line," said Nate.

Carlos groaned. "No one is killing Aiden. I just want some moral support and manual labor for when I get my stuff out of his place."

"You gonna rent a storage unit or what?" Ty asked.

"I actually don't really have that much stuff. I ditched most of my furniture when I moved. So it's mostly clothes and personal stuff, nothing big."

"But you're staying at Nate's little apartment?" Ty asked.

"For now, yeah." Carlos was starting to wonder how wise that was given the prospect of a maybe-romantic relationship between him and Nate, but he couldn't think of anyplace he'd rather be, and the thought of having to find an apartment in the current competitive real estate climate gave him hives.

"You can keep anything you need to at our place," said Ian. Ty balked, but Ian turned to him and kept talking. "We have plenty of space, and that way he doesn't have to cart it all back to Manhattan. It's just temporary. Until he gets settled."

"Yeah, all right," said Ty.

"Really?" said Carlos. "I'd be grateful. It would just be a couple of boxes, and only until I figure out where I'm going to land permanently."

"It's no problem," said Ty.

Nate got up to get everyone another round. Carlos said, "I do appreciate your help."

"This thing with Aiden," Ian said. "I mean, what he did. It's such a surprise. I never imagined… I mean, did you see it coming at all?"

"I keep thinking I should have," Carlos said, leaning forward on his elbow. He was tired of thinking about this, and he wanted to be able to shut off the part of his brain that was still obsessed with analyzing the past few months for signs. "I keep thinking of things that in retrospect make it seem clear that something like this was bound to happen, but I didn't see it at the time."

Ty nodded. "I thought we knew Aiden pretty well. Who would have guessed he had this in him?"

"Are you going to press charges?" Ian asked.

Carlos sighed. He really didn't want to. He felt enough hurt and shame where Aiden was concerned; drawing it out with the police and a potential court case sounded like Carlos's worst nightmare. "No. I just want to put it behind me. Nate keeps arguing I should, but I really don't want to."

Ian rubbed Carlos's shoulder. "Well, whatever you decide, we support you."

"Thanks. Really, guys, thank you, both of you. I do appreciate it."

"Of course," said Ty.

"It's over now." Carlos watched Nate talk to the bartender from across the way. Nate was making some flirty hand gestures, or else Carlos was reading into it. "It's over."

Everything seemed so different now. Carlos found himself overanalyzing everything. It wasn't just the past few weeks with Aiden, it was the past few months, the past years, with Nate. Had he been dropping hints about his feelings that Carlos just missed all along? Now he carefully watched everything Nate did for some hidden meaning, which meant that the way Nate sometimes talked with his hands—gestures that made him read a little fey, something Carlos had always thought of as one of his gay tells—took on a whole new character. Nate was doing it now with the bartender as the bartender made four drinks, and Carlos wondered if he was flirting or just being friendly.

"I can't help but notice that you are staring at our auburn-haired friend," Ty said.

"Ugh, I know. Sorry."

"Hey, don't apologize to me. Something going on between you two?"

"No. Well, not really. We kind of had… I mean, there was a moment a few nights ago, but Nate thinks we should wait until I've sorted out everything with Aiden."

Ty narrowed his eyes. "That is remarkably levelheaded of him."

"He said he doesn't want to be just a rebound thing for me." At Ty's expression, Carlos asked, "What?"

"I'm just surprised, is all." Ty's lazy Texas accent rolled off his tongue. "This must be hard for him."

"Hard for *him*?" Carlos said.

"Oh boy," said Ian.

"What?" said Carlos.

Ty shrugged. "It's nothing. Since you had a moment, I'm guessing the secret is out there."

"Secret?" Carlos glanced back at Nate. He was still out of earshot. "That Nate has feelings for me? Yeah, he told me."

Ty raised an eyebrow. "Oh, honey. Feelings? Nate's had it bad for you for quite a while. I'm surprised he's being so rational. Not sure I could be in his shoes."

Carlos went back to watching Nate. How long had this been going on? Nate had admitted to feelings, sure, and Carlos was starting to get the picture that these were intense, but had Nate felt strongly enough to confide in his other friends about how he felt? "You guys knew?"

"He wasn't subtle," said Ty.

That was news to Carlos. "I had no idea."

"Look, it's not my place to say much. You should talk it over with Nate. Just, you know."

Ian rolled his eyes. "I think what my boyfriend is trying to say is that you and Nate could potentially make each other very happy. But it's probably best not to rush into anything. So good for Nate for not pushing you. He cares about you a lot."

"I know." And Carlos did know that. "Does the whole team know?"

"I don't know if *everybody* knows," Ty said, "but Nate's friends do. So us, Mason, Josh, probably Joe."

"Geez. I feel like Lois Lane."

"Huh?" said Nate, setting down a little tray with four beers.

"Lois Lane is always the last to know anything," Carlos explained.

"Oh, yeah." Nate sat back down. "I mean, come on, glasses are a stupid disguise. Some investigative journalist she was. And I mean, remember in the nineties when Superman had a mullet in the comics? She should have figured that out. Like, 'Oh, Clark, nice mullet you've got there, it's just like Superman's. Hey, wait!'" Nate handed everyone their beers.

"You're a weirdo, Nate," said Ty.

"Thanks." Nate took a sip of his own beer. "Anyway, I was thinking. Maybe we should also tell Josh about this. The situation with Aiden, I mean."

"What? Why?" Carlos's pulse kicked up at the mere thought of having to tell more people. As if getting beaten up by one's boyfriend wasn't mortifying enough.

"To get Aiden kicked out of the Rainbow League," Nate said matter-of-factly.

"No, wait, whoa," Carlos said. "You don't think that's taking it too far? He didn't do anything wrong."

Nate leveled his gaze at Carlos. "Except hit you. Repeatedly."

Carlos rolled his eyes. "Yeah, I was there. I remember that part. But I meant in the league. Aiden and I are over. Isn't that enough?"

Nate frowned. "I just thought that… I mean, you don't want to see him again, and this would make it easier, wouldn't it? I'm sure if we talked to Josh, he would—"

"Let's not bring more attention to this, okay?" Carlos practically spat out the words, but he needed Nate to get off the high horse. He appreciated having a defender, but Nate didn't need to take it that far. "I just want to end it all quietly and *privately* so we can all get on with our lives, all right? I'm going to have to face Aiden again anyway. Let me figure it out, okay?"

Ty and Ian exchanged a look. Carlos didn't know what it meant, but he didn't like it. He wondered what they knew that he didn't.

"Okay," said Nate. "Whatever you want to do."

"What I want is to get my stuff out of Aiden's apartment with as little hassle as possible."

"Deal," said Ty. "How's Tuesday morning?"

"That's perfect," said Carlos.

OPERATION: GET Carlos's Stuff Back commenced on Tuesday morning with Nate, Carlos, Ty, and Ian standing in front of Aiden's building. Ty hit the lock button on the remote to the van they'd rented, and the locks clicked on with a short honk of the horn.

"Are we sure he's not home?" Nate asked.

Ty grinned. "I might have called his office. He's there."

"You called his office?" Carlos guffawed.

"Might have been a prank call." Ty rocked on his heels.

Carlos shook his head. "Wow, guys. You're the best friends a fifteen-year-old boy could have."

"I try," said Ty.

"Let's get this over with," said Carlos.

After Carlos let everyone into the apartment, he saw that Aiden had started doing the work for him. He'd stacked five boxes in the living room, each labeled *Carlos*. The boxes hadn't been taped up yet, so Carlos opened one and saw that it contained the towels and bedding he'd brought from his previous apartment. The one next to it had a bunch of his clothes. The one under it was full of Carlos's books. And so on.

"This might be easier than I thought," Carlos said. "Let's start with these."

Ty nodded and grabbed one of the boxes. "I'll bring these to the van."

Most of the living room had been divested of Carlos's stuff, and near the TV Carlos found a box full of his knickknacks and framed photos. The photo on top showed Carlos and Nate posing with Derek Jeter. The glass was broken and the photo was scratched. "Well, that's just perfect." Carlos showed the photo to Nate.

"Classy guy, Aiden," Nate said. He looked around. "I've never been here, you know that?"

"Aiden sort of forbid you from helping when I moved. And then I just didn't invite you over here after that because Aiden didn't want you here."

"Really?" Nate's eyebrows shot up.

"Yeah. Said that because you hated him, you weren't welcome in his home." Carlos grabbed the tape gun from Ian and started sealing up the open boxes. "I didn't say anything because you and I weren't on great speaking terms at the time either."

"I'm sorry."

"I know. Me too. Hand me one of those empty boxes?"

Nate did as he was told. Carlos taped up the bottom of the box. Then he stopped and sighed, glancing at the bedroom door. He said, "Please come with me to the bedroom." If there was a single spot in the apartment in which he'd need the most moral support, that was it.

"Sure."

Carlos led Nate into the bedroom. Aiden had already shoved a bunch of Carlos's clothes into his old, banged-up suitcase, which he'd left open on the floor. He gestured, and Nate got down and zipped it up. Carlos started filling the box with the remainder of his stuff that was still out in the open, though there wasn't much of it. There had never been much of Carlos's stuff in this apartment.

Then Carlos noticed an envelope tucked into the frame of the mirror over Aiden's dresser. *Carlos* was scrawled across the envelope in Aiden's messy handwriting. Carlos took a deep breath and grabbed the envelope. Inside was a letter written on spiral notebook paper with the torn edge still attached. Carlos unfolded it.

Dear Carlos,

I figured you'd come in here when I was at work to take the rest of your stuff. I started packing it up because I assume there's no hope for us now. I fucked up too much. I just want you to know that I really am sorry and I know that what I did was wrong and I never should have done it. I have no excuse and I acted in a horrible way. Maybe in time you can find it in you to forgive me, but I understand if you can't. If you do, though, you know where to find me.

Love,
Aiden

"That guy's got balls," Nate said, reading over Carlos's shoulder.

"Nate."

"Sorry. Rude of me."

For a moment Carlos felt a pang of sympathy for Aiden. He'd still been texting Carlos about once a day with an apology and a plea to at least talk this out. Carlos had thought back with some fondness on better times, because he knew Aiden had it in him to be a great man and a great boyfriend. Of course, he'd also had it in him to hit Carlos. Carlos had finally texted back to reiterate that their relationship was over and he'd be coming for his stuff soon.

"Do you want me to do something?" Nate asked.

Carlos shook his head. "It's enough that you're here."

Nate nodded. "Okay. Just tell me if you need anything."

"I will." Carlos looked around. Aiden had left a few of his things around in the bedroom. This would take less time if Nate helped him collect those things. "Actually, could you grab those photos propped up on the taller dresser?"

"Sure thing." Nate walked over and grabbed the three framed photos off the dresser. He looked at one of them for a long time. "Wow. If I'm the enemy, I'm amazed he let you keep this one in here." Nate showed Carlos the photo he meant: Nate and Carlos with Don Mattingly at the World Series dinner.

"Maybe he didn't recognize you." Carlos might not have if he hadn't remembered so well what Nate looked like as a kid. He'd been skinny at twelve, all elbows and knees, and his hair was always kind of a mess, but it was worse here because it had been under a hat until about thirty seconds before the photo was taken.

Nate had since grown into his body and filled out nicely—despite Carlos's ribbing, Nate did actually have an athletic body and a decent amount of muscle definition on his chest and abs—and he'd been much more self-conscious about his hair since he'd started dating boys in college.

"He probably wouldn't have recognized Don Mattingly either," Nate said, carefully placing the photo in the open box.

"True. He doesn't watch sports. He asked me once if the guy with the mustache in that photo was one of my uncles."

Nate balked. "Uh, Mattingly was up there with Ruth and DiMaggio as one of the greatest Yankees ever. How can Aiden not have—"

"Make yourself useful," Carlos said. "Look in the bathroom for any more of those yellow towels. You know, the ones that Mom got me as a housewarming gift when I moved into the place on Eighteenth Street?"

"You mean the ones with the little ducks embroidered on the corner?"

Carlos sighed. "Those would be the ones."

Nate laughed. "Mama Lulu is my favorite."

Carlos felt a pang then as he realized he still hadn't told his mother or his sisters that he and Aiden were over. He'd been avoiding it because he hadn't wanted to explain why, but he knew they loved him and would accept whatever he told them. He could probably just say the relationship had fallen apart once they started living together, which was the truth.

All told, it only took them about an hour to get the rest of Carlos's stuff out of the apartment. Carlos gave the room one last look and then took the keys off his keychain. He left them on the coffee table and flipped the lock on his way out the door. Now it was well and truly over.

Once they loaded the van, Ty drove it over to his and Ian's place, just eight blocks from Aiden's, and unloaded everything except the clothes, shoes, and one box of personal items Carlos wanted to take with him to Nate's. Ty stacked the boxes neatly in a little alcove off their living room that they weren't currently using for anything.

"Anytime you need anything, just let us know," Ian said.

"I will. And I promise to take everything once I figure out where I'm going next," Carlos said.

Nate was behind the wheel of the van when Carlos got back. He stared out the windshield pensively.

"So that's done," Carlos said.

"Yeah. How does it feel?"

"Good. You sure you can drive this thing to Manhattan?"

Nate waved his hand. "I learned to drive on the streets of the Bronx. I can drive anywhere."

"Uh-huh. Can you drive it without killing any pedestrians or totaling a taxi?"

Nate put the car in gear. "I'll certainly try. I can't make any promises."

NATE SAT at his mother's bedside and watched her breathe.

The doctors were not optimistic. It was anxiety-inducing, watching each intake of breath, half-convinced it would be her last one.

Still, they'd had a brief conversation when he'd first arrived, before she fell asleep. He'd explained that Carlos had gone through a bad breakup and was currently crashing at his place. He didn't tell his mother that the sleeping arrangements had gotten weird. Now that Carlos's bruises had mostly healed, they were switching off between the couch and the bed. It was too much bother to change the sheets on the bed every night and Carlos said he didn't mind, so now Nate was falling asleep every other night on sheets that smelled like Carlos, and it was slowly driving him mad with lust.

But that was not an appropriate thought for his mother's deathbed vigil.

When visiting hours ended, a nurse came to check on Nate.

"She's stable," the nurse explained. "She's been awake on and off, but it's mostly been this for a week."

"Yeah, that's what Dr. Lefkowitz said."

"If you want to sit with her, that's all right, but if you have somewhere else to be, I'll give you a call if anything changes."

Nate nodded. He thought that a good son would have vowed to stay at her side through the bitter end, that a good son would already be torn apart by grief. Nate must not be a good son, because looking at her irritated him. The nurse letting him off the hook offered some relief, yes, but mostly he felt angry. He was angry at her for not telling him the cancer was back. He was angry because she was about to leave him. And suddenly it felt like his whole life, she'd been taking steps away from him.

"I, um," he said to the nurse. "Do you think anything will change today?"

"Hard to say, but I doubt it. Her vitals are as good as can be expected. She even ate a pretty hearty breakfast. It was nice to see her appetite up."

"That is good." But Nate knew it was a short-lived victory. She wouldn't recover from her current relapse. The malignant cells had taken over a number of her internal organs, and now it was just a question of how much longer she'd hold out.

And Nate fucking hated hospitals. He hated the acidic smell of death and bleach, hated the sadness that seemed to permeate every wall of the oncology ward in which his mother now resided, hated the false cheeriness of the nurses in their jolly pink scrubs.

And he hated that he was now dealing with all this alone.

He needed Carlos. He needed to be back home where Carlos offered him some modicum of hope instead of the hopelessness that seemed to reign here.

"I do need to get home," he told the nurse, "but please call me if anything changes. I'll come straight back if that's the case. Otherwise, I'll be by tomorrow."

"Sure. I've got your number."

He nodded. "All right. Just give me a second to say good-bye. Then I'll get out of your hair."

The nurse nodded and left.

Conscious of the fact that this could possibly be his last visit, Nate took a moment to soak it all in, every detail, from her white-blonde hair to her sallow face to her skin, which had wrinkled and aged far beyond her years. The cancer had started destroying the outside of her just as surely as it was destroying her inside. Her eyes were closed, though her eyelashes fluttered as if she were in a dream. Her breath seemed labored, but she kept on breathing. She was hooked up to three different monitors and had an IV in the back of her hand, which rested calmly at her side. The flowers he'd brought on his last visit sat on the side table, starting to wilt. He'd brought her a stack of paperback romance novels a couple of weeks ago too, and a few of them showed signs of being read—they had cracked spines and dog-eared pages—so Nate supposed not all was lost. Not yet.

"Bye, Mom," he whispered. "Just… in case this is the last time, I love you. I hope you're comfortable."

Feeling overwhelmed, he swallowed and left the room.

He felt drained when he walked into his apartment sometime later. He'd grabbed a pizza on his way home and slid it onto the coffee table in front of Carlos, who was wearing pajamas and watching TV.

"How'd it go?" Carlos asked.

"She's the same. Stable."

"Want to talk about it?"

Nate appreciated that Carlos asked, but he wanted to put it out of his mind. "No. Not much to say. I got sausage and mushroom."

"My favorite! You're the best, Nate."

"What are you watching?"

Carlos smiled, obviously understanding Nate needed a distraction. "Oh, it's this terrible reality show about real estate agents in New York. The people on it are the worst kind of pretentious. But one of the agents on the show is really hot." He paused and looked at the TV. Then he pointed. "That one."

The guy talking on screen had short brown hair combed just so and was wearing a very nice suit. He was okay-looking if you liked corporate banker types. Or real estate moguls, as the case might be.

"He's gay too," Carlos said through a mouth full of pizza. "Alas, he's dating a model. Of *course*. And not even, like, an aspiring model, but a real model who has done magazine spreads and stuff. Although the model is kind of a butterface."

Nate nodded and grabbed a slice. "Well, what's the point of that?"

"Dunno. Maybe he's got a big cock."

Nate laughed.

"Oh, and after this is the cooking show you like. I'm rooting for Janine. She's a little snobby about food, but she's spunky."

"I like Rich, even though he puts pork in everything."

"Oh yeah. He's good too. I really thought when they showed him calling his wife and kid at the beginning of the last episode that he was getting the loser edit, but then he won the challenge. Keeping us on our toes, I guess."

"Carlos?" Nate said, already feeling better.

"Hmm?"

"Thank you."

Carlos grinned. "Anytime."

Chapter 14

THE CALL came when Nate was at work two days later. "She's having trouble breathing," Dr. Lefkowitz said. "You'd better get here as soon as you can."

Nate grabbed a cab and directed the cabbie to take the route with the least traffic, and by some miracle, Nate arrived at the hospital when she was awake and lucid.

"Hi, Mom," Nate said as he sat in a chair at her bedside.

"Nathan," Rebecca wheezed.

"We had to put a tube down her throat to help her breathe," the nurse said. "We took the tube out when she started breathing on her own, but her throat is probably a little raw."

He nodded. He looked at his mother, at her thin, fragile frame, and realized he had nothing to say to her.

It was a terrible thing to realize at the bedside of his dying mother. Worse, he knew he'd been using the bullshit with Carlos—as high-stakes as it felt in the moment—as a distraction from all this. Because no matter how strained their relationship had grown over the years, she was still his mother. She'd saved money to pay for balls and gloves and uniforms so he could play baseball, something that had made him happy. He had no doubt that she loved him and had done the best she could.

And now she was dying.

He knew that the cancer wasn't her fault, but it was hard not to feel like she was leaving him.

Like everyone had left him. Like his lovers had. Like Carlos had left him for Aiden.

He knew he was being unfair and maudlin, but he choked out a sob anyway.

Rebecca reached over and placed her hand on his where it rested on the side of the bed.

"Oh, Mom," he said, unable to keep the tears from stinging his eyes.

"Tell me about work," she said.

He sighed. "Nothing to tell, really. I'm working on online math tutorials for middle school students now. Editing and doing some of the coding. It's kind of fun, actually."

She nodded. "And you said Carlos has moved in with you?"

At least she'd listened. "Well, just temporarily. He broke up with his boyfriend and needed a place to stay."

"Oh." She took a deep breath. "That's all? I thought you and Carlos—"

"No." Realizing the word was too harsh, he said, "I mean, not yet, anyway. Maybe. I don't know."

She nodded. "You like him."

"Of course I do."

"I know."

Nate nodded. He understood that she did know all of it.

She took a deep breath and then whispered, "I know I haven't always been the most accepting."

"Mom, it's fine."

"It's not. I want to make sure you're taken care of."

"I'm fine. I have a good job. A good home. I have friends and baseball."

She shook her head. She propped herself up on her elbows, which clearly took all her strength. He could see it in the way her arms shook. "You were so young when your father left us. I was so young. I let it make me bitter. I want better for you. I want you to have love and happiness."

A rock seemed to lodge itself in Nate's throat. He managed to say, "Even with a man?"

She nodded. "Even then. It took me a long time to work through what I knew from church and what was before my own eyes." She frowned. "I know now that nothing is so simple. Husbands are supposed to honor their wives, and yet mine filed for divorce and wanted nothing to do with his own son."

This was a story Nate knew well. His father had taken off when Nate was three, before he'd formed any lasting memories of the man. All Nate really knew about him was that he and his mother had been college sweethearts and that his father had felt overwhelmed by the prospect of raising a child. He'd panicked one day and left forever. Or this was Nate's mother's version of events; Nate suspected the truth was worse. Carlos used to ask him if he was curious about his father, but he genuinely wasn't. Any man who could abandon his wife and child was not worth Nate's time.

Rebecca wasn't done talking. She touched Nate's hand again to get his attention. He looked at her and their gazes met. Her eyes were blue and watery, tired, paler than they should have been. But she was still alive, and she clearly had something she wanted to say. So Nate listened.

"Father Egan said for years that gay people were wrong, and I believed him. But you're gay, and there's nothing wrong with you. You're my son, Nate. *My* son. You grew up to be a good man." Her eyes crinkled a little as she gently squeezed is hand. "It took me longer to realize it than it should have. But you're the best thing I ever did with my life. I'm so proud of you." Then, as if that took everything she had, she relaxed and sagged against the pillows.

Nate was too choked up to speak.

Rebecca squeezed his hand again. "If I had it to do over, there are things I'd do differently," she whispered. "I'm sorry for that."

Nate understood that she needed absolution, and he recognized too that she was contrite enough to deserve it. They both knew what was happening here. "You did your best," Nate said. "I'm grateful. I had a good childhood, Mom. There was nothing I needed that you didn't provide."

She nodded. "I did try." She took a deep breath and then let it back out shakily. "Maybe I hoped you and Carlos were together because I want to make sure someone is looking out for you. He cares about you so much. Him and Mama Lulu and all of the Ruizes. I know they will take care of you. But Carlos is special."

"He is, yes. I… maybe something will happen. I want for us to be together. If we can work out how, I think we will be."

"You'll figure it out. I want that for you," she whispered.

She gasped suddenly. The monitor beeped, and the nurse, who must have wanted to give them a private moment, rushed back into the room and started fretting over the equipment.

Rebecca held it together long enough to wheeze, "I love you."

He felt that deep in his gut and knew it was true. He touched her hand softly. "I love you too. I'll miss you."

That seemed to satisfy her. She gasped again and settled against her pillow, though her face scrunched up in discomfort.

"It's her lungs," the nurse said.

Nate nodded; he knew the cancer had gotten there too. He'd already talked to her doctor about it. The doctor thought the malignant tumor on her lung would have been operable if the cancer hadn't weakened her system so much already. She'd never survive surgery. Nate had agreed that the best course of action was to make sure her last weeks were comfortable. Most of the time, that meant she was drugged to the gills and barely able to speak. He wondered if she'd had the will to fight through the drug-induced fog to talk to him today because she knew the end was nigh.

He watched her features relax as whatever the nurse put in her IV eased her to sleep.

"Did you talk to Dr. Lefkowitz?" the nurse asked.

"Yes. I think I'll stick around today, if it's all right with you."

The nurse nodded and patted his arm. "I'm so sorry."

He was too. No one should have to spend an afternoon watching his own mother slip away.

IN ONE of his more morbid moments, Carlos tried to picture what would happen if one of his parents had fallen ill. His father in particular was less active these days than he'd once been, and Mama Lulu was always after him about what he ate, so Carlos knew he was mortal, but he'd never had to face the possibility that they wouldn't be around indefinitely. He made a mental note to make time to see his parents soon.

He did call his mother after Nate texted that Rebecca had taken a turn for the worse, and he was headed to the hospital. He finally told her what had happened with Aiden, although he kept his explanation to the fact that they'd been arguing a lot since they moved in together and couldn't make it work.

"So you're at Nate's now?" she asked before he could even explain.

"Yeah. How did you know?"

"You didn't come here."

Fair enough.

He had called Nate when he left his office to make sure he was all right.

"I'm hanging in there," Nate said. "So is she, so far."

"Do you want me to come to the hospital?"

"No… honestly, I'd really rather you didn't. The idea of you being in this awful place… no."

"Are you sure? Even just to hold your hand?"

Nate sighed heavily. "Oh, sweetheart, I…. It's tempting, but I have to face this on my own. I'll come home tonight and you can hold my hand all you want."

"All right. Can I at least send Mama over there with some real food? You probably haven't eaten all afternoon."

"No, I… I mean, I guess, if she's not busy…."

"I'll call her right now. You're sure you don't want me to come too? I'll bring pizza."

"No, really. Please just… be home when I get there?"

That Carlos could do. "I'm headed there now."

Carlos didn't have to wait long. After setting his mother in motion—she promised to bring Nate and Rebecca some of her famous chicken soup—Carlos stopped at the store to buy some comfort junk food before heading home.

That evening he sat on the couch, flipping through channels but not really seeing anything on the TV, fretting about Nate more than anything else. Nate's texts had not sounded optimistic. Carlos couldn't help but think about what Nate must be experiencing, if his mother would even live out the day. It was hard to wrap his head around.

Nate got home a little after eight. He looked haggard.

"Well?" Carlos said, holding his breath as he waited for the answer.

Nate shook his head and walked toward the sofa. "She's gone."

"Oh, *mi corazón*. Come here."

Nate sat on the couch and leaned on Carlos's shoulder. He let out a shaky breath. "That was one of the hardest things I've ever done."

Carlos put his arms around Nate and held him there. He rubbed Nate's back.

Nate started shaking. Softly, he said, "We had this nice talk, and then she fell asleep, and then she just… eventually she stopped breathing. We had decided, you know, weeks ago, not to resuscitate. And I didn't want to let her go… I mean, after all these years, we talked and I finally felt like we understood each other." Nate let out a sob. His next words were almost a wail. "And then she died."

"Nate. I'm so sorry."

"She left, Carlos. She's gone. But she was in so much pain. I could see it on her face. In her shoulders. She was all tense at the end, and then suddenly she… wasn't."

"Now her pain is over."

"I know. But she's my mother, you know? And now she's… she's gone."

Nate broke then. He started weeping, big sobs wracking his body and making him shake. He lurched forward, falling practically into Carlos's lap, and he cried in the way that Carlos supposed only someone who had just lost his mother could. Carlos tried to murmur comforting things, but mostly he just held Nate and let him cry.

Nate kept whispering, "She's gone," over and over.

So Carlos held him and stroked his back and let him cry. Nate pressed his face into Carlos's chest and gathered some of Carlos's shirt in his fist and seemed to hold on for dear life. Carlos could only hope that he could offer some comfort, and in a way, he was glad that circumstance had led him to be here, because Nate shouldn't have been alone when he'd just suffered one of the worst losses of his life.

"I'm here," Carlos said. "I'm here for anything you need. You want to talk, I'm here. You just want to cry, anything, I'm here. Anything for you, Nate."

And Carlos meant it. He would be or do anything Nate needed. Because he loved Nate, and not just as a friend. He loved Nate best of everyone in the world, with his whole heart, with his soul.

He hated that it had taken a crisis to make him realize that.

And now was certainly not the time to say anything. No, Nate needed some time to mourn his mother. And Carlos intended to give him that. So instead of speaking any more, he held Nate as Nate cried. The rest could wait.

Chapter 15

NATE CALLED out of work. He was sitting at his tiny kitchen table eating a bowl of cereal and staring off into space when the cavalry arrived.

Carlos had called out of work too, so he was in the process of setting the sofa to rights after he'd slept on it when the buzzer rang.

"I think it's the casserole brigade," Carlos said as he walked over to the intercom.

Indeed, a few minutes later, Mama Lulu, followed by her husband and Marisol, paraded into Nate's apartment bearing grocery bags.

Nate stood to greet her as she walked toward him. She said, "Oh, *mi hijo*!" and smothered him in a huge hug.

"You didn't have to come," Nate said.

"Nonsense," said Mama Lulu. "Of course we did. We're here for you."

Nate sighed and sank into her fleshy hug. "You didn't have to come, but I appreciate that you did."

She squeezed him again and then took a step back. "Marisol, please put those bags in the kitchen."

"Did you bring me food?" Nate asked.

"Just a few things."

Carlos wandered in to help Marisol unpack. "Just a few things? There's enough here to feed me and Nate for two weeks."

Mama Lulu shrugged. "I know how you boys are. You're both too skinny. And Nate here is going to be too upset to want to cook anything. All you have to do is heat those up. Put the blue Tupperware in the freezer for later."

"Thank you," Nate said.

He took in the whole picture. Mama Lulu and Carlos's father, Juan, were both dressed in head-to-toe black. Marisol was wearing a red blouse tucked into black trousers, but she had a black scarf in her hair.

They'd come to help him mourn.

Juan approached and slapped his shoulder. "You must be overwhelmed. I had to make arrangements for my own mother not too long ago, and it's very difficult. We've come to help if you need it."

Nate nodded slowly. "Yeah. I think I do." He took a deep, shuddery breath. He wasn't pleased to have his morning interrupted, but it was nice knowing he had help. Juan was right; Nate felt completely overwhelmed. "Father Egan from St. John's came to the hospital yesterday to perform last rites, so I talked to him. The funeral will be there on Thursday. And that's as far as I got."

"We're here to help, *mi hijo*," said Mama Lulu.

"You almost got the whole clan here this morning," Marisol said. "I explained to Mom that even just the immediate Ruiz family would not fit in your apartment. Plus, the last time Lourdes's kids came to my place, they got into my unmentionables drawer." Marisol raised her eyebrows and shook her head.

Nate laughed despite the situation.

"They will all be at the funeral, though, of course," said Mama Lulu. "You don't have to go through this alone."

Marisol walked over to Nate and gave him a hug. "That I can agree with. We're all here for you. Lourdes and Gabriela too."

"Thank you, guys. I don't know how to even express...." The outpouring of love overwhelmed Nate, the tide of emotion was hard to stop. He was sad and out of sorts but so grateful to his surrogate family for coming through when he needed them. He swallowed a sob, unable to continue speaking. His throat stung.

Marisol was closest, so she hugged him again.

"Should we start making phone calls?" Mama Lulu asked. "There's that funeral home near St. John's that could probably do a wake. What is the name of it, Juan?"

"Brayer's?" said Juan.

"A wake?" Nate asked.

Mama Lulu nodded decisively. "We will pray for Rebecca to have an easy passage to heaven."

It was no less than a woman who had worked hard and been a good Catholic all her life deserved, so Nate nodded. "All right."

Rebecca deserved it, but Nate wondered about the fate of his own soul. Yesterday afternoon, Father Egan had offered a few opinions on the "lifestyle" Nate lived, informing him that he and Rebecca had had a number of in-depth conversations about Nate's choices and the state of his soul. Nate wasn't altogether convinced he wouldn't burst into flame when he entered the church for the funeral. But he'd long ago tossed off his mother's religion, choosing to live his own life without apology, and if Father Egan didn't like it, well, he could take his own advice.

But Nate knew his mother would appreciate the trappings of a Catholic funeral, from the wake to the mass, so he spent the afternoon mostly agreeing to Mama Lulu's suggestions. They had so much to negotiate, from the timing of the wake to what flowers Nate would buy to the color of the casket. And Nate's angrily tossed off "It's a box we bury her in, I don't care about the color" got him an angry glare, so it wasn't all smooth sailing, either.

"You have keys to your mom's place?" Marisol asked at one point.

"Yes." And that was one more thing. "I'm going to have to clean it out, aren't I?"

"We'll help," Mama Lulu repeated.

So maybe it wouldn't be terrible, but then Marisol pointed out that they'd have to pick out a dress to bury his mother in, and that choking feeling he'd been experiencing on and off all day resumed.

"I don't know if I can do this," Nate said.

Carlos took his hand and gave it a squeeze. "You can. We'll get through it."

That simple sentiment probably shouldn't have soothed Nate so well, but it did. He let out a breath and nodded. "Thank you," he whispered, meaning it just for Carlos.

Carlos smiled. "Anytime."

THE NEXT few days were a blur. On Tuesday and Wednesday nights, Nate kept vigil at a funeral home in the Bronx. Carlos sat out Tuesday night's Rainbow League game with him, keeping near his side or close to it the whole time they were in the funeral home. On Tuesday most of the Ruiz family and a few of Rebecca's friends came to pay their respects. Mama Lulu sat near the casket and quietly prayed, worrying rosary beads through her fingers as she did, but she'd stop and greet anyone who came up to her. Wednesday most of the Hipsters and a few of Nate's other friends and coworkers came by, as if they had all figured out at the same time that these rituals were for those left behind more than they were for the deceased.

Although Nate didn't burst into flames when he entered the Catholic church he'd attended as a kid, he still felt uncomfortable as he made his way to the front pew for the funeral mass. He'd hated this place for so long. When he was a kid, it was mostly the location of boring masses and CCD classes made bearable only because Carlos attended them with him. Then it was the place that had convinced his mother something inherently sinful was in him, putting a rift in their relationship that only seemed to heal at the end of her life.

Still, he lit a candle for his mother before the mass began and then he sat in that pew, Carlos beside him, both of them flanked by various members of the Ruiz family. And they had *all* shown up for the mass. Mama Lulu and Juan came, as did Marisol, now seated beside Carlos. Lourdes and her husband and their kids came, and Carlos's baby sister, Gabriela, sat with her fiancé. A smattering of Carlos's aunts and uncles and their kids had come too. None of these people were strangers; Nate had been attending Ruiz family events, including funerals not unlike this one, since the early days of his friendship with Carlos.

He was so grateful to have everyone there with him. Nate's biological family was down to just himself now that his mother was gone, but the Ruizes were his family just the same. There were no words for how much he needed and appreciated their support. How very like them all to rally in his time of need. He belonged with them.

He belonged with Carlos.

Carlos was coming around to that idea, because as the mass began, Carlos took Nate's hand and pressed it between both of his own. When Nate started to feel like he might lose it again, when he thought he might choke or when his eyes stung with unshed tears, Carlos was right there, his presence comforting Nate. He'd squeeze Nate's hand or nudge him with his shoulder. He handed him tissues when he needed them and murmured consoling words when Nate started losing his grip.

They buried Rebecca in her favorite green polka dot dress, one Nate remembered she'd loved and that Marisol had helped him find in her closet. Marisol had also taken it upon herself to box up a lot of those old clothes to take to a women's shelter she volunteered for. He'd let the Ruizes have free rein to take any of his mother's old things that they thought might be useful. He sold most of the furniture on Craigslist hoping to offset some of the funeral costs and took only a few things for himself, mostly what remained of his childhood in his old bedroom and all of the photo albums and a few of her more cherished pieces of jewelry. By the time the funeral began, they'd pretty much cleaned out the apartment. The rush was mostly to gratify the impatient landlord, who wanted to find another tenant.

Still, Nate reasoned it was best to get it over with.

Now that he was sitting in the pew at church, he felt drained. He was surprised that the compulsory words of the funeral mass brought so much emotion to the surface. He really did hope his mother was in a better place now, a place where she could finally rest after so many years of working herself to the bone to take care of the two of them.

So maybe they hadn't had the best relationship, but he was still grateful to her.

He was surprised, too, that he still remembered the rhythms of the mass, remembered when to stand and when to kneel and when to pray. He wondered how much of that was muscle memory from having the rituals drilled into him as a child. He kept an eye on Mama Lulu and her rosary. If prayer alone were enough, Rebecca was likely enjoying smooth sailing into heaven. Not that Nate believed in any of that, but he was grateful to Lulu for her prayers just the same.

For the funeral procession, Nate was herded into a Town Car owned by the funeral home. He pulled Carlos into the car with him.

"That was hard for you," Carlos said softly once the car was moving.

"I think, actually, that the next part will be harder."

"You know, my parents go to Sacred Heart instead of St. John's these days. Mama doesn't have a lot of nice things to say about Father Egan after he gave a sermon a few years ago saying all the heathen gays would burn in hell."

Nate sighed. "I've already endured two lectures from the man himself. He only agreed to do the funeral because he liked my mother so much."

Carlos took Nate's hand again and kissed his knuckles. The gesture warmed Nate. "This will all be over soon," Carlos said.

The graveside service was really a blur, because Nate spent a good portion of it weeping uncontrollably. He fought to gain control, but the harder he worked to keep the tears at bay, the more forcefully they came.

When he mentioned later that he'd thought it unmanly to fall apart so publicly, Lulu told him that the death of one's mother was one of those times it was perfectly acceptable for a man to cry in public.

"What's another time?" Nate asked, unsure if he wanted the answer.

"His wedding," she said with a wink.

NATE WAS quiet on the cab ride home after the funeral, and Carlos figured it was better to let him brood than to try to fill the silence. He found the quiet unnerving, though, and around the time the cab passed from the Bronx into Manhattan, Carlos said, "If you want to talk, tell me. Even if you want me to just talk about stupid stuff. Or if you want me to stay quiet, I can do that too."

Nate took Carlos's hand. He threaded their fingers together. "After all that, I feel like I have nothing left to say. I just want to get home as fast as possible, eat some of that potato and chorizo thing your mother left for us, and then sleep for three days."

"Reasonable."

"Tomorrow I will send your mother the biggest bouquet ever. Maybe also a box of chocolates and some of that herbal tea she likes."

"She really does know how to rally the troops."

Nate squeezed Carlos's hand. "I never would have gotten through this week without her, without all of you."

"That's family for you."

"No, Carlos, don't you see? My blood family wasn't like that at all. Your family is special. I'm honored you all consider me a part of it."

"You're my best friend."

Nate nodded, though he resumed his silent contemplation for the next few blocks.

The cab dropped them near Nate's building after what felt like a million years and a million blocks. Carlos kept his grip on Nate's hand as they walked to Nate's apartment. It wasn't something they would have dared in the Bronx, but here in Chelsea, with rainbow flags dangling over the doors of almost every business, and several other male couples holding hands as they walked down the street, it was safe.

When they finally arrived at Nate's apartment, Carlos told Nate to sit on the couch while he heated up dinner. He slid the whole dish into the oven, as there were really only two servings left anyway. He and Nate had been working their way through the small feast his family had left. Stressful situations tended to zap Nate's appetite, but Lulu had known perfectly well that he couldn't resist the siren call of her cooking.

While Carlos waited for the dish to heat up, he sat next to Nate, who was now staring at the blank screen of the TV.

"Nate?"

Nate looked at Carlos, his face still registering the day's pain.

Carlos cupped Nate's face. "The thing with family is that they love unconditionally, you know? When you need something, they're there for you."

"Yes," said Nate.

Carlos swallowed, not sure how to say what he wanted to say. "I wish I had seen… I wish I hadn't had my head so far up my own ass that I didn't know you were going through this sooner. I'm so deeply sorry that I ever let Aiden get between us."

"It's over. That's all in the past."

"I know, but that doesn't mean I'm not sorry."

"You were here for me this week, when I really needed it. That's what counts."

"You're family."

Nate sighed and leaned into the touch of Carlos's hand. "Is that all?"

Carlos knew what Nate was asking. "For so long, we were brothers. I never thought of you in any other way."

"And now?"

Carlos shook his head. "This is maybe the worst time to say this, but now? Honestly? Well, I'm realizing we're not actually related."

"Oh."

Nate's disappointment hung in the air between them as he lowered his head and ducked away from Carlos's touch.

Carlos put his hands on Nate's shoulders, causing Nate to look up again. Carlos said, "No, that's not what I meant. I just meant… we're not actually brothers. Because if we were, the things I've been thinking about you recently would be incestuous and gross."

Nate closed his eyes.

"But it's not just that," Carlos went on. "It's not just lust or a fleeting attraction or whatever. It's that you're the most important person in my life, and this week, you were suffering. I would do anything to ease that suffering."

"Carlos...."

"I love you, Nate, is what I'm trying to say. Not just as a brother."

Nate opened his eyes wide and met Carlos's gaze. The air around them seemed to freeze for a moment, as if time had stopped.

Carlos broke the moment by leaning forward and kissing Nate.

Nate responded instantly, burying his fingers in Carlos's hair. Nate's lips parted, inviting Carlos in, and Carlos took the invitation.

Kissing Nate really was a revelation, unlike kissing anyone else. It was beautiful and comforting and exactly what Carlos thought they both needed. Nate's lips were salty and soft. He gripped Carlos's hair, showing his passion.

Nate eased away slightly. "Carlos, I...."

"It's okay, *mi corazón*. You don't have to say anything."

"No, I do. Carlos, I have loved you for so long. These things you're saying, they're perfect. And yet."

"And yet your mother just died and the timing is terrible."

Nate looked down and let out a tired laugh. "Yeah. If I thought myself capable of being with you right now, we'd already be in bed."

"It's okay. Dinner is almost ready."

Nate nodded.

They ate together at the little table off the kitchen. Nate was still mostly quiet, but he seemed thoughtful now. Eventually he said, "This sucks."

"That seems like an understatement for today," said Carlos. "In what specific way does this suck?"

"All of it. This week. Mom. Father Egan. The fact that I can't stop thinking about Mom and her last day. You and Aiden. You living here. You kissing me the way you just did and me feeling unable to do much more than crawl into bed and sleep forever."

"If it's meant to be, everything will work itself out."

"I never had your faith." Nate ate a forkful of potato and then put his fork down. He rubbed his forehead. "I needed you this week and you came through for me. I hope that Mama Lulu is immortal and this never happens to you, but if it does, I can only hope that I can come through for you in the same way."

"You will."

Nate nodded, though he didn't look convinced.

They cleaned up; then Nate announced that he was going to sleep.

"You take the bed, *papi*," said Carlos. "You look like you could use a more comfortable sleep."

Nate went into his bedroom, but he returned a few moments later wearing a T-shirt and boxers. "Do you think you could also sleep in the bed?"

"What?"

"Not for sex. Just, I don't want to be alone right now."

"Yes, of course. Anything you need."

Carlos went through his nightly ritual, and by the time he was ready to crawl into bed, Nate was already there, the covers pulled up to his chin, the air conditioner rattling in the bedroom window. Carlos lifted the covers and got in beside him.

"Is this awkward?" Nate asked.

"Not for me. Is it for you?"

"No." Under the covers, Nate grabbed for and caught Carlos's hand. "I just... I need a friend right now."

Carlos thought this might straddle the line between mere friendship and something more, but he held Nate's hand and settled into the mattress. "Then I'm here for you," he said.

Chapter 16

NATE THOUGHT the next week went by like a Disney movie montage, lacking only the plucky young heroine's catchy "what is this feeling?" song. On the other hand, he'd questioned his own feelings plenty, perhaps enough to write a whole song himself.

He'd lost his mother, which seemed to be a Disney hero requirement, so there was that. That was hard enough, but he hadn't expected to feel so unmoored by it. He'd been living on his own without much support except for an occasional phone call for almost fifteen years. But something about being orphaned, even at the ripe old age of thirty-three, made Nate feel like the foundation of his life had just fallen out from under him.

That was one thing. Still having Carlos in his space was another. He certainly didn't mind, but the situation with Carlos wasn't playing out the way he'd expected. Since coming to the unwelcome realization that he was in love with Carlos, Nate had spent a not-insignificant amount of time imagining what their life would be like when they were together. In his head, it was all smiles and sex. It was their relationship as it has always been, just with more nudity.

The reality was that even though there was no nudity—yet—Nate's feelings had changed in a way that was more subtle and complex than he thought possible. It wasn't the same. It was deeper. Every time he looked at Carlos, he had the sense that they were on the same team, just as he'd always felt, but he also felt gratitude and warmth. There was so much love in him he thought it might be coming out of his pores.

At Nate's insistence, no one slept on the couch, but nothing happened in bed either. They just slept. Nate was too drained for any funny business at the end of the day anyway. That Carlos seemed unfazed by this and didn't push him for anything was both a relief and kind of unnerving. Didn't Carlos feel all this passion too? Nate only wished he could summon the energy to rip Carlos's clothes off, because part of him wanted to see what could happen between them. But part of him was terrified of that too.

So much was changing. And it was changing so fast.

But Carlos was there with a hug whenever Nate started to think he needed one, often without being asked. Two days after the funeral, as Nate was staring dumbfounded at the box of cereal in his hand and the bowl on the counter, utterly mystified by the process of preparing breakfast, Carlos gave him a tight hug and took over. When he had to finish paperwork regarding Rebecca's estate, Carlos reminded Nate that he was a lawyer and translated the legalese. When Nate put on the Yankees game one evening but missed a key play because he'd spaced out, Carlos put an arm around him and brought him back to reality.

But it wasn't just hugs. It was also kisses. So many kisses. Toothpaste kisses over the sink first thing in the morning. I'm-leaving-for-work kisses. Do-you-need-anything-from-the-store kisses. The-Yankees-win kisses. Just-because-I-caught-you-smiling kisses.

It left Nate feeling fluttery. And yet he also felt grounded, as if his grief were a hot air balloon straining toward the sky, but Carlos was the sandbag holding him down. He needed the sandbag or he'd risk floating away.

So maybe, if he'd planned it, this wasn't how a romantic relationship with Carlos was supposed to start, but this reality had weight to it. It felt real in a way nothing else did. Love, then, was maybe not just gratification, which Nate realized was how he'd been picturing it. He'd always imagined one day he'd kiss Carlos and confess how he felt and then they'd live happily ever after. No, love was having an anchor, having someone to hold you when you felt yourself drifting away. Love was giving of yourself easily and freely. Love was what Carlos had given to Nate in the week after Nate's mother died. Love kept Nate from falling to pieces. Nate was humbled by it. He could only hope to be able to give that back to Carlos.

ON THE subway ride to practice Sunday, Nate was quiet, as he had been since Rebecca's death, though he didn't seem as morose as he had been all week. Josh had even called that morning and told Nate it was cool to sit out a few more games if he felt he needed to. But Nate insisted he wanted to play baseball again, that he needed the familiarity and the distraction. He planned to head back to work Monday too. Carlos was glad Nate was surfacing, but it was still hard not to worry.

"Carlos?" he said after a long silence between stops.

"Yes, *papi*." Carlos took Nate's hand.

Nate stared at their joined hands and smiled briefly before he said softly, "Thank you for everything. I don't know how to even begin to repay you."

"No payment needed. It was nothing. I wanted to help."

"I know, but I've been so out of it, and you've been amazing. I don't even have words to really thank you or tell you how much it means to me."

"You'd do the same."

Nate nodded. "I'd certainly try."

Carlos put his fingers below Nate's chin. He gently pushed up so Nate would face him. "You already have. When everything went down with Aiden, you offered me a place to stay."

"It's not the same."

Carlos shook his head. "It's not a contest. Life isn't orderly or predictable like that. Shit happens, and all we can really do is be there for each other. I did all this for you because I love you and I wanted to help. I trust you and know you'd do anything you could if I suffered a loss like this." He took a deep breath. "I don't know what's going to happen with us, but something has definitely changed."

"I know."

"Hopefully for the better." Carlos dropped his hand.

"Yeah. I think so." Nate spoke so softly it was hard for Carlos to hear. "Not a conversation for the subway, though."

"No, probably not."

Nate let out a breath. "I love you."

Carlos patted Nate's shoulder. "I have faith everything will work out the way it's supposed to."

Nate smiled sadly. "I love your faith. I wish it were catching."

Carlos laughed. "Well, now you've made it sound like a disease."

Once they got to practice, Nate threw himself into it with aplomb. During batting practice, he threw nothing but fastballs straight through the strike zone, and no one could hit them. Scott was apoplectic with frustration over everyone's lack of batting skills, but toward the end, he walked up to Nate and patted him on the back.

That touching moment over, Scott barked, "We're playing the Queens on Tuesday. You bums could beat them in your sleep, but come prepared anyway."

"Oh, shit!" Carlos said aloud.

"What?" Nate asked as he resumed his place next to Carlos.

"Uh, Aiden plays for the Queens."

Nate frowned. "Hey, Josh!"

"Nate…," Carlos started.

Josh jogged over and smiled at them. He gave Nate a big hug. "Oh, Nate. I'm so sorry about your mother."

"Thank you."

"Tony offered to make you a lasagna. It's his way. He's so Italian he bleeds marinara, so he copes with hardship by cooking."

"I wouldn't say no to Tony's lasagna…."

Josh smiled. "Did you need something else?"

"Just a question. Does the Rainbow League have a policy on domestic violence?"

Josh narrowed his eyes and looked confused. "We're against it? I don't know. What do you mean?"

"Let's say," Nate said with a glance at Carlos, "*hypothetically*, that two players were dating each other and one of them beat the other. If someone else in the league found out about it and reported it, could the league kick out the abuser?"

Josh frowned. He glanced at Carlos, which Carlos figured meant he'd seen the bruises at practice the week before. Josh was a smart guy and probably didn't need much to put the pieces together. "I don't know that we really have a policy on that. Will is usually pretty adamant that what happens off the field is none of our business. I mean, look, we're a bunch of gay men and women and we often drink together. There's bound to be drama. Breakups are pretty common. Will and I always tell players to keep it off the field. We don't generally get involved." Josh looked troubled by this and glanced at Carlos again. "Hypothetically, the victim in question would be forgiven for sitting out a game against his ex-boyfriend's team."

"It's not that big a deal," Carlos said. "I just want it all behind me."

Nate crossed his arms. "You won't press charges, but surely we should do *something*. I want him out of the league."

Josh shrugged. "I want to help. If what I'm reading between the lines is true, I'm shocked and appalled. He probably does deserve to get kicked out of the league, at minimum. But unless a grievance is filed because of an incident on the field?" He paused with a raised eyebrow. Carlos shook his head. "Unless a grievance is filed, there's nothing to be done. It sucks and I'm sorry."

"I don't want to sit out the game," said Carlos. He glared at Nate. "I can handle it. What can he do when the field is full of other players?"

"I don't like it," said Nate.

"And I appreciate that," said Carlos, though he was annoyed at Nate for intervening. He didn't know how to make Nate hear what he wanted. "But let's just let it lie. I don't want to cause more drama. He seemed sorry, it's over between us, let's all move on with our lives."

Nate sighed and dropped his arms. "All right."

"Thank you. And thanks, Josh, for listening, but… maybe don't tell anyone?"

"I won't. Again, it's off the field. In a professional capacity, it's not my business. But if you need to talk as a friend, I'm here." Josh turned to Nate. "You guys coming out with us tonight?"

"I'm pretty tired," Nate said.

"Do you want to go home?" asked Carlos.

"Yeah, kinda. But you can go out if you want to."

"No, it's all right. I'll keep you company. We can just order a pizza or something."

Josh looked between them, an amused smile playing on his lips.

Chapter 17

TUESDAY EVENING was muggy and hot the way only New York City could be. As Carlos walked from the train to the East River Park ball fields, the stench of garbage rotting on the sidewalk assaulted him and every bit of grime in the air stuck to his skin. He'd only been outside about three minutes, but he already wanted a shower. Well, what he really wanted was to not be walking to this game, but he couldn't let Aiden win.

He thought of poor Nate, who just that morning had been waffling about whether he could play or not. He hadn't slept at all the night before, and so neither had Carlos, who woke up every time Nate tossed or turned.

The two of them were quite a pair, weren't they?

Still, Nate had texted Carlos that afternoon to say he wanted to at least be at the game to support Carlos, who would be seeing Aiden for the first time since he'd walked out, something he hadn't given much thought to in the past few days because Nate was so out of sorts. And Nate had ultimately pointed out that since he was a pitcher, if he played terribly, he could get Eddie or Travis to pitch in his stead.

Carlos hit the park and made his way to the ball fields, anxiety kicking up to a flutter in his belly as he made his way across the lawn. Happily, Nate was the first person he saw. He caught Carlos's gaze as he practiced tossing a ball in the air and catching it in his glove. Nate was talking to Ty, though he seemed subdued; usually this particular tableau looked more jovial and upbeat.

In his peripheral vision, Carlos could see the Queens setting up at their bench, but he kept his gaze forward, unable to face them quite yet.

Nate smiled as Carlos approached, but then his smile wavered. "You okay?" Nate asked.

"Yeah. He's over there, right?"

"Yup."

"So this is a whole dome of awkward," Ty said. "Great."

"I'm sorry," said Carlos.

"Not your fault, bro," said Ty.

"Still. I should probably go over there and say something to defuse the situation. Unless you already have?"

"Nope," said Nate. "I decided to wait to see if he wanted to talk to me, but I'm apparently beneath his notice."

"Well, whatever you decide," said Ty to Carlos, "we've got your back. The whole team."

Carlos nodded. "I know. Thanks, guys."

That was somewhat reassuring, to know that the Hipsters would defend him, that they'd all be there for him after the inevitable confrontation.

Nate would be there for him.

Scott clapped his hands a couple of times, his sign that he wanted the game to get started. Carlos looked at Nate, who looked just as sad now as he had for the last week. Carlos leaned over and gave him a kiss. No tongue or anything, but it was definitely more than a peck.

"What was that for?" Nate asked with a quiet smile.

"I think we both needed that."

"Carlos, I—"

"We're up first, Hipsters!" Scott bellowed.

"We'll talk after the game," Nate said.

Nothing really happened—nothing outside the awkwardness so thick you could cut it, that is—until the third inning when Aiden, who was late in the order, finally came up to bat.

From his vantage point in right field, Carlos couldn't see Aiden's facial expression, but his body language was like a cat who met a foe he didn't like: his back up, his hair standing on end. Carlos couldn't imagine that Nate was helping matters from the pitcher's mound; Carlos could easily picture Nate's sneer.

But he pitched fair, no errors. A clean fastball soared through the strike zone and into Joe's glove. A curveball veered slightly away from Aiden, though he swung for it and the ump ruled it a strike. Nate wrapped it up with another fastball that, again, soared right through the center of the strike zone and past Aiden. Aiden said something Carlos couldn't hear, though it sounded like a growl from Carlos's spot on the field. He tossed his bat in the air as he gave Nate the finger and walked back to the Queens' bench. The Hipsters and a few of Aiden's teammates booed from the field or cried of unsportsmanlike behavior. The Queens' coach pulled Aiden aside and had a word.

Then, in the fourth, Aiden succeeded in snagging Carlos's arm as the teams switched places for the bottom half of the inning.

"Are you with *him* now?" Aiden hissed.

"That is no longer your concern," Carlos said, though he didn't feel nearly as haughty or confident as he sounded.

"So I was right."

"I didn't say that." Carlos tried to pull his arm free, but Aiden held firm. "You need to let me go. We were over...." He looked around, not wanting to draw attention. He whispered, "We were over the moment you hit me. What I do now is none of your fucking business."

Aiden let go, so Carlos walked away thinking—hoping—that it was over.

But then in the seventh, Carlos got a triple off the Queens' pitcher and landed at third out of breath. Aiden, who held court over third base, glared at him.

Josh caused a delay when he walked up to the plate—apparently his cleat was untied—so Carlos took the opportunity to say, "This is probably not the last time we'll run into each other, so we need to find a way to be civil."

Aiden sighed, though his brows still furrowed like they did when he was angry. "I know."

"You're still mad at me? After everything?"

"I heard you were living with him."

"He's my best friend. Your jealousy where he's concerned is part of why I left, you know."

"We could have been great."

Carlos sighed and looked toward home plate, where Josh was still fussily fretting over his shoelaces. "I wanted us to be great. But I have boundaries and deal breakers. A boyfriend who decides to take out his anger on my face? That pretty well crosses the line. I won't be forgiving you for that, nor do I want any kind of future relationship, and if I could just make a clean break, if things could have ended the minute I got the rest of my stuff out of your apartment? That's what I would have wanted. But we're both a part of this league, and we're going to see each other again, so look. I can be civil if you can."

Nate was late in the batting order and probably wouldn't be up that inning—although that was hard to determine, as the Queens' pitcher was throwing balls all over the place—but he stood and took a step away from the bench. He met Carlos's gaze and motioned in a way that Carlos read as him asking if he should come over. Carlos shook his head.

Aiden saw it and grunted.

"I was angry," he said, "and I apologized. I'm sorry for hurting you."

"All right. But if I accept your apology, it doesn't change anything. We're over. It's done. I'm not coming back."

Aiden sighed.

Josh finally got his cleats sorted out and stepped up to the plate. He whiffed the first pitch but hit the second one at the ground toward third. As it rolled, Carlos moved to take off, but Aiden snagged him by grabbing his shirt. Carlos tried to pull away, jerking his arms, terrified now that he wouldn't be able to get away from Aiden's firm grip. As panic started to subsume him, memories of his last night with Aiden flooded his mind. He could feel Aiden's unrelenting hold on him all over again, could see those fists flying at his face. He found it hard to move, and he kept reliving each terrible moment, terrified it would happen again. He flailed his arms and tried to get enough leverage to kick Aiden, but Aiden held firm. He said something Carlos couldn't quite hear, but it sounded like "You should be mine."

Then Carlos was falling. Aiden must have let go or Carlos must have tripped, but the ground was coming up awfully fast. Carlos fought to get his hands in front of him, but he didn't quite make it and landed hard on his right arm. He let out an "oof" as his shoulder hit the dirt.

"Time out!" Scott called as he ran across the field.

"You okay?" a familiar voice asked. Carlos rolled onto his back and looked up at Nate's face. "Carlos? Did you hit your neck? Where are you hurt? Anything broken?"

"Just bruised, I think," Carlos said. He sat up. He was still too stunned to feel anything, though he suspected he would once the adrenaline wore off. "Fell on my arm, but I'm all right."

"Aiden, get the hell out of here," Josh was saying. "As the league official here, I'm ruling that you're suspended from play until we get this sorted out. This is interference and unsportsmanlike behavior." Josh leaned down and helped Carlos stand. "I'm sorry, honey. I should have done something sooner. But now it's on the field, so it's within my purview."

"It's okay," Carlos said as he dusted himself off. "It's over. Right?"

Aiden's shoulders slumped as he gave up the fight. He nodded and walked toward his team's bench. Everyone watched in near silence as he collected his things and walked off the field.

"You better ban his ass, Josh," Nate said.

Josh nodded. "I'll see what I can do. He could have really hurt you, Carlos. Are you sure you're okay?"

"Yeah." He rotated his arm experimentally. It hurt, but not more than the rough ache from being slammed into the ground. "Yeah, nothing's broken. It'll probably bruise, but I'll be all right."

And then he was in Nate's arms, his face pressed into Nate's shoulder, and Nate was stroking his hair. "I should have moved faster. I saw him looking at you like he wanted to hit you again, but I really didn't think he would do something like that with this many of us here."

Carlos's heart was still pounding as the rush subsided. He held on to Nate for a moment, feeling for an anchor and finding that Nate's voice, his body, his words gave him the pull he needed to settle down. He took a deep, shuddering breath, but then he pulled away. "I'm okay. Let's give the Queens a moment to replace Aiden at third and then finish this game."

Josh nodded and ran back to home plate to talk to the ump. Scott moved away to yell everyone back into position. Nate lingered and gave Carlos a long look. Then he grabbed the back of Carlos's head and pulled him in for a fierce kiss.

When Carlos eased away, he said, "What was that for?"

"We both needed it," said Nate. Then he kissed Carlos's forehead and walked back to the bench.

Chapter 18

WHEN CARLOS got home Friday night, Nate was sitting on the couch, still dressed for work in a wrinkled oxford shirt and khakis, his left loafer still on its proper foot but the right one kicked aside as if Nate had started to take his shoes off and then gotten distracted. He was staring at the TV, but the TV was off.

"Nate?"

Nate looked up. "Hi."

"Hi. You okay?"

Nate looked around and nodded slowly. He smiled faintly. "Yeah. But I've been thinking."

Carlos slowly put his briefcase down and took a step toward the sofa. "Okay."

"I think we should have sex."

All air rushed out of Carlos's lungs. He couldn't speak for a moment, could only stare at Nate, into his blue eyes and that open, earnest expression on his face.

That Carlos had wanted this for weeks was not entirely accurate, or it certainly didn't feel that way now that his whole body seemed focused on this one moment, on those words from Nate's mouth. The truth was that Carlos had wanted Nate, subconsciously or otherwise, for the better part of a year, or, hell, probably for many years, for his whole life. It had taken a very long time for those desires to become conscious thoughts, because Nate was his buddy, his friend, his favorite person on the planet. Nate was also, as it was impossible to deny now, attractive—no, he was gorgeous, beautiful, sexy. His reddish brown hair was tousled in a cute way, sticking out a little above his forehead, stubble shadowed his jaw, and his eyes, those unnaturally blue eyes, stared back at Carlos, waiting for an answer.

"Yes," Carlos whispered, the syllable long like a hiss. Then he came back to himself all at once. "But what brought this on today? I thought you wanted to wait."

Nate leaned forward a little, resting his elbows on his thighs. "I did."

Carlos wondered if he should sit on the couch or keep his distance. "And?" He wobbled on his feet as he decided, and then stood near the arm of the sofa, two feet from Nate.

"And okay, there are some things we should talk about."

"You think?"

Nate looked over at Carlos. "Would you sit? Your hovering is making me nervous."

"So you can have your wicked way with me?"

Nate sat up and laughed softly. "No, sweetheart. Sit on the goddamned couch so that I can have a goddamned conversation with you before we get naked."

So Carlos sat, suddenly nervous, his heart beating erratically.

"I will be honest," Nate said. "I've put this off because I was worried it would change things."

"It will change things."

Nate sighed and rolled his eyes. Was he really getting frustrated? Carlos's heart was about to beat right out of his chest and Nate was *annoyed*? But Nate said, "No, I *know*, and that's… this is a big deal, okay? I mean, obviously, once we actually sleep together, things will probably be a little different, but it feels risky to me. I haven't wanted to do it yet because… well, what if it's terrible? What if I disappoint you?"

Wait, what? "That's not possible."

"Oh, believe me. It *is* possible."

"Nate, *mi corazón*, let's review. We love each other, right?"

"Yes. Of course."

"And you think I'm foxy, yes?"

Nate laughed. "Obviously."

"We love each other and we're attracted to each other, so the rest will sort itself out."

Nate raised an eyebrow. "It's good of you to think so."

Had Nate always been this insecure? Carlos scooted over on the sofa so that he was actually sitting next to Nate. He put a hand on Nate's thigh. "What are you really worried about?"

Nate stared at Carlos's hand. The gesture had been unconscious, but now that they were actually touching, Carlos realized how hot Nate's skin was under his pants, how warm and electric their connection could be. He rubbed Nate's thigh softly, just enough to make Nate's skin tingle, he hoped.

"I'm worried about a lot of things," Nate said. "Like, okay, I want to have sex with you. I want to be making out on this sofa right now instead of talking. But before we do this, I have to know that neither of us will regret it after. Or that you won't, really."

"I won't."

"You say that, but we've never.... I mean, I haven't seen you naked since we were kids, which doesn't count. We've never done anything remotely sexual with each other. We don't even really talk about sex, except in the abstract. We may not be sexually compatible at all. And then where will we be? All this buildup, all these nice words and these feelings, and I love you so much, but what if this sucks?"

Carlos put his arms around Nate, hugging him close. Nate hugged Carlos back. Carlos said, "Is *that* what you're worried about?"

"I know it's stupid. But this just seems so complicated. There's a lot about this part of you that I don't know about."

Carlos laughed softly and stroked Nate's back. Then he leaned away. "You never asked."

"I never wanted to know. Because then I'd have to picture you doing it with somebody else."

Carlos understood that. He nodded as he played with Nate's hair. He'd never brought it up with Nate either, for pretty much exactly the same reason. "We're both idiots, you know? Didn't see the good thing in front of us. My sisters have been trying to get us together for years, and I was all, 'No, Nate's like a brother, gross,' but I never *really* thought that. I guess I just assumed you did and filed it away."

Nate nodded and leaned his forehead against Carlos's. "Have you ever pictured it? Us together?"

"Pretty much constantly for the last month."

Nate let out a surprised laugh. "Oh, really? What did you picture?"

Carlos considered. He lowered his voice and whispered, "Us in bed. Me on top and you writhing beneath me." Nate shivered, so Carlos moved closer to lean in his ear. "Or me pushing you over your desk and fucking you from behind until you scream. Or maybe you straddling me, throwing your head back as you come."

Nate leaned back, his eyes wide. With fear or desire, Carlos couldn't tell. "So you're a top."

Carlos shrugged. "I have toppy tendencies, I guess."

A bead of sweat ran down Nate's forehead. He leaned away from Carlos and played with his fingers. These were sure signs Nate was really nervous now. "Well, then there's definitely something I have to tell you."

"Uh-huh. You're also a top, huh?"

"No, actually. I'm… well, I'm really not into anal at all."

Carlos was so surprised by that he balked.

Nate bit his lip, but then he said, "And see, this is kind of what I was worried about. Most of the guys I've been with have been okay with it. Not all of them, though, and, like… ugh. I couldn't take it if you rejected me."

Carlos stroked Nate's face with his thumb. "I would never reject you. So you're not into it? It's fine."

"Are you sure? Because it really squicks me out and always has. I mean, you know what comes out of there, right?"

Carlos laughed. "Yes."

Nate shivered, not in a sexy way but like he was legitimately grossed out by the prospect. "I tried. A couple of times. Both on top and on the bottom. It just never… I don't understand it, I guess. It was either too painful or I was too grossed out to stay hard."

Something in Carlos's brain shorted. He tilted his head, tried seeing Nate with this new information in mind.

"What?" Nate said.

"I was just picturing… I mean, you with an erection."

Nate groaned and shifted away from Carlos. "Ugh, this is a terrible idea. We'll go back to being friends or we'll just be a chaste couple or something. Forget I said anything."

"No, Nate. Stop it. No. It was a good mental image. Thinking about you this way is a new thing for me, and it was a little strange for a second, but in a good way. The reality is different from the fantasy. I guess I'm still not quite all the way there with seeing you as more than my best friend, but if we had sex, I'd get all the way there quickly, I bet."

"Right. But I'm not… I can't bottom for you. I won't."

"That's fine. I mean it. There are plenty of other things we can do." And Carlos really wasn't bothered by it at all. Truth be told, it had never been his favorite act either.

Nate nodded. "I've been picturing us together for a long time."

A space of six inches separated them, so Carlos moved a little closer and took Nate's hand. Nate was pretty well cornered, pressed against the arm of the sofa, but he didn't look uncomfortable. "What did you picture, *papi*?" Carlos asked, curious now that anal was out of the equation.

Nate sighed. "At first it was just touching. You know, when you started dating Aiden, I was just starting to realize I was in love with you, and anytime I saw you together, he'd touch you, just, like a caress? He'd touch your arm or hold your hand and I'd think, *It should be me touching him that way*. Then I wanted to kiss you. God, more than anything, and almost constantly, I would think about kissing you. Watching you kiss Aiden broke my heart."

Carlos put a hand on Nate's shoulder and pulled him close again. "That long ago?"

"Yeah."

"You never said anything."

"I was terrified. I'm still terrified. What if I told you everything but you didn't feel the same way? That would have killed me. It seemed better not to risk that."

"Is that why you wanted to wait to have sex? Were you afraid I wouldn't like your… preferences?"

"Yeah, kind of, but the whole thing. I mean, it's terrifying. I love you, I really do, and I have for a long time. It's been this pure thing, you know. But now things are different. It makes me so happy that you love me too, that you want me. I like feeling this way. I don't want to fuck anything up."

"You won't."

"Aren't I, though? I told you when you walked in that I thought we should have sex, because I think we need to, or I need to, so I can just get over myself. I'm tired of holding back. I'm tired of keeping my mouth shut. I'm tired of hoping that one day you'll turn and look at me the way you used to look at Aiden. But I'm forever my old self, aren't I? I tell you we should have sex, but instead we've been talking for an hour."

"Really only, like, ten minutes."

Nate rolled his eyes. "You know what I mean." He let out a breath and squeezed Carlos's hand. "I came home from work today and I was itchy, you know? Itchy and horny for the first time since before Mom…. Well. I feel like I'm finally coming back to myself. So I was thinking as I came home that, you know, we've been sharing a bed for a while, and maybe tonight's the night we finally…. But then I started panicking, because what if you…. What if we…." Nate let out a disgusted grunt. "I suck at this sort of thing. So I thought, no, I'll just be assertive for a change. I'll tell Carlos what I want."

"I hope it's more than kissing."

"Oh, it is." Nate smiled.

Carlos reached up and stroked Nate's hair. It was soft and disheveled. He met Nate's gaze; Nate still looked worried. "We'll make it good."

Nate nodded, not looking entirely convinced.

Carlos decided to pull Nate away from his worries. He leaned close and lowered his voice. "So what do you want?"

Nate leaned closer to Carlos as well. "I've been wondering what your cock looks like for a long time. How it would feel in my hand." He put his arms more fully around Carlos and whispered in Carlos's ear, "In my mouth."

It was Carlos's turn to shiver. In the good way. "Yes," he whispered.

"Carlos?"

"Mm-hmm." Carlos rubbed Nate's back, felt Nate's warm skin through the smooth fabric of his shirt. Nate smelled clean and warm and a little sweaty.

"Kiss me."

Carlos was happy to comply. He kissed Nate hard, taking the time to savor, to taste, to think about the pressure of their lips together. Nate parted his lips and snaked his tongue into Carlos's mouth, so Carlos leaned in closer and licked at Nate's teeth. The proximity of Nate, the smell of him, made Carlos's heart pound again, and within seconds his skin was tingling and his cock was hard and he was pressing Nate against the arm of the sofa.

Nate gasped and threw his head back, but when Carlos leaned closer to kiss his neck, he said, "Hang on, I think I'm sitting on the remote."

Carlos backed off a little as Nate wriggled and pulled the remote out from behind a sofa cushion. Then he started laughing.

Carlos laughed too. "This is going to be weird, isn't it?"

"Probably." Nate laughed harder, clearly unable to get control of himself. He kept giggling. "So weird."

"It's not *that* funny."

"I know." Nate wiped his eyes, still giggling.

"Let's go to the bedroom." Carlos stood and stepped away from the sofa.

Nate nodded and stood as well, a smile still on his face. He took Carlos's hand and led the way.

IT WAS strange for something Nate had wanted for so long to appear right before him. It didn't seem real; it felt more supperreal, everything in sharp focus, everything grounded, present. He stood in his bedroom with Carlos, and the two of them stood staring at each other, each waiting for the other to make a move.

"Carlos," Nate said.

"This shouldn't be awkward."

"No. I just... I love you and I want this to be perfect."

Carlos smiled. "I know, but I don't think it can be perfect. Just like our friendship isn't perfect. Our relationship isn't perfect. We've both made mistakes. So this will be what we make it."

Nate stroked Carlos's shoulder. Carlos was right. Strangely, it took the pressure off. "Come here," he said, finally making the first move.

Carlos put his hands on Nate's waist. They kissed. This, at least, was familiar. The way Carlos was touching him, moving his palms against his waist, that was new, but it felt nice, and combined with the slick slide of their lips together, it was like a prelude to a whole symphony of sexual potential.

Nate pulled back suddenly. "I just thought of something stupid."

"Nathan O'Sullivan. You are ruining the mood."

Nate laughed. "No, just... so, okay, we've never really done anything sexual together, but for whatever reason, I just remembered that you lost your virginity to Kevin Baylor in eleventh grade."

Carlos took a step back and crossed his arms over his chest. "So? You lost your virginity to that Dmitri guy senior year. Who cares?"

"I don't, I just can't help but think about these things. Like our whole histories are sort of woven together with each other, even our sexual histories, even though we haven't had sex yet. It's still kind of weird, I don't know. I'm adjusting."

"You think too hard, *papi*."

Carlos took a step back and whipped his shirt off. Being confronted with Carlos's finely sculpted chest did take the words from Nate's lips. Because Carlos was so undeniably masculine, the skin of his shoulders smooth, his pecs nicely developed, his abs defined. A smattering of black hair kept his skin from being too smooth. The sight of Carlos's body pulled at something primal in Nate, and his animal brain finally took over. He ran his hands over those perfect pecs, feeling the coarseness of Carlos's chest hair against his palms. Carlos's nipples hardened under Nate's touch; feeling Carlos's body was interesting and a little weird but certainly not bad.

Carlos kissed Nate, distracting Nate further as he sank into the salty sweetness of Carlos's mouth, the softness of it. Carlos didn't touch Nate in return, but he shifted slightly, so he was up to something. Nate pulled away from the kiss and looked down to see what was going on.

Carlos had taken off his pants, and they lay pooled at his ankles. He was wearing white boxer briefs, which seemed stark against his naturally tan skin, but that was irrelevant, because Carlos's erection was tenting those briefs, and nothing else mattered.

Nate reached down and cupped Carlos's erection, rubbing it, and it seemed to fit right there in Nate's hand as if Nate were meant to touch this man this way. He groaned and kissed Carlos again, any reservations fleeing. Nate pushed all of his confusion and misgivings aside and surrendered himself to this man in this moment.

Carlos sighed and sank into Nate, kissing his lips, his jaw, his ear. He pressed his face into the crook of Nate's neck and thrust his hips against Nate's hand. He whispered something Nate couldn't hear, a Spanish love word maybe.

Nate kissed Carlos's face in kind. Against his cheek, Nate whispered, "I need to see your cock." Because suddenly nothing in the world was more important. Just the two of them, raw, naked, making something new together.

Carlos nodded and backed toward the bed. He peeled off his underwear and then lay down, totally and completely naked. He crooked a finger at Nate, beckoning him toward the bed.

Nate's heart pounded as he took in the sight. He'd never seen Carlos this way, naked and hard, but he'd thought about it plenty. All those old mental images were fuzzy photographs compared to the real thing, here with him and waiting for him and calling out to him.

So Nate started to take off his own clothes. He undid the top few buttons on his shirt before he pulled the whole thing and his undershirt off in one go.

Then he was self-conscious. He crossed one of his arms over his chest.

"Stop it, Nate," Carlos said. "To me, you are sexy. Don't be nervous. I want to see you. You won't disappoint me."

So Nate took a deep breath and undid his pants. He took them off. Now all that remained was his own briefs. His animal brain was taking a break, apparently, because he was nervous enough that his own erection had flagged.

"Come here, *mi corazón*," Carlos said.

Nate went to the bed. As soon as he crawled onto the mattress, Carlos took him into his arms and kissed him hard. Carlos's cock was hard against Nate's thigh, and that bit of rubbing, the knowledge that Carlos was now *naked* and in his arms, made Nate's own cock rise to the occasion again.

"I'm nervous," Nate said, hoping the confession would help the nerves go away.

"Of course you are, my love. This is important."

"You don't seem nervous at all."

"Feel this." Carlos took Nate's hand and put it on his chest, near his heart. That very heart was beating so hard and fast, Nate could feel it vibrate against his hand.

"Oh," said Nate.

"Lay back. I want to see you."

Nate rolled onto his back. Carlos propped himself up on one elbow and looked down at Nate for a moment before grabbing the waistband of Nate's briefs. He pulled them down and Nate's cock flopped out. He felt self-conscious again, but Carlos just looked. And looked.

"You're staring."

"It's weird," Carlos said.

Nate laughed. "Not something a guy likes to hear when he's naked."

Somehow that cut the tension. Carlos laughed too. "Not what I meant."

"I know."

"It's a very nice cock, in fact."

Carlos took it in his hand, his touch soft, the heat of his palm dancing lightly over Nate's skin. Then he tightened his grip and stroked. And like that, arousal passed through Nate in a wave so fast he shivered. Carlos stroked more forcefully and Nate got hard again, his blood rushing through his body.

"A *very* nice cock," Carlos said before he took it in his mouth.

Jesus Christ, but Carlos had a nice mouth, hot and slick, his lips pressed against the shaft of Nate's cock and just *right there* and dear Lord, it felt good. Nate watched in awe as currents of pleasure zipped through his body. Carlos was sucking on him. His cock was in *Carlos's* mouth. And it was *amazing.*

Carlos used some trickery with his tongue, tracing patterns and then dipping into the space below the head of Nate's cock. Nate cried out, the sheer pleasure of it forcing all thought away. Nothing mattered but the silky feeling of Carlos's mouth on Nate's cock.

Nate groaned and pumped his hips a little, wanting more. Carlos held him down, pressing his hands against Nate's pelvis, and then he went to town, licking and sucking on Nate's cock. This was good, but it wasn't *right*, because Nate wanted Carlos in his arms.

"Carlos," he said.

"Mmmph."

"Carlos, sweetheart, come here."

Carlos moved back up Nate's cock, giving it a long lick. The expression on his face was reluctant, but he complied and settled into Nate's arms, giving him a quick kiss. Then he said, "Was that okay?"

"That was more than okay. That was amazing. But I didn't want to come just yet. I want to be holding you when I do. And I want you to come too."

Carlos kissed him, so Nate took the opportunity to wrap his hand around Carlos's cock. He was hard and it was hot, and it felt good against Nate's hand. He stroked a few times, getting used to the sensation of touching his old friend in this new way, but he liked it. Carlos moaned and humped against Nate's hand.

But they could do this together. Nate took both of their cocks in his hand, rubbing them together. And *that* was awesome, all that hot flesh pressed together. Carlos licked into Nate's mouth as Nate stroked them. They moved their hips in unison, seeking friction, making music, blurring together. Both of them were moaning. Carlos and Nate pressed their bodies together, kissed, tangled their tongues. Carlos thrust one hand into Nate's hair and wrapped his other around Nate's hand to increase the pressure.

Nate's very skin felt alive. The scent of Carlos's cologne, so familiar, was the scent of sex now, arousing Nate that much more. It was just animal grunting, the two of them together, seeking release in each other, and the two of them and the place where their hands joined were all that mattered.

"Oh, Nate, *mi amor*, I'm going to come."

Nate felt that, deep in his chest, love and arousal and all of it, and he knew he would come soon too.

"Carlos, I love you."

Carlos kissed him fiercely. "I love you too."

And then it happened. They were rubbing together, increasing speed, creating pleasure, and then the orgasm hit Nate all at once, rushing through his body. Nate threw his head back as he came, pumping against Carlos and their joined hands, spurting everywhere. Then Carlos let out a moan and hot stickiness poured over Nate's fingers and he didn't care one bit because it was essential and he was with Carlos. He kissed Carlos, both of them panting. They breathed into each other's mouths as they came down.

Carlos leaned away a little, but he kissed Nate softly as he rubbed their combined fluids against Nate's belly. Nate pulled Carlos close to kiss him hard, to taste him.

Nate eased away from the kiss and held Carlos close. Carlos laid his head on Nate's chest. Maybe it wasn't quite lovemaking, but it was good, whatever it was. Nate felt raw, exposed, like he'd let Carlos see the one part of himself he'd never shared before. Not with Carlos, not really with anyone. He felt good about that, though. He trusted Carlos with his secrets. He trusted Carlos with his heart.

"Nate?" Carlos said, stroking Nate's chest.

"Yeah?"

"I have no regrets. Do you?"

"No. Never. Once we… well, once the animal part of my brain took over, it wasn't weird anymore. It felt… natural. It felt right."

Carlos squeezed Nate a little. "I agree. I think we're right together."

Nate kissed the top of Carlos's head. "Yeah. I love you so much. My whole life I've loved you, I think."

Carlos kissed the nearest bit of skin, near Nate's nipple. "Me too. I've always loved you. Not to get all mushy, but I am pretty sure I will for the rest of my life."

"Me too. There will never be anyone like you to me."

They lay there for a long time, just breathing. Nate would have thought Carlos was asleep had Carlos not periodically traced lazy patterns on Nate's stomach with his finger. Nate felt content and at ease for the first time in a very long time. He closed his eyes and simply felt all of it: his body sinking into his old mattress, Carlos's hands on him, Carlos's scent now embedded in his own skin.

"Maybe it's not perfect," Nate said softly, "but whatever it is we made together is pretty fucking amazing."

Carlos lifted his head and smiled. "Amazing," he murmured before closing the space between them for another kiss. "I think we should make it together again very soon."

Nate's body seemed to agree. "Yes. God. Come here."

Chapter 19

THEY LAY tangled up in each other the next morning. Nate was trying to decide if he absolutely needed to eat breakfast or if he could just have sex with Carlos, again, some more, for the rest of the weekend. He was so comfortable, his body snug under the covers with Carlos, Carlos's even breathing lulling him back out of consciousness. This felt right. It felt perfect, regardless of what Carlos had said. He kissed the top of Carlos's head, which earned him a happy murmur and more snuggling.

But then Carlos's phone beeped and vibrated against the nightstand. Carlos cursed in Spanish. "Just a text message. Unless it's from you, it can wait."

"Okay." Nate shifted his legs so that he could link knees with Carlos, which felt silly and a little childish but for all the nudity. He hugged Carlos and Carlos buried his face in Nate's neck, and they held each other until the damn phone beeped again.

"Nope," Carlos said.

It beeped again.

Nate sighed. "It's probably one of your sisters."

Then Nate's phone, sitting right next to Carlos's, started to buzz.

"Do you think it's an emergency?" Nate asked.

"They'd call if it were an emergency."

"So are they just going to keep annoying us unless we look?"

"Probably. Dammit."

Carlos peeled himself away from Nate and reached for the nightstand. He grabbed both phones and then rolled onto his back before handing Nate his.

So Nate looked at the message. It was from Marisol. *Gabby is unreasonable.*

Nate chuckled. That was likely true. He texted back, *Why?*

Carlos hasn't responded to her texts. Told me to ask u if he was home.

He is.

Then Carlos groaned. "Gabriela really needs to know *right now* what color tie I'm wearing in her wedding? I don't even know. Whichever one comes with the tux I'm renting." He stabbed at the touch screen keyboard with his index finger.

"Do they match the bridesmaid dresses?"

"I don't know. I don't care. I'm only in the wedding because Gabby guilted her fiancé into asking me." Carlos's phone buzzed again. "You're going, right?"

"Yeah. At least I don't have to wear a tux."

Carlos looked at Nate. "Are you wearing your blue suit?"

"I hadn't really thought about it." Nate owned three suits. He figured he'd just wear whichever one struck his fancy on the day of Carlos's sister's wedding.

"Wear the blue one. You look good in it. Color brings out your eyes." Carlos went back to typing on his phone.

Nate rolled onto his side and propped his head up on his elbow. "You've noticed how I look in suits?"

Carlos looked at Nate with lowered eyelids. The expression seemed to say, *Duh.* He went back to texting. When his phone beeped again, he frowned. "Shit."

"What?"

"Now she's asking if I'm bringing another date instead of Aiden."

"Are you?" Nate asked.

"I'm with you now, dumbass, so I—" Carlos stopped abruptly and frowned. "Should we go together? Like, as a couple."

"Aren't we a couple?"

"Yeah, but are we ready for my family to know that?"

That was a valid point. Nate wasn't sure he was quite ready to stomach all the hugs and *I told you so*s. "Let me get an expert opinion."

To Marisol, he texted, *I have a serious question.*

Is it about vest colors or flowers? If so, I'll scream.

He considered how to ask.

"Are you asking Marisol?" Carlos asked.

"I think she'd be honest. And she can keep a secret."

Carlos furrowed his brow. "Since when?"

Nate reached over and ran a hand through Carlos's hair. "She's known about my feelings for you since before I did. And she didn't tell you, did she?"

Carlos grumbled and shook his head. "She always liked you more than me. She's *my* flesh and blood."

"It's because I'm so cute."

Carlos laughed. "Sure, okay."

"Is it okay if I tell her?"

Carlos kissed Nate's temple. "Sure. She's gonna find out anyway."

Not about vests, Nate texted. *Hypothetically, if I came to the wedding as Carlos's date....*

Nate hit Send because he couldn't think of how to finish the sentence.

Marisol texted back a yellow smiley face with its mouth hanging open in shock. Nate showed it to Carlos, who rolled his eyes.

So Nate texted, *Hypothetically. Would your whole family die or what?*

I'm gonna have to go to another Ruiz family wedding soon, aren't I?

Nate bristled. *Hypothetically.*

Marisol said, *Hypothetically, you're sleeping together now, aren't you?*

Nate glanced at Carlos, who read over Nate's shoulder and shrugged. "Tell her whatever you want to tell her."

Yes, Nate wrote.

Gross. But congratulations.

Then, *Mom has been planning your wedding since 1994, so you probably won't have much work to do.*

Nate choked out a laugh. Carlos read the text and sighed. "That's probably true." Carlos's phone buzzed. "Oh, now Mari is yelling at me over text about not telling her you and I were together."

"What are you going to say?"

"That it's none of her beeswax."

"That's mature."

Carlos sent the text and then tossed the phone aside. "I told her to shut up and stop texting us so I can make out with you."

Nate put his phone back on the nightstand. "Well, that should give her nightmares for a while."

"Seriously, though, the wedding's not that far away, right? Let's go together. It'll give me an excuse to dance with you during the slow songs."

Nate couldn't help but smile at that. He put his arms around Carlos. "Like you need an excuse. All you ever had to do was ask me."

Carlos rolled over on top of Nate and kissed him soundly. Then he said, "Guess I'll have to tell Mason and Patrick to readjust their seating charts too."

"Do we have to tell everyone right this minute?"

"Do you want to wait?"

"I want to spend my weekend with just you."

Carlos smiled. He leaned down and kissed Nate's nose. "That sounds excellent, *papi*. We'll worry about everyone else next week."

CARLOS HAD noticed Nate's arms before, but he hadn't really *seen* them. They were powerful from having thrown so many pitches. Not bulky, but undeniably strong. They felt good wrapped around Carlos's body, holding him close, loving him. Nate had the best arms.

Carlos ran his tongue along them, licking the muscles, tasting Nate's skin. He pushed at Nate's arm until Nate lifted it up, and then Carlos licked the underside. Nate gasped when Carlos buried his face in Nate's armpit and licked him there too. Nate smelled so good, so intense here in particular, and Carlos wanted that scent imprinted on himself, in his brain, forever.

A part of him wanted to be inside Nate too, but he respected Nate's desires. Instead, he pushed Nate down into the mattress and then crawled over him, straddling his legs. He moved his hips until their cocks lined up. And that was pretty fucking good, to be pressed against Nate, their cocks rubbing together. Nate had a gorgeous cock, pink and nicely sized, and Carlos liked how it looked next to his own erection.

He leaned down to kiss Nate, pressing their bodies together from shoulders to knees, and found a surprising amount of intimacy in this. It was like their whole bodies were connected to each other. Nate groaned as if he agreed. Then Nate put those amazing arms around Carlos and held him close as they kissed and thrust against each other.

It was different this time, slower, less urgent. They'd gotten the initial nervous first encounter out of the way and were free now to just enjoy each other. Carlos certainly enjoyed Nate, who had a beautiful body and those amazing arms. More than that, though, Carlos was with Nate, the man he loved best in the world, and there was nowhere else he wanted to be than in this man's arms.

Warmth spread across his chest as surely as arousal moved through his body in waves. He thrust against Nate's cock, pulling hisses and sighs from Nate, and then he kissed Nate because he felt their connection, their years of friendship, their trust in each other, and their deep love all at once. It nearly overwhelmed him to the point of tears, but he blinked them back. Instead he kissed Nate, touched Nate anywhere he could reach, and kept moving his hips in a crazy rhythm. Nate bucked back, creating the sweet friction they both needed to get off, but this wasn't about getting off. This was about expressing how they felt with their bodies, this was about finally coming together in all ways.

Nate trailed a hand down Carlos's back, his fingertips lightly touching his spine, and Carlos shivered and broke out in goose bumps everywhere. He sighed and kept kissing Nate, even as his grip on the moment loosened and arousal took over. He wanted to tell Nate he loved him, but he couldn't speak, and it didn't matter anyway, because Carlos was saying it with his body, and Nate already knew. They'd never had to speak much to make themselves understood, and this was no exception. The language here was in body movements, in the scrape of teeth against skin, in the soft press of a hand, in the electricity that sparked every place their bodies connected.

Carlos loved Nate in the depths of his soul, and as he thrust his hips against Nate and pressed as close as he could get, he felt Nate's love for him radiating back. With every stroke of Nate's hands, he felt cared for. With every thrust, he felt desired. And when Nate's arms came around him, he felt loved.

They didn't speak, they merely continued to move, to make love in the only way possible, the gentle press of their bodies slowly building into something explosive. Carlos felt that orgasm hovering, felt the tingle in his balls, in his limbs. Nate kissed him, brushed his teeth against Carlos's lower lip, and Carlos was warm everywhere, electric everywhere. And then one last thrust and Carlos was white-hot everywhere, pumping his hips against Nate until he cried out and came all over Nate's belly. Nate held him close and thrust his own hips until he too was moaning and coming. Nate was so fucking beautiful, the expression on his face as he came blissful. How had Carlos never known this about Nate, that he was this beautiful? How had he overlooked it for so long?

They sank into the mattress together, their feet tangled in the sheets, but Carlos didn't care, because he had Nate now and they loved each other. He ran a hand over Nate's chest and then settled into those arms.

"I love you," he told Nate.

"I know, sweetheart. I know. I love you too."

"I mean, just in case."

Nate's chest vibrated as he took a deep, shaky breath. "I never want to leave this bed. I just want to stay here with you forever."

"That's not how the world works."

"I know. It's a nice dream, though."

"We still have the rest of the weekend. That's, like, a day and a half before we have to face the rest of the world."

Nate laughed softly. "We do have that."

Chapter 20

THE SUN blared down on the Hipsters as they got ready for their Tuesday night game. Nate squinted up at it as he tied his cleats.

"It's fucking hot," Ty said. "And I'm from Texas, so I know hot."

"Thanks for that astute observation. I never would have noticed the heat if you hadn't said something." Nate stood and wiped the sweat from his forehead before he started warming up his arms.

"Ha-ha, asshole," said Ty. "Just let me be a whiny bitch for a few minutes."

Nate chuckled. "Hey, I got an e-mail from Will that he wants me to join the traveling team."

"Of course he does," said Ty. "You're the best pitcher in the league."

"Apparently the Gay Baseball World Series or whatever they're calling it is in Chicago this year."

"Yeah, there was a rumor it would be played in Wrigley Field, but Josh told me that's bunk. Wouldn't that be awesome, though?"

"You make the team?"

"Yup," Ty said with a grin. "So did Joe, since he's your catcher, and so did Mason, because obviously."

Nate nodded. Carlos hadn't, although Carlos didn't want to be on the traveling team. But this meant a week of baseball in Chicago in September, without Carlos. Unless Carlos could be persuaded to take the week off work and make a vacation of it. Or unless the New York team got eliminated quickly. They'd figure it out; it was still six weeks away.

It occurred to Nate, as it had frequently for the past week or two, that this was another thing to negotiate. A romantic relationship was not all fun and games.

"It's still only August," Nate said. "This summer is endless."

Ty stopped smiling abruptly and looked at Nate. "Oh. I'm so sorry. I keep forgetting… I mean, you've had a really rough summer."

Nate nodded. "Mostly I'm just anxious to put it behind me."

Carlos walked over with a broad grin. "You'll never guess what just happened."

"Andreas sucked you off behind one of those bushes?" Ty guessed.

Nate guffawed. Carlos furrowed his brow. "What? No. Gross. What?"

Ty laughed. "I was kidding. You just looked so happy, I figured sexual gratification was involved, and since everyone on this fucking team seems to think our German friend hung the moon, I extrapolated."

"Do you not think he's hot?" Nate asked. "I mean, your eyes are in good working order, right?"

"Ha," said Ty. "He's fine. I mean, I get it, he's conventionally attractive. But he is not actually responsible for putting the moon and stars in the sky. I just don't think he's all that."

"Ian must have mentioned he thought Andreas was pretty," Carlos said to Nate in a conspiratorial whisper.

Ty rolled his eyes.

"I bet he's bad in bed," Nate said.

Ty choked out a laugh. "Oh. I thought you would know for sure by now."

Nate raised an eyebrow at Ty.

Ty sighed. "Oh, right. I forgot what a fussy prude you are."

Carlos giggled—giggled!—and then put an arm around Nate, giving him a quick hug. "That's our Nate."

"Look, I'm sorry I didn't sleep with the hot German guy so that you all could live through me vicariously. Have either of you actually talked with him? He's nice, but his looks are pretty much all he's got."

"We never said you had to marry him," Ty said.

"He'd probably be selfish in bed," Nate said. "What would be the point?"

"You know he's standing right there?" Carlos asked.

Nate followed Carlos's gaze and saw Andreas chatting up Joe, all smiles and handsomeness. Sure, he was hot, but less so now that Nate had spent a whole weekend naked with Carlos.

"Eh," said Ty. "Whatever. Do what you want."

"What happened that we'll never believe?" Nate asked, trying to find the thread back to normal conversation. He wasn't eager to discuss Andreas in front of Carlos.

"Oh! See, now it seems lame."

"Just tell us."

"That guy Doug on the Devil Gays brought his dog with him, and it can do tricks." Carlos gestured toward Doug, who was petting a medium-size dog that looked like some kind of collie mix. "So Doug was showing me how the dog can catch a treat off his nose. Cute, right? Then he said conversationally that they played the Queens last week, and Aiden came to the game because I guess his suspension is over, and the dog bit him!"

"What?" Nate said, surprised by Aiden interrupting what had otherwise been a pretty good evening so far.

"Doug said Aiden was okay. The bite didn't even draw blood. So maybe it wasn't the karmic retribution I would have wanted, but...."

Nate was all righteous indignation now. "Aiden's suspension is over? He didn't get kicked out of the league?"

Carlos sighed and put a hand on Nate's arm. "Nate, don't."

"Josh!" Nate bellowed.

Josh walked over, looking irritated, as if he already knew what Nate was about to say. But he said, "What?"

"Aiden's still in the league?"

"Nate...," said Carlos.

Josh bristled. "The Queens needed him to play because both of their spare players were sick last week, and anyway, Will wants to further investigate the incident before making a ruling." Josh glanced at Carlos. "What's likely to happen is that he'll play the rest of the season—and honestly, the Queens' chances of making the playoffs are slim, so it probably won't be much longer—and then be asked not to come back next season."

"Will's right over there," Nate said. "I'll go talk to him."

Nate moved to march over to Will, but Carlos grabbed his arm and held him back. "Nate, no. Stop it. Don't do this for me."

"Carlos, everyone here saw what happened that day. Aiden has no right—"

"I don't want to draw more attention to him, okay? I want to just let this go and move on. If the league doesn't let him play again next season, that's enough for me, okay?" He grunted. "I don't need you to defend me. I know you want to, but I really just want for this to be over. Can we do that without starting a war?"

Nate looked at Carlos, at the pleading look on his face, and relented. If this was how Carlos wanted it, this was what they'd do. "All right. But if you change your mind, I'll go kick Aiden's ass myself."

Josh let out a breath. "I know this whole situation sucks, and I'm sorry, I genuinely am, for how everything played out. But as soon as I filed an incident report with Will, the whole Queens team showed up at Will's office to defend Aiden, so Will was inclined to think I'd overreacted. Asking for him not to come back after this season was the best compromise I could negotiate."

"That dog bit him, at least," said Ty.

"What?" said Josh.

Carlos waved his hand. "Never mind. Thank you, Josh, for doing what you could."

Josh nodded and patted Carlos's shoulder. Then he said, "I gotta…," and gestured back toward the bench where the Hipsters were setting up.

"You sure about this?" Nate asked.

"Yes. I appreciate your loyalty, but down, boy. It's over."

Nate nodded and went back to his warm-up, feeling a little dissatisfied. He supposed not everything could or should end with a lot of drama; perhaps situations just petered out sometimes. It didn't even matter anymore, because Nate had won. The one bright spot in his otherwise completely crappy summer was that Carlos was just as in love with Nate as Nate was with Carlos.

Maybe that was why Nate was so quick to defend what he finally had. That, and he wanted Carlos to be safe.

Nate wasn't at his best that game, pitching a little wildly, but Scott kept him in and the Hipsters eked out a victory over the Hell's Kitchen Devil Gays by a single run. It was a hard-won victory, but the mood was somewhat subdued on the walk to Barnstorm afterward.

"So," Carlos said sotto voce on the walk to the bar. "Maybe we should tell our friends about us? That it's official now?"

"Probably. I mean, I thought they already knew, given that I kind of made out with you at the last game, but if Ty's making jokes about you hooking up with Andreas, they don't really *know*."

"Yeah. I don't want to hook up with Andreas. I mean, just for the record."

Nate smiled and took Carlos's hand. He gave it a brief squeeze and let go. "I appreciate that."

Still, the task remained to tell everyone that they'd moved their relationship from "friends" to "maybe?" to "oh, yeah, definitely together now." Nate wasn't sure why the prospect unsettled him, but thinking about telling Mason and Ian and especially Ty made him nauseous.

"You okay?" Carlos asked.

Nate shrugged, trying to seem casual, but he hung back a little so they could talk without being overheard. "You should probably know that I spent a lot of time—I mean, really a *lot*—moping about you in the company of these guys while you were off with Aiden."

"Really?" Carlos seemed taken aback by that. He frowned and adjusted his bag on his shoulder. "You moped about me?"

"Sweetheart, I realized I was in love with you about five minutes before you went out with Aiden. Can you imagine?"

"Yes." Carlos sighed. "I know exactly how you are. You had that crush on Brad Marsden sophomore year."

Well, now Nate was just embarrassed. He groaned. "Don't remind me."

"Didn't you write him a series of plaintive love letters?"

"That I never gave him, thank you very much."

"No. Why would you tell anyone how you feel when you can just mope about it?"

"What's that supposed to mean?"

Nate realized suddenly that he'd raised his voice, so he took a deep breath and watched Carlos, whose face was turned determinedly ahead.

Carlos said, "Why didn't you ever tell me you had feelings for me?"

"I didn't think you returned them."

"But did you really spend two years, the entire length of my relationship with Aiden, moping about me?"

"Well, not the *entire* time."

Carlos sighed. "I love you, I do, but it's so like you to mope about something rather than put your heart out there. If you had just said—"

"If I had told you I was in love with you two years ago, how would you have reacted?"

"I don't know. You never gave me the opportunity to think about it."

Nate scoffed. He didn't want to be a dick, but he was pretty sure if he'd said "I love you" two summers ago when Carlos was spending so much time pining for Aiden, he and Carlos would no longer be friends.

"Look," Carlos said. "I can't honestly say how I would have reacted. I probably would have been surprised by it. But maybe if you'd given me the chance…."

Anger flashed white-hot in Nate. Part of his moping had long been over the fact that he hadn't said anything before losing Carlos to Aiden, and he'd thought to himself many times over the past couple of months that if he had, all of this could have been avoided, so he took some responsibility for that. But to hear Carlos say it with those words in that tone, as if it weren't something Nate had been agonizing over for such a long time….

"I can't change what happened," Nate said, bitterness putting an edge on his tone. "Maybe I should have said something. But I didn't and I have to live with that."

"I'm not saying it to be a jerk, just your MO has always been—"

"I know," Nate said sharply. They'd fallen a fair distance behind the pack of baseball players walking to the bar, so they were at least out of earshot. Nate slowed his pace to hang back even more. "Yeah, I get it. There's a pattern. I never speak up for myself and choose to brood about it. Right? Ever since Brad fucking Marsden and his stupid long eyelashes in tenth grade. Yes, I did write him letters that I never intended to send him and I only told *you* because you were my best friend and I had to tell *someone*. He's not even gay, by the way. We're friends on Facebook. He married a woman."

"Yeah, but—"

"I was fifteen. I was terrified of putting myself out there. Hard enough to be a teenager, right? Like any teenager is good at just speaking honestly when emotions are on the line. And I'm gay on top of everything else, and I had a horrible crush on a straight guy sophomore year, and yeah, I got pretty angsty about it. But, again, I was *fifteen*. Now I'm over thirty, and if nothing else, this summer has taught me that I'm too old to wait for things. Maybe my MO has always been to hang back and not speak up for myself and then mope about it afterward. But I'm done with that now. I have been totally honest with you for weeks now. I'm in love with you, I have been for a long time, and now you know about it."

Carlos stopped walking and turned to face Nate. "That's all I want, you know. For you to be honest. I wish I had known. When I told Ty you admitted to your feelings, he said it was obvious, but I didn't see it. I really never suspected."

"Yeah, well." Nate met Carlos's gaze.

Carlos put his hands on his hips and looked up at the sky. "I'm not trying to pick a fight with you. But bringing this up reminded me of how you can be sometimes. Maybe you forget that I know you better than you know yourself." He touched Nate's hand briefly before pulling his arm back. "The two of us are making something new, you know? I don't want to repeat old patterns."

"No, I agree. I don't want to repeat my mistakes."

"You're mad at me."

Nate glanced down the sidewalk. They were on a rather cute, quiet residential block on East Sixth Street. No one seemed to be around, save for a woman pushing a stroller in the distance. The rest of the team had turned onto Avenue B to go to Barnstorm.

"I'm not mad," Nate said.

Carlos pulled a face, tilting his head and raising his eyebrows as if to say, *Come on, now.*

"I'm *not* mad, but what you said did hurt a little, okay?"

Carlos nodded. "I didn't mean to hurt you. I didn't even realize I wasn't kidding until the words were out of my mouth. Because you do have a tendency not to speak up for yourself, but I want you to be able to speak to me. I mean, come on, Nate, it's *me*. If there's anyone you should be able to be honest with, it's me."

But Nate hadn't been. For years he hadn't been, not completely. And look at where it had gotten them. "I know," he said. "I understand that. I'm sorry."

"Being in a romantic relationship sure complicates things, doesn't it?"

Nate pointed down the sidewalk, and they resumed walking. "I expect this is not the last argument we'll ever have."

"I'm sorry too, for what it's worth."

"I know. Just…. While I was moping, when I was fantasizing about what a relationship with you would be like, I pictured us happy all the time. But that wasn't realistic, was it?"

"The people we love most also have the greatest potential to hurt us, I guess."

Nate sighed. "This whole summer has been a goddamn disaster, but at least we made things right between us, right?"

Carlos stopped walking again. He put his hands on Nate's shoulders. "I don't mean to put a negative spin on all this, like I'm resigning myself to my fate or whatever, because you and I could make each other very happy. Will we fight sometimes? Probably. Will we say hurtful things? Yeah, I'm sure we will. But as long as we can talk it through and come back together afterward, I think we will be very happy together."

Nate nodded slowly. "I think so too. I don't mean for it to sound like I'm resentful that our relationship is not just us hopping around on clouds with puppies and kittens and rainbows all the time, because that's not what I think. What we have feels *real*. And that's more important. I just.... God." It was a lot, this summer. Aiden, Nate's mother, all of it had just been so much piled on top of them, and it seemed like a miracle that they'd come through it together. "When I first brought this up three blocks ago, all I meant to say is that when we tell our friends about us, expect some ribbing."

"I would expect no less," Carlos said. "Are you sure you're okay?"

"No."

Carlos glanced both ways and then pulled Nate into his arms, holding him close and stroking his back. "What's wrong?"

"Everything. I don't know. Mom. Aiden. It's hot outside. The jock I'm wearing is digging into my skin and making it itchy downstairs. I really want a beer, but we're not at the bar yet."

Carlos laughed softly. "Come on, *papi*, let's get a beer." He took a step away and then offered his hand, so Nate took it, and they walked to the bar together.

CARLOS WASN'T sure of the right tack to take. Nate seemed content to stay mum, sitting at the bar and sipping his beer while Carlos devised a strategy. They'd been sitting there for about ten minutes, and maybe it was just the intense air-conditioning, but Nate seemed in better spirits already. Carlos found that unnerving.

"I like this new IPA Tom has on tap," Nate said. "Rich and hoppy without being too bitter."

Carlos stared at him for a moment. "Since when are you such an expert on beer?"

"I had to find something to occupy my time while you were—" He stopped abruptly and put a hand over his mouth. He sighed. "Sorry. Didn't mean to bring it up again. Last fall, this bar near my apartment started doing beer and cheese tastings on Wednesday nights as this kind of gay singles meet-and-greet. So, like, you go and end up sitting at tables with a bunch of other guys, and they give you a plate of cheese and craft beer in Dixie cups and tell you what you're eating. I didn't really meet anyone interesting, but I learned a lot about beer and cheese."

"You went to a gay singles thing?"

Nate shrugged. "You were with Aiden. I figured I had to move on."

"Bro." Carlos patted Nate's knee. He could hear the pain and resignation in Nate's voice but decided to let it go instead of turning it into A Thing.

"I know." Nate took a sip of his beer and seemed to let it sit on his tongue while he thought. He swallowed and said, "I was lonely, I guess."

Nate left a lot unsaid. He had been lonely because Carlos had been off letting Aiden manipulate him. Carlos had neglected Nate at a time when Nate was going through so much. Some of that was directly related to Carlos, of course.

"I'm so sorry," Carlos whispered.

Nate nodded. He put his now empty glass on the bar. Tom surreptitiously got him a refill. Nate said, "I have a much clearer picture of everything now. I know what mistakes I made and what things were out of my control. If I had it all to do over, the last two years would have played out differently." Nate glanced at his refilled glass and did a double take. He shook his head and said, "We've both made mistakes, and we both got suckered by circumstance, so all we can really do moving forward is learn our lessons. Be honest with each other. Talk things through. And don't linger on the past too much because it's the past and we can't change it."

Carlos leaned forward a little. "Very mature of you."

"See? I can grow."

Carlos grinned. "What am I going to do with you?"

"Love me," Nate said matter-of-factly.

Carlos leaned over and gave Nate's nose a quick peck. "Should we tell these clowns we're dating?"

"I dunno. This is not the most direct group. We found out about Mason and Patrick because we caught them making out here after a game once. Of course, Mason didn't formally introduce us until, like, two weeks later. But seriously, Ty, Ian, and I were having a drink over by the retired jersey wall and there was Mason, sticking his tongue down the throat of some guy. We were all mildly shocked by it."

"I hate that I missed it."

Nate shrugged. "I'm sure there will be other opportunities to catch our teammates in compromising positions. I mean, I've been watching Andreas awkwardly flirt with Joe for, like, ten minutes now, and he's not really getting anywhere. Joe seems skeptical."

Carlos glanced behind him, and sure enough, Joe was leaning against the wall with a raised eyebrow while Andreas rubbed his arms.

"Doesn't Joe have a boyfriend?" Carlos asked.

"Yup. Andreas's failure is inevitable."

Mason wandered over and ordered a beer. He smiled. "Are you guys conspiring?"

"Mocking Andreas," said Nate.

Mason nodded. "And here I thought you and Andreas would hook up."

Nate balked. "No. Why does everyone assume that? Did I drool?"

"No, it was just clear he was really into you," said Mason. "And since you were both single…."

"Oh."

"You're not ugly, Nate," said Carlos.

Nate rolled his eyes. "Gee, thanks."

Carlos smiled. "What, am I supposed to tell you you're dreamy?"

Nate adjusted his position on his stool and took another sip of beer. "Hey, I know I'm not as pretty as Andreas, but it would be in your best interest to butter my ego occasionally."

Carlos's grin got wider. "Oh, I see. In my best interest?"

Nate glanced at Mason. He sat up a little straighter. "Oh, hey there, Mason. I was about to say something inappropriate."

"Oh, don't keep it appropriate on my account." Mason rocked on his heels, looking amused.

Nate smiled at Mason sheepishly. "So, Mason, there's something you should probably know, especially if you're still working on seating charts for the wedding."

Mason frowned. "The moms are working on that, actually. I made the mistake of implying that maybe we could tone it down a little, that we didn't need to make this the event of the season, and now I've been banned from planning my own wedding. As a result, this is now the biggest, most ostentatious wedding New York City has ever seen." Mason shivered.

Nate chuckled. "Aren't you just renting out a party room at a restaurant?"

"No, we're renting out the whole restaurant." Mason sighed. "Patrick's delighted and is just as bad as the moms now, so I guess this is my life. I want him to be happy. Of course, now he keeps asking me questions about colors and flowers and I am mystified, but...." He shrugged. "Our parents are getting along and I'm marrying the man I love in three weeks, so I guess I shouldn't complain."

"Well, pass along to your mother that Carlos and I would like to sit together."

"Oh, right," said Mason. "I don't know if I told the mothers to take out Aiden, and originally, I had you across the room from each other because I thought Aiden would try to...." Mason shrugged and smiled sheepishly. "Well, anyway. *That's* over, so yeah, I think something can be arranged."

"Good," Carlos said. He threw an arm around Nate. "Because we're together now."

Mason balked, his eyes going wide. "Wait, really?"

Nate nodded.

"Oh."

Carlos couldn't tell if that was a good "oh" or a bad "oh."

"See, what did I say? I thought this would happen," said Nate.

Carlos felt like there was an inside joke here he wasn't privy to. How much pining had Nate really done? Mason, Ian, and Ty all knew about it, right? And, well, here was Mason motioning Ian and Ty over.

"Guys, really. Here's the whole story," said Nate, holding up his hands. "We've had a completely shit-tastic summer. Right? Carlos and Aiden's spectacular breakup. My mother. All of it has sucked. Carlos is the one bright spot in my life right now. He's my best friend. And he knows the whole story, with the pining and the angsting and the brooding behind his back. Somehow, he loves me in return. So we're giving this whole relationship thing a whirl, and please don't make fun of me too much because I've been this close"—Nate held up his hand, his thumb and index finger about half an inch apart—"to losing my goddamn mind for weeks now. Don't take this from me, okay?" He threw his arms around Carlos and hugged him tightly.

Ty leaned forward and tilted his head. "Wait, what?"

Carlos hugged Nate back. "We're together now."

"I… oh."

Everyone just stared for a moment.

Well, this was not at all how Carlos expected this to go. He took a deep breath and pulled away from Nate. "I get how this probably looks," Carlos said, "but it's real and you should be happy for us."

"We are," Ian said. "It's just that…. I mean, with everything that's been going on, are you really sure that…."

"Yes," Carlos and Nate said in unison. Carlos turned to look at Nate, who suddenly cracked up and started laughing. He put a hand to his forehead like he thought it would help him hold all the laughter in. He looked just as crazed as Carlos felt.

"Man, I love you," Nate said to Carlos.

Carlos couldn't help but grin in response.

"Well, I'm happy we won't have to listen to Nate whine anymore," Ty said.

Nate let out a heavy breath. "Was I really that bad?"

Ty made the tone of his voice a little higher and did a fair imitation of Nate's mild Bronx accent. "Oh, Ty, I'm so sad to watch the love of my life Carlos make out with Aiden, I'm all emo about it and will drink this beer sadly and mope all the time."

Nate shook his head. "I was not *that* bad."

Ty raised an eyebrow. "I've never seen anyone moon the way you do. Except maybe Andreas. I bet he'd be real broken up to learn you were going out with Carlos after all."

Across the bar, Andreas had moved on to flirting with another player. "I'm sure he'll be devastated," Nate said.

"I'm looking forward to the look on Scott's face when we tell him there's another couple on the team," said Mason.

Ty laughed. "He'll threaten to separate us all, probably."

Ian draped his arms over Ty's shoulders from behind and gave him a gentle hug. Ty lifted his hand and rubbed Ian's forearm. Ian said,

"If Scott didn't want people on his team hooking up, he should have become a Little League coach."

"Little League? Not Major League?" asked Ty.

Ian just raised an eyebrow.

Nate laughed. "Are you implying that Major League players are hooking up with each other?"

"Seems logical," said Ian. "I mean, if you had to spend every day of the summer in a locker room with a bunch of professional athletes…. I mean, you know a couple of them are probably totally doing it in the showers after everyone else leaves."

Everyone turned to look at Mason, the ex-Yankee, who held up his hands. "I plead the Fifth."

Carlos felt some relief that this crowd was so easily distracted. He turned to Nate and admired his profile before Nate turned to him and smiled.

"Aw," said Ian. "Congratulations, you two."

"Yeah," said Mason. "Let's toast this." He made sure everyone had drinks, and then they all clinked their glasses together.

Nate got a little sauced on the beer people kept buying him, but by the time they got back to the apartment later, he was calm and quiet.

"Everything all right?" Carlos said as he changed out of his uniform.

"Yes," Nate said. "I've just been thinking. I guess it really hit me tonight as we were telling our friends that we're together that this is a *relationship*. You know?"

Carlos shook his head. "What do you mean?"

"I mean, when I pictured us together, I only ever saw the good. I never thought about how hard some things would be. Like, we had a fight today. We won't always communicate well. I've been keeping my feelings for you a secret for so long that it's a habit, and it still feels strange sometimes to be public with them. So I'm bound to fuck some things up, and we'll probably fight again, and things between us will not always be so easy."

"Relationships can be hard," Carlos said, still not really sure what Nate was getting at.

"It's not all snuggling on the couch while watching a game, I guess."

"But it's better, right?" Carlos took a step toward Nate and ran his hands up Nate's arms. "This is better, what's happening between us. Not just because of the sex, although that's pretty awesome." Carlos paused for acknowledgment. Nate smiled and nodded. "But, like, we're closer now than we ever have been, and it feels good, doesn't it?"

"It does, yeah."

"So you don't have any regrets, do you?"

"Only that I didn't tell you how I felt sooner."

Carlos hugged Nate. "Nothing to be done about that now."

"No." Nate put his arms around Carlos and held him firmly. "But I want to do right by you going forward. For the rest of our lives, if you'll have me."

"I know. I will. Thanks, Nate."

"You are so very welcome."

Chapter 21

NATE THREW the lock on the men's room door and raised his eyebrows at Carlos.

"We're going to get caught," Carlos said.

Nate grinned. He tugged on the door handle. "That is a deadbolt, my friend. No one is getting in here unless they have a key."

"All it would take is Tío Felipe and his weak bladder to complain to hotel management, and a whole SWAT team will be banging the door down to let him in."

"What I have in mind should go quickly. We'll have our pants back on before the troops arrive."

Carlos rolled his eyes, though secretly he was pleased. Nate's sex drive had come back slowly, and then suddenly this past week he'd been insatiable. Carlos loved it and was having fun exploring Nate in new ways, and it was wild to see usually cautious Nate be spontaneous this way.

In fact, Nate was already unbuckling his belt.

Carlos looked around. The black tiles on the floor and walls, the dark marble counters, the dark green stall doors—this was a classy bathroom. "It's nice in here."

"Don't care. Take your pants off."

The crisp tan suit Nate wore might as well have disintegrated with how quickly he pulled it off. He tossed his tie, then his jacket, then his pants toward the sink. Carlos laughed as Nate stood there in just his white shirt and a pair of blue briefs.

"You're crazy," Carlos said.

"You love me," Nate said, walking toward Carlos, his hand outstretched toward the fly on Carlos's pants.

"That's true, but it doesn't make you any less crazy."

Nate smiled wide and undid the button holding Carlos's pants up.

"Keep in mind that this is a very expensive suit," said Carlos. "You get anything on it, I'm making you pay the dry cleaning bill."

"Why do you think I'm making you take it off?" Nate unzipped Carlos's pants slowly, letting his fingers graze the length of Carlos's cock. That got Carlos's blood pumping, and he hardened quickly under Nate's soft touch.

They'd been doing things like this all week, sneaking in kisses and make-out sessions and sex in weird places, and Carlos's body knew the drill. Nate was near naked, and Carlos's animal instincts took over. He grabbed Nate's head, pulling him in for a big, sloppy kiss while Nate made quick work of the rest of Carlos's clothes. Once they were both down to their shirts and their underwear, Nate grasped Carlos tight and thrust his hips forward. When their cocks pressed together, Carlos groaned.

"Some quickie if we're naked," Carlos said, though speaking was a challenge given how aroused he was. "Shouldn't we be banging against the stall door with only our pants undone?"

"You want to negotiate this or you just want to have sex?" Nate said, reaching into Carlos's underwear to pull out his cock.

"Mmm, sex."

"Then shut up."

Nate gave Carlos a hard kiss and then pushed Carlos against the wall. Carlos hit it with a grunt, but he couldn't be bothered to think about whether it hurt. He tugged on Nate's hair and licked into his mouth. Nate groaned as he stroked Carlos's cock. Then Nate leaned back with a grin and sank to his knees.

Carlos moaned Nate's name as Nate took Carlos's cock into his mouth.

He slid back a little, pressed his lips against the tip of Carlos's cock, and then reverently licked the whole length of it before enveloping it in his mouth. Those soft lips pressed against Carlos's shaft, and Nate licked and sucked and kissed. It was still a little bit strange to see *Nate* doing these things, but it felt so good it didn't matter. Carlos's skin tingled as Nate continued to go down on him, as Nate reached up to cup and tug on his balls, as Nate drove him wild with lust.

"Fuck, that's good," Carlos whispered, thrusting his fingers into Nate's hair. And it was good, both watching the way Nate worshipped his cock and the sensations Nate's clever mouth and tongue gave him. Nate's mouth was hot, his tongue rough, his lips soft. It was an expert blow job, all texture and pressure and friction. Carlos lifted his hand and bit into his palm to keep from screaming, because he was about to—

But then it stopped abruptly. Before Carlos could even figure out what was happening, Nate was kissing him again.

Carlos smiled against Nate's lips. God, he loved this man.

Carlos reached between them and pulled their cocks together, stroking them, close now that Nate's cock was pressed against him. He knew from the frenetic nature of Nate's kiss that Nate was close too. They thrust against each other, finding a rhythm easily, and they kept on kissing, and everything felt choreographed, but then, Nate and Carlos had always excelled at communicating without words. Hand gestures, grunts, meaningful looks, and now thrusting and kissing, and Carlos knew exactly what Nate was feeling because he felt it himself.

Warm arousal spread through Carlos, and tingles and electricity, and he knew things would soon get messy. "Nate, I—"

Nate knew, and he jerked as he grabbed a wad of tissues from the box on the counter, but then he returned and they writhed against each other. Nate jerked again, and then he was coming, groaning out Carlos's name as he pressed the tissues against both of their cocks.

How thoughtful.

But Carlos didn't have time to consider it further, because then his mind flew apart, and he thrust against Nate, begging for more. Nate grabbed him and squeezed and then stroked him quickly, getting the pressure and force just right to finally pull that orgasm through Carlos from his toes, and Carlos shot into the tissues and he leaned forward to kiss Nate as the orgasm tore through him. They continued to kiss as it subsided, as white-hot pleasure melted into something softer but no less wonderful. Nate tossed the tissues in the trash and then pulled Carlos into his arms, and the two of them held each other and kissed and panted into each other's mouths.

Carlos pulled back and slumped against the wall. "That was hot."

Nate smirked. "I know."

"We should probably get back."

Nate glanced at the clothes piled on the counter. "I suppose."

"Do you really want Mama Lulu to decide to hunt us down? Can you imagine her finding us together in a men's room?"

That seemed to motivate Nate, who backed away from Carlos and started sorting through the discarded clothes.

When they were mostly set to rights and Carlos was trying to fix his hair in front of the mirror, the door jiggled.

"Why is this locked?" barked Tío Felipe.

Carlos laughed and gave up. He checked that Nate was dressed—he was, and though his hair was a little disheveled, he looked just as he had when they'd first walked into the men's room, curse him—and then went to the door.

"Sorry, Felipe, must have hit the lock by accident on my way in."

Tío Felipe grumbled as he walked to one of the stalls.

Carlos looked at Nate and their eyes met. Nate put a hand over his mouth, probably suppressing a laugh. It was just like the thousand other times they'd nearly been caught doing something they probably shouldn't have been doing.

Carlos reached for Nate's hand and tugged him toward the restroom door. "Come on, lover boy," he whispered. "Let's go see what's going on at this party."

"I HAVEN'T seen this many ball gowns since that crazy birthday party Mom threw for Gabriela when she turned fifteen," Carlos said, standing on the edge of the dance floor in the hotel ballroom. "It's like a prom on steroids."

"I know," said Nate, taking in the scene. "Even Lourdes's wedding wasn't this insane."

In a way, it was comforting to Carlos not to have to explain Ruiz family custom to Nate. Aiden had been intimidated by Carlos's large family and overcompensated by mocking or deriding its traditions. Nate was unfazed by them, probably because he'd been taking part in them for so long.

In the time since they'd snuck out of Carlos's cousin Lana's Super Sweet Sixteen—and Nate and Carlos had made their little side trip to the men's room—the whole Ruiz clan and a smattering of people Carlos didn't recognize had filled a hotel ballroom. The DJ was squawking over the microphone about getting all the kids dancing, so everyone crowded around the dance floor to watch. Carlos looked on, not sure how to act. Nate had been invited to the party, but not as Carlos's date.

The DJ switched to a slow song so that the gathered teenagers could grope each other in an officially condoned way. Nate stood beside Carlos and then reached between them and took Carlos's hand.

The moment was actually kind of romantic, between the tinkly piano ballad the DJ was playing, the teenagers awkwardly dancing with and smiling at each other, and Carlos's hand folded into Nate's. Carlos looked over at Nate, who was in profile against the weird spotlights in the ballroom, gazing across the floor. Nate was so handsome tonight in his neatly tailored suit. Even his hair looked tidy—Lana's mother, Carlos's Tia Lola, had fussed over them when they'd emerged from the bathroom, actually, because heaven forbid anything be out of place— and his face was freshly shaved. He looked a bit more polished up than usual, but he looked wonderful. Carlos felt stupid with love for him, felt stupid he didn't see this thing between them sooner.

Nate turned and caught Carlos looking. He winked.

"Now, if we could get some of the grown-ups out here…," the DJ started.

Marisol wandered over and grabbed Carlos. He let go of Nate's hand as she pulled him through the crowd onto the floor. Carlos held his arms up. Marisol smiled and put her hands on his shoulders.

"Some dance, huh?" she asked. "Worse than Lourdes's wedding."

"Yup. Speaking of which, if what I hear about a certain banker is true, you're up next after Gabby."

"Uh-uh, bro. You and Nate finally worked your stuff out. The banker and I are just having fun. *You* will have to be the shining star of the next Ruiz wedding."

"When you say it that way, it sounds like a death sentence."

Marisol laughed. "Hush. It's a good thing. I like you and Nate together."

"I hope Mama and Dad feel the same."

"You still haven't told them?"

"I'm still working out how. It just…. It feels like such a big thing. And part of me wanted to keep it private for a while. I know I have to tell them, but I don't know how."

"You'll figure it out. And I'm sure they'll both approve."

"Are you sure?"

"Hey, everyone, find someone else to dance with!" said the DJ.

Marisol smirked. "I think they're about to find out, either way."

Suddenly Nate appeared beside them. "Mind if I cut in, Mari?"

"Not at all." Marisol pulled away from Carlos and stepped back. "And hey, here's my date!"

Carlos narrowed his eyes at the tall guy who walked up to Marisol. He couldn't remember the guy's name—Rick? Rich? Rock? Oh, right, Dirk—and he was instantly distrustful, but Marisol grabbed his arm and pulled him away. This was the banker she'd been dating, and he definitely had something slick and moneyed about him, but Marisol seemed to like him, so Carlos let it go.

"Will you dance with me?" Nate asked.

Carlos smiled, Marisol's date forgotten. "Of course, *mi amor.*"

Carlos, being just slightly shorter than Nate, put one hand behind Nate's neck and pulled him close. With his other hand, he took Nate's. Nate put a hand on Carlos's waist. And then they danced. Really, Carlos was leading, using his feet to pull Nate around the dance floor. Nate followed, matching his rhythm and his pattern of steps. It was like they'd been dancing with each other for years. Maybe they had. Probably some of Lana's friends and other family members were scandalized. Carlos didn't care.

Really, he didn't care who saw or who judged them, because he knew in his heart that what he had now with Nate was real. Not only was it real, but it was the sort of love that spanned the ages, that had been building between them for nearly thirty years, and Nate, above all others, was the person Carlos loved best in the world. Nate was his closest friend and now was his lover.

The DJ broadcast some crooner through the speakers, the voice soft and warm, so Carlos pulled Nate closer until their chests nearly touched, and his pulse kicked up to a new speed as excitement zipped through him. God, he loved Nate, loved being with Nate this way, public but intimate, and a warmth spread through his chest as he looked up and met Nate's gaze. Nate smiled, his blue eyes twinkling, and everything Carlos felt was reflected right back at him.

The song ended and the DJ switched to a faster-paced pop song. Nate laughed softly and pulled Carlos into a tight hug. It was so wonderful to be in Nate's arms, like coming home after a long time away. Which, Carlos supposed, was an accurate assessment of the situation.

They wriggled out of the crowd of dancers and, by some unspoken agreement, walked hand in hand to the bar. As they waited for the bartender to mix their cocktails, Mama Lulu walked up to them.

"Is there something you'd like to tell me, *niños*?"

Her glare was stern. Carlos had often found himself under that glare as a boy, and it made him nervous now. Part of that was habit or instinct, some kind of Pavlovian reaction to that glare that instantly made him feel guilty, even though he hadn't done anything wrong. Part of it was just nerves. He wasn't sure how he'd cope if his mother did not approve of his relationship with Nate.

But he didn't care *too* much, because he loved Nate.

"Nate and I are together now," Carlos said. "I mean, we're dating."

That gaze persisted, got worse when she raised one eyebrow, but then the façade broke and she grinned. She pulled both of them into a hug. "Oh, boys, I am so happy for you. Finally, you figured it all out." She pulled back and patted Nate's cheek. "And you I already love like a son."

"It means a lot for you to say so," said Nate a little stiffly, like he still didn't believe her reaction. Carlos didn't blame him.

"You both looked so handsome dancing together," Mama Lulu said, her smile broad.

The bartender slid glasses onto the bar. Nate picked his up and took a sip. He glanced at Carlos, who couldn't help but smile back. He looked back at his mother.

"I take it you approve," Carlos said.

Mama rolled her eyes. "You have to give me a little time to plan the wedding. Gabby's is only a few weeks away, and we can't have so many of them so close together."

Carlos rolled his eyes, but just as he was about to crack a joke, he realized Nate was staring at him.

"What?" Carlos asked.

Nate frowned. He shot Mama Lulu a sidelong glance. "Not that I'm not rolling my eyes on the inside, since both your mother and Marisol seem to be taking it for granted that we'll get married. And, well, I'm like a hairsbreadth from dropping on one knee right here and asking you if you want to. But we've only been dating a few weeks, and this summer has been so crazy."

"Nate, it's fine," said Carlos. "I know."

"It's not that I don't want to marry you. I just… want to be sure."

"No, I know. It's too soon."

Mama Lulu made a little squealy noise. "That's why I know you'll be all right. You boys love each other. You will figure out how to be with each other for good, and then you will tell me so I can start planning your wedding."

This time Nate did roll his eyes. That made Mama laugh.

Two hours later, as Nate and Carlos retired to their room at the hotel—they were staying up in Westchester near Tia Lola's house, and Carlos had made a unilateral decision that going back to the city so late at night was unreasonable—Carlos said, "Nate?"

Nate fumbled with the lock on the door. His need to lock hotel room doors was an affectation Carlos had forgotten about, but then he remembered the rare times they'd shared rooms at weddings and school trips and could easily picture a much younger Nate fussing over the door. When Nate seemed satisfied, he turned around and looked at Carlos. "Yeah?"

"You want to be with me forever, right?"

"Of course."

Carlos motioned Nate over to the bed and they sat down next to each other. "I get why it's too early for us to talk something more permanent, but I'm not opposed to the idea either. For the record."

"Good to know."

Carlos put an arm around Nate. "I kind of see us as two people teaming up against the world, just like we did when we were with kids, just with more sexy times."

Nate laughed and shook his head. "Oh, if only it were that simple."

"It is."

"No. There's so much more at stake now. I love you and I want to be sure we get our relationship right."

"We will. I love you."

Nate leaned over and kissed Carlos briefly.

"That's all we need," Carlos said.

Nate sighed and pressed his forehead to Carlos's. "We have to go to Patrick and Mason's wedding in a week and we'll probably have to answer these questions all over again."

"Well, or Patrick will be so incandescent no one will notice us. You know the Hipsters have a pool going for what color Patrick's hair will be at the wedding? My money's on hot pink."

Nate laughed. He pulled away, but then he hugged Carlos tightly. "Oh, you're the best. I think blue, though."

Chapter 22

MASON SPENT most of the afternoon frowning at his phone and not carrying Carlos's boxes down from Ty and Ian's apartment.

"See, the reason I asked for your help is your big strong arms," Carlos said.

"Just a sec." Mason thumbed the screen of his phone. "Last-minute wedding nonsense."

"If this is how wedding planning goes," Nate said to Carlos, "I'm not marrying you."

Mason grunted and pocketed his phone. "I'm sorry. My mother's having a breakdown because the florist can't get the lilies she wanted, and Lord, I do not care about flowers."

"Not marrying you either," Carlos said to Nate.

"Uh, boys," Ty said, carrying the last box out to the sidewalk. "I love you all, but I don't know how *I* ended up doing all the work."

Carlos jogged over and took the box from Ty. "Seriously, thank you, guys."

"So you're moving in with Nate permanently?" Ty asked.

"Looks that way." Carlos looked over at Nate, who was now organizing Carlos's boxes into a pile. The plan had been to call a cab, although there was more stuff than Carlos remembered leaving at Ty and Ian's place. "And not that I'm seeking your approval, but you all are fine with it, right?"

Ty smiled. "Yeah. You guys are good together. Just, you know. Ian's influence or something. He never makes a decision without considering every angle and talking it over with me for three hours. I just didn't want you guys to rush into anything. If it blew up in your faces…."

"I know."

Ty nodded. "I know you do. That's why I wish you guys the best."

"Thanks."

"Oh, speaking of happily-ever-afters, I have news," said Ty. "Josh told me Aiden is officially out of the league. They told him not to come back next season."

"That's something," Nate said. He glanced at Carlos.

Carlos was glad Nate was finally willing to leave it alone. Carlos just wanted to move on with his life. "I'm happy if I never have to see him again."

"As comeuppances go, this one's a little disappointing," said Ty. "We'll all go kick his ass anytime, though. You just say the word."

"Thanks, guys. I appreciate it."

"Are we calling a cab or what?" Nate said, staring at the tower of boxes. "And did these boxes breed with each other? I don't remember carting this much stuff out of Aiden's apartment. Where are we going to put all of this?"

Ty laughed. "There he is."

Carlos grinned. "Yeah."

"What?" asked Nate.

Ty walked over and slapped Nate on the back. "You've been either subdued or blissed out for the last few weeks. It's nice to see you come back to yourself. Fretting over Carlos's shit is kind of your natural way of operating."

Nate scowled for a moment, but then he sighed. "Yeah," he said wearily. "And now there's a lot more of it."

"Most of this is books," Carlos said. "That bookcase by the kitchen is half-empty."

This was one of those practical things they'd need to negotiate. Carlos and Nate had never lived together before, and there had been something temporary about Carlos staying at Nate's place over the summer. Strangely, Carlos felt more at home at Nate's apartment than he ever had at Aiden's, but he thought bringing all of his stuff there would make it seem more so. He thought about asking if Nate was willing to move as well, so that they could get a place that was *theirs* and not *Nate's*, but Nate had such a sweet deal on the place and it was in such a great neighborhood that Carlos didn't want to tempt real estate fate. He really did like the scones at the bakery near Nate's apartment. Carlos planned to pay half the rent, though, at least until they figured out the next step.

They still had so much to negotiate. Strange how falling in love with one's best friend wasn't as easy as it looked on TV.

Carlos walked over to Nate and examined the box pile. There were five in all. He put an arm around Nate. "It'll be fine."

"I know," Nate said. "Or I guess we could get a bigger place one of these days. My place was only ever meant to be a bachelor apartment. I mean, I know couples who live together in tiny studios, but they always seem just about to divorce each other. I love you, but I don't know that I want you all up in my business *all* the time."

Carlos laughed. "Yes, *papi*. We'll work it out."

PATRICK SURPRISED everyone by dying his hair blond for his wedding.

Nate watched from his vantage point near the faux hearth on one wall of the restaurant. The room had been cleared of tables and instead had two sets of chairs arranged in rows. Nate and Ty were decked out in matching tuxes with purple ties and vests as Mason's groomsmen. Carlos had insisted they looked handsome, but Nate was really unsure about this color, which was... vivid. To have Patrick walk down the aisle looking so plain by contrast was kind of a punch in the face.

Well, plain was relative. Patrick wore a white tux that had silver piping on the sleeves and lapels and what might have been glitter near the cuffs. It was tasteful, not too Liberace, but it still seemed rather tame for Patrick. His hair, though only blond and not the riot of color it usually was, was still spiked out and a little crazy. He beamed as he walked down the aisle on his mother's arm.

Mason rocked on his heels as he waited for his groom to walk down the aisle. Mason had on a black tux, and Patrick's attendants included his best friend Valerie in a gown the same color as the groomsmen's ties, completing the wedding tableau. Nate thought it was all a lot, but it was beautiful in its way. Despite his protests about the wedding being too big and too grandiose, Mason had been grinning like an idiot all day.

Nate glanced toward the chairs and saw Carlos and Ian giggling together. Nate would be with them now if it hadn't been for Mason's estranged brother, Odell. After a long silence, Mason and Odell had been talking and trying to repair their relationship, but when Odell said some unkind things about Patrick, he'd been taken off best-man duty. Mason had given him an ultimatum: he could come to the wedding with a promise to behave or he could stay at home with his hate. Nate scanned the room but didn't see Odell.

Mason, meanwhile, had made Ty his best man and asked Nate to be a groomsman as well, so here Nate was. It wasn't the first gay wedding he'd attended, but it was the first in which he was a direct participant. It was a little surreal.

Nate rolled his shoulders as Patrick made his way down the aisle. Nate ran a hand over his poor disheveled hair. He'd gotten it to look just so that morning—Carlos had teased him the entire time he'd been futzing in the bathroom—but it had been drizzling on his walk from the subway to the restaurant earlier, and now his hair was a lost cause. Mason had pointed out that everyone would be looking at sparkly Patrick, which Nate hoped was true, because he was sure he looked stupid.

The ceremony was short, mercifully. Nate's mind was all over the place and he had trouble paying attention. In the middle of the ceremony, when the officiant was talking about the meaning of the promises Mason and Patrick were making to each other, a murmur went through the crowd. Nate looked around to figure out what was happening; everyone's attention had shifted away from the happy couple toward the window. It took a moment, but Nate saw it.

A wide rainbow spread across the sky over the Hudson River.

It was perfect.

Nate looked toward those assembled and, trying not to draw attention to himself, made eye contact with Carlos, then tilted his head toward the window. Carlos winked and smiled.

The officiant paused and also looked out the window. "Well, will you look at that rainbow?"

Sure, a rainbow over a gay wedding was a bit of a cliché, but that didn't make it any less magical.

Then the ceremony was over and everyone was ushered onto a terrace that overlooked the Hudson for cocktails. Nate hunted down Carlos in the crowd. He found him talking to Ian near a little bar. When Carlos turned and saw Nate approach, his face broke into a wide grin.

"Hey, *papi*," Carlos said. He puckered his lips, so Nate kissed them. "Guess we both lost our bet."

"Yeah. Patrick said he didn't want to look ridiculous in photos that were probably going to be circulating for all time."

"Were you betting on hair color?" Ian asked. "I mean, I had ten bucks on green, but I should have known Patrick would surprise us all."

"They look cute together, though, don't they?" Carlos said, nodding toward the other side of the terrace, where Mason and Patrick had their arms around each other, all smiles.

"They do," Nate said.

"I'm glad the sun came out," Ian said, looking up.

Nate looked at the sky. A few wispy clouds drifted by, but otherwise there was no evidence that it had drizzled all afternoon. He patted his head.

"Are you still freaking out about your hair?" Carlos asked. He swatted Nate's hands out of the way and started finger combing it. Nate closed his eyes and surrendered himself to the feel of Carlos's fingers rubbing his scalp.

"You look fine, Nate," Carlos said softly.

"Just fine?" Nate asked, cracking one eye open.

Carlos laughed. "You're hot, *papi*. Best-looking guy here. Happy?"

"Yes. So my hair doesn't look too stupid?"

"No. Not *too* stupid."

Nate pushed Carlos's hands away while Carlos laughed.

"Love you," said Carlos with a grin.

Ian laughed. "Scott's going to kick us all off the team. Too much sappiness."

"Does Scott have a boyfriend?" Carlos asked. "I can't remember."

"Is it possible for robots to find love?" Nate asked.

"Can you imagine how bossy he is in bed?" asked Ian.

Everyone laughed. Carlos said, "I just wondered. I mean, if he got paired off with someone, maybe he'd be less grouchy all the time."

"Are you saying that all our coach needs is to get laid?" Nate asked.

"Maybe."

Carlos looked at Nate and Nate met his gaze. Carlos said, "So what do you think? Is this whole wedding thing an entirely terrible idea or what?"

It sent a giddy thrill through Nate to contemplate his own wedding. And not just a wedding, but one to Carlos. "Not a terrible idea," he said, throwing an arm around Carlos. Carlos patted his chest in return. It wasn't a real plan, but it was a promise.

Nate turned to Ian. "So not to be an ass, because I bet you've heard this before, but what about you and Ty? Think you'll ever get married?"

Ian shrugged. "It's fine. We talked about it. We're not in a hurry. If we're both happy, what's the rush?"

Nate smiled. "Sure. Hell, I'd be happy if Carlos consented to slow dance with me during the most romantic bits of the reception tonight."

Carlos hugged Nate. "Not a problem."

"Aren't we all just so sappy and sweet?" said Ty as he approached.

"We were just saying we'll make Scott miserable next season precisely because we're all coupled and cute," Ian said, greeting his boyfriend with a quick kiss.

Ty grinned. "That's great. I live to make Scott miserable."

Mason and Patrick approached hand in hand. Patrick had taken off his tux jacket to reveal a white vest embroidered with little silver flowers.

"Congratulations!" said Carlos, giving them both hugs. "Although I'm surprised Patrick didn't wear an amazing technicolor dream tux."

Patrick grinned. "I couldn't let you all win your bets."

Mason laughed. "I think you look gorgeous."

Patrick preened, grinning widely. "Thank you, darling. I wanted to look fetching. All eyes should be on the bride at her wedding, right?"

Mason chuckled and kissed Patrick's cheek. "Anyway," Mason said, "thank you all for coming. We should be able to move back inside for dinner in a few minutes. I, for one, am looking forward to dancing with my husband."

"Mmm, that sounds perfect."

It was all pretty sappy, Nate thought as he looked at his friends, but here with Carlos in his arms, he didn't mind it one bit. He kissed Carlos's temple and couldn't remember a time he'd been this happy. For such a horrible summer to end so well was a blessing.

Then, out of the corner of his eye, Nate spotted Odell cautiously walking onto the terrace. Mason must have spotted him too, because he gasped.

"Miracles can happen after all, huh?" Patrick said, certainly knowing how much Mason's brother's presence at his wedding must have meant to him.

"Don't count on it quite yet, but… he's here."

"Yeah," said Patrick. "Let's go talk to him."

Mason and Patrick moved on to talk to Odell. Ty and Ian had fallen into their own little conversation, so Nate turned to Carlos. "If we do ever get married, it doesn't need to be this fancy."

Carlos cocked an eyebrow. "Have you met my family? Mama Lulu will have the opportunity to throw the big gay wedding to end all big gay weddings. She'd rent out Central Park to do it, you know."

Nate did know. He sighed and tried to portray his annoyance with that, though secretly he liked the idea of a big wedding celebrating his love for Carlos.

"I know," Nate said. "Doesn't matter as long as you're there, sweetheart."

"Aw, Nate." Carlos leaned over and kissed Nate's nose. "I love you, you big cheeseball."

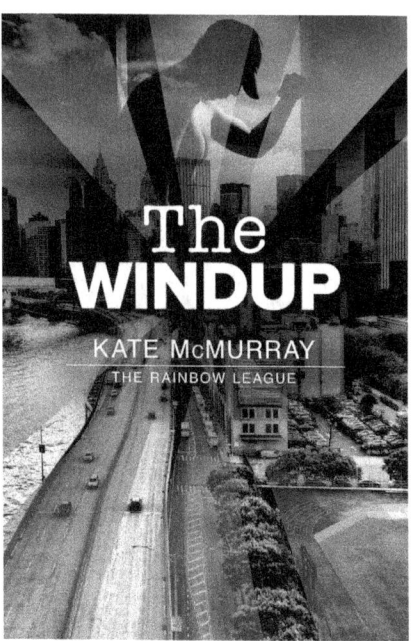

Ian ran screaming from New York City upon graduating from high school. A job offer too good to turn down has brought him back, but he plans to leave as soon as the job is up. In the meantime he lets an old friend talk him into joining the Rainbow League, New York's LGBT amateur baseball league. Baseball turns out to be a great outlet for his anxiety, and not only because sexy teammate Ty has caught his eye.

Ty is like a duck on a pond—calm and laid-back on the surface, a churning mess underneath. In Ian, he's found someone with whom he feels comfortable enough to share some of what's going on beneath the surface. The only catch is that Ian is dead set on leaving the city as soon as he can. Ty works up a plan to convince Ian that New York is, in fact, the greatest city in the world. But when Ian receives an offer for a job overseas, Ty needs a new plan: convince Ian that home is where Ty is.

www.dreamspinnerpress.com

Mason made headlines when, after his professional baseball career was sidelined by an injury, he very publicly came out of the closet. Now he's scratching the baseball itch playing in the Rainbow League while making his way through New York's population of beefcakes, even though they all come up short. Plus, he's still thinking about last summer's encounter with hot, effeminate, pierced and tattooed Patrick—pretty much the opposite of the sort of man he has long pictured himself with.

Patrick hasn't been able to forget Mason either, and now that baseball season is back upon them, he's determined to have him again. Mason is unlike any man Patrick has ever been with before, and not just because he's an ex-Yankee. All Patrick has to do is convince a reluctant Mason that their one night wasn't just a crazy fluke and that they could be great together… if only Mason could get past his old hang-ups and his intolerant family.

www.dreamspinnerpress.com

KATE MCMURRAY is an award-winning romance author and fan. When she's not writing, she works as a nonfiction editor, dabbles in various crafts, and is maybe a tiny bit obsessed with baseball. She is active in RWA and has served as president of Rainbow Romance Writers and on the board of RWANYC. She lives in Brooklyn, NY.

Website: www.katemcmurray.com
Twitter: www.twitter.com/katemcmwriter
Facebook: www.facebook.com/katemcmurraywriter

Kate McMurray
BLIND
ITEMS

Columnist Drew Walsh made his career by publicly criticizing conservative, anti-gay politician Richard Granger. So when a rumor surfaces that Granger's son Jonathan might be gay, Drew finds himself in the middle of a potential scandal. Under the guise of an interview about Jonathan's new job teaching in an inner-city school, Drew's job is to find out if the rumors are true. Drew's best friend Rey is also Jonathan's cousin, and he arranges the meeting between Jonathan and Drew that changes everything.

After just one interview, it's obvious to Drew that the rumors are true, but he carefully neglects to mention that in his article. It's also obvious that he's falling for Jonathan, and he can't stay away after the article is published. Still, Jonathan is too afraid to step out of the closet, and Drew thinks the smartest thing might be to let him go—until Jonathan shows up drunk one night at his apartment. The slow burn of their attraction doesn't fade with Jonathan's buzz, but navigating a relationship is never easy—especially in the shadow of right-wing politics.

www.dreamspinnerpress.com

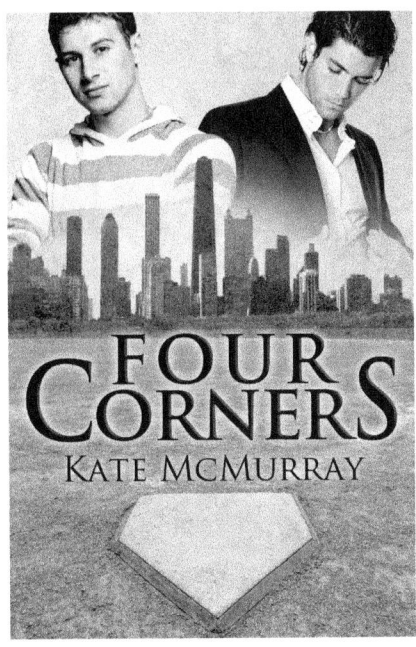

Since childhood, Jake, Adam, Kyle, and Brendan have been teammates, best friends, brothers. Then one day, when they were twenty-five, Adam disappeared without a word, devastating his friends—none more so than Jake, who had secretly loved Adam since they were teenagers.

Now, five years later, Adam is back, and he has his mind set on Jake. But those years of anger, hurt, and confusion are a lot to overcome, and Jake doesn't find it easy to forgive. He isn't sure they'll ever fit together the way they did. Jake, Kyle, and Brendan have moved on with their lives, but Adam's high-profile career keeps him in the closet—the same place he's been for years. Still, his apologies seem sincere, and the attraction is still there. Jake desperately wants to give him a chance. But first he has to find out why Adam left and if he's really back for good.

www.dreamspinnerpress.com

Weathermen are predicting an incredible blizzard for New York City, but with old snow melting on the sidewalk, Seth Roland is a little skeptical. Despite moping over his ex-boyfriend Evan, who recently dumped him, Seth pretends all is well as he steps into his regular local bar, where he's surprised by a blast from his past. Enter Kieran O'Malley, Seth's very first boyfriend, in the city for a conference.

It might have been just a chance meeting, but first a train derailment and then the predicted blizzard keep Seth and Kieran in close proximity. It's enough time for old feelings to surface, rekindled attraction to take hold, and new hopes for a future together to fill them both. But once the storm passes, the real challenge begins. Will Seth and Kieran work to make the relationship last, or will they let it melt away like snow in the sun?

www.dreamspinnerpress.com

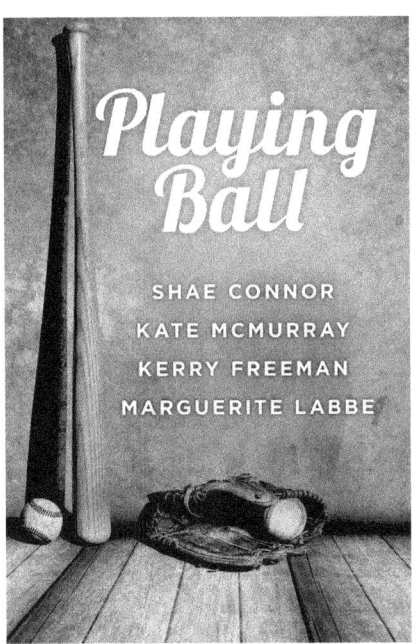

Baseball—America's favorite pastime—provides a field wide open for romance. A Home Field Advantage may not help when Toby must choose between the team he's loved all his life and the man he could love for the rest of it. In 1927, Skip hides his sexuality to protect his career until he meets One Man to Remember. Ruben and Alan fell victim to a Wild Pitch, leaving them struggling with heartache and guilt, and now they've met again. And on One Last Road Trip, Jake retires and leaves baseball behind, hoping to reconnect with Mikko and get a second chance at love.

Home Field Advantage by Shae Connor
One Man to Remember by Kate McMurray
Wild Pitch by Marguerite Labbe
One Last Road Trip by Kerry Freeman

www.dreamspinnerpress.com

Giovanni Boca was destined to go down in history as an opera legend until a vocal chord injury abruptly ended his career. Now he teaches voice lessons at a prestigious New York City music school. During auditions for his summer opera workshop, he finds his protégé in fourteen-year-old Emma McPhee. Just as intriguing to Gio is Emma's father Mike, a blue-collar guy who runs a business renovating the kitchens and bathrooms of New York's elite to finance his daughter's dream.

Mike's partner was killed when Emma was a toddler, and Gio mourns the beautiful voice he will never have again, so coping with loss is something they have in common. Their initial physical attraction quickly grows to something more as each hopes to fill the gap that loss and grief has left in his life. Although Mike wonders if he can truly fit into Gio's upperclass world, their bond grows stronger. Then, trouble strikes from outside when the machinations of an unscrupulous stage mother threaten to tear Gio and Mike apart—and ruin Emma's bright future.

www.dreamspinnerpress.com

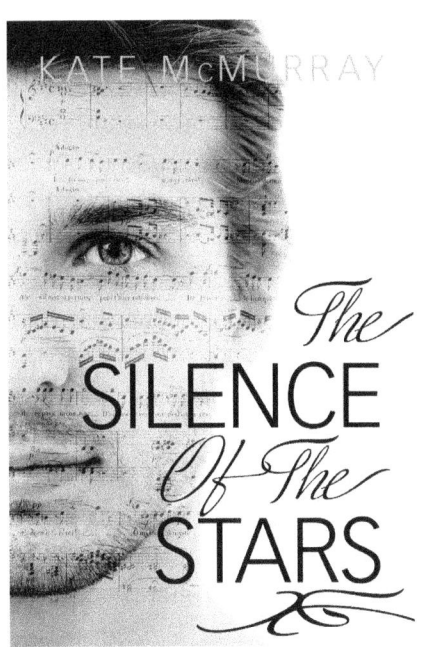

Sandy Sullivan has gotten so good at covering up his emotions, he's waiting for someone to hand him an Oscar. On the outside, he's a cheerful, funny guy, but his good humor is the only thing keeping awful memories from his army tours in Afghanistan at bay. Worse, Sandy is now adrift after breaking up with the only man who ever understood him, but who also wanted to fix him the way Sandy's been fixing up his new house in Brooklyn.

Everett Blake seems to have everything: good looks, money, and talent to spare. He parlayed a successful career as a violinist into a teaching job at Manhattan's elite Olcott School and until four months ago, he even had the perfect boyfriend. Now he's on his own, trying to give his new apartment some personality, even if it is unkempt compared to the perfect home he shared with his ex. When hiring a contractor to renovate his kitchen sends Sandy barreling into his life, Everett is only too happy to accept the chaos… until he realizes he's in over his head.

www.dreamspinnerpress.com

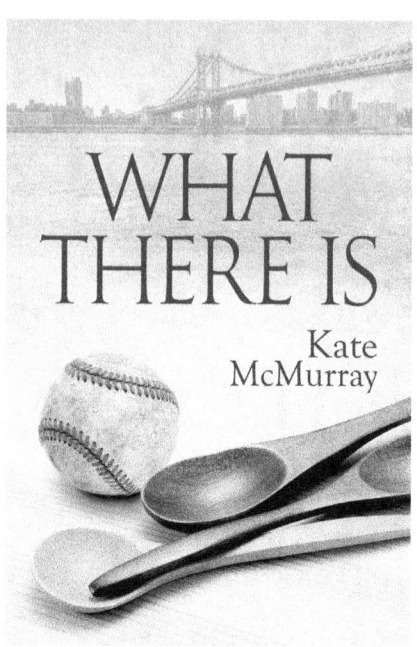

Former professional baseball player Justin Piersol needs a new life after a career-ending injury, and his job as a high school baseball coach isn't exactly fulfilling. Still, things are looking up: he finds the perfect room in an apartment in Brooklyn with Mark, who writes a popular column on sports statistics.

Mark is nerdy and socially awkward and intensely shy, and he immediately develops a terrible crush on Justin, who barely seems to notice him. As they get to know each other, Justin admits he misses playing baseball, that coaching doesn't scratch the itch. Mark confesses he thought he'd be married by now, that he wants a serious relationship. So they make a pact: Justin will help Mark find a man, and Mark will help Justin find something he loves more than baseball.

They put their plan into action... and then life gets complicated. Mark meets a nice guy named Dave, and Justin is suddenly crazy with jealousy. Justin realizes he wants to let go of the past and focus on the present, but as Mark and Dave become an item, Justin fears he's too late.

www.dreamspinnerpress.com

Best friends Michael Reeves and Simon Newell always lived within ten minutes of each other, but somehow they're never in the same place at the same time.

Brash, outgoing Michael's unwavering confidence that he and Simon are meant to be carries him through some hard times. When Simon moves to New York, Michael dutifully follows. Quiet, practical Simon loves Michael as a dear friend, but he's not ready for anything romantic.

Several years and several failed relationships later, Simon realizes he's been in love with Michael all along. Only now Michael has moved on. Though Simon offers everything Michael's ever dreamed of, the timing is all wrong. Confusion, betrayal, and secrets from the past threaten their friendship until it might be time for them to go their separate ways. Or maybe the planets will finally align, and Michael and Simon will find themselves in the right place at the right time to take the next step.

www.dreamspinnerpress.com

FOR **MORE** OF THE **BEST GAY** ROMANCE

DREAMSPINNER
PRESS
dreamspinnerpress.com

www.ingramcontent.com/pod-product-compliance
Lightning Source LLC
Chambersburg PA
CBHW060052260626
47160CB00005B/1659